What People Are Saying about

The Demas Revelation

Looking for a great weekend read? If you like archaeological adventure stories and entertainment that still makes you think, you'll love *The Demas Revelation.* Not since *A Skeleton in God's Closet* has a Christian novel thoughtfully addressed a what-if question that might endanger everything we believe … and make us stronger for the process.

—LISA T. BERGREN, BEST-SELLING, AWARD-WINNING AUTHOR OF *THE BEGOTTEN AND THE BETRAYED*

The Demas Revelation is a compelling, mind-boggling story that keeps you turning the pages. You find yourself seeking resolution with the revelation, as well as resolution within your own faith.

—NANCY MOSER, AUTHOR OF *MOZART'S SISTER* AND *THE GOOD NEARBY*

Journey to Italy and its archaeological wonders in Shane Johnson's historical twist that pivots on the incredible power of one man's words. As you walk in the footsteps of the apostle Paul, you'll be convinced that everything is not always what it first appears to be. It's a descriptive story that challenges what you believe … and why.

—AUSTIN BOYD, AUTHOR OF *THE PROOF* AND *THE MARS HILL CLASSIFIED SERIES*

A NOVEL

The Demas Revelation

SHANE JOHNSON

Good News in Fiction

COOK COMMUNICATIONS MINISTRIES
Colorado Springs, Colorado • Paris, Ontario
KINGSWAY COMMUNICATIONS LTD
Eastbourne, England

RiverOak® is an imprint of
Cook Communications Ministries, Colorado Springs, CO 80918
Cook Communications, Paris, Ontario
Kingsway Communications, Eastbourne, England

THE DEMAS REVELATION

Published in association with the Steve Laube Agency, 5501 N. 7th Ave., #502, Phoenix, AZ 85013.

This story is a work of fiction. All characters and events are the product of the author's imagination. Any resemblance to any person, living or dead, is coincidental.

First Printing, 2007
Printed in the United States of America

Cover photo of woman by Angelo Cavalli/Getty
Cover design by studiogearbox.com
Interior design by Lisa A. Barnes

1 2 3 4 5 6 7 8 9 10

ISBN 978-1-58919-090-0
LCCN 2007921093

This book is dedicated in loving memory to Zola Levitt
For decades an untiring soldier for Christ,
he did much to light the path for Jew and Gentile alike
and set many on the course for home.

Now when Jesus came into the district of Caesarea Philippi, He was asking His disciples, "Who do people say that the Son of Man is?"

And they said, "Some say John the Baptist; and others, Elijah; but still others, Jeremiah, or one of the prophets."

He said to them, *"But who do you say that I am?"*

Simon Peter answered, "You are the Christ, the Son of the living God."

And Jesus said to him, "Blessed are you, Simon Barjona, because flesh and blood did not reveal this to you, but My Father who is in heaven."

—Matthew 16:13–17

Prologue

A glint of silver.

With that, a veiling of centuries would come to a sudden end, there in a deliberate darkness, hidden away, lost to the world.

The moment had come.

The air became thick and still. Three pairs of young, wind-dried eyes opened wider as the passage narrowed, the light-drenched world falling behind. A handful of other caves explored that morning led them on forays that had proved all too brief, the caves' depth and promise less than had been hoped for. But now, more than a dozen feet of gently sloping rock had already been conquered, with more lying before them, shrouded in mystery, taunting the meager beams of their flashlights.

The trio, two boys and a girl, slowly continued their search, their lights sweeping ahead as their classroom chairs, many miles away, sat noticeably empty. Words spoken just the day before, as the children sat transfixed and listening, had not been lost on them—words embodying the kind of adventure that had long been the substance of their dreams.

A minor earthquake lasting less than a minute had shaken the area a decade before. Loosened rock had fallen away from the cavern's entrance, allowing access, but for ten years afterward, no one had noticed the exposed crevice. The youths' choice of that particular opening in the tawny rock had been random, or so it had seemed. The cavern was just another of many, one of thousands cut by millennia of natural forces into a vast, mountainous land. While hundreds of such caves had, over the decades, given up whatever secrets they held, there were simply too many for any significant number to have been cataloged. Too many to have been explored and mapped and known.

Treasure, the children were sure, was there for the taking. Perhaps not the kind of plunder they had seen in the movies—glittering booty wrested from lords and ladies by loutish, laughing pirates, who held it aloft before scattering and hiding it away—but treasure nonetheless.

The wisdom of the ages, recorded by hands long ago turned to dust.

Twenty-five, then fifty, then a hundred feet into the mountainside the children ventured, sometimes crouching, making their way where no one had been for a very long time. *Or maybe never,* they feared. Breathing was a labor, the air cramped and oppressive and thick like the stone all around them—their lungs, as if drowning, fought against taking another breath. The earthy scent soaked into them, pervading their clothes, coating their tongues, crawling into every pore. Their clothes were dusty, their faces smudged.

Every few feet the smallest and youngest of their number complained to his brother, a fear of the heavy darkness tearing at him as it so often did, rising as the sunlight dwindled and finally vanished behind them. Each protest, however, brought only the promise of "Just a little farther."

Then, in the distance, from within the cool, palpable solitude of a chamber not altogether naturally formed, something shone in their searching beams.

Silver.

Excitement propelling them forward, the three emerged from the tunnel into a roughly circular chamber, its higher ceiling allowing them to stand. The boy in the lead rushed quickly toward the glint he had seen, his fingers sweeping away the shallow layer of sand that still partly concealed the object. His heart leaped. He knew the object for what it was—or thought he did. He had seen pictures in a storybook.

He turned with his find and showed the others, straining under its weight as he held it out for all to see. It was as long as he was tall. Their cheers echoed loudly off the chamber walls. Uncounted generations had been born and had passed into history since a glimmer of light had last found the polished contours of the ancient treasure. Wars, rumors of wars, and rare sprinklings of peace had flared and fled away. Nations had risen and fallen. All the while, there in the darkness, it had waited, untouched but never forgotten.

And now, finally, its wait was over.

The three took a quick glance around. Then their small hands burrowed into the smaller, loose chips of flat stone that covered much of the chamber floor. They found nothing else, though the broken shards—seemingly deliberately placed—whispered of more treasure, perhaps just beneath the surface.

But they had no tools. They had been hoping to find clay jars, like those once famously and accidentally discovered by a shepherd boy elsewhere among those same hills. Instead, they had stumbled upon something very different, with no way to dig, to understand, to properly explore their find.

But they knew someone who could.

A veil of mystery, concealing an artifact forgotten by the world, hidden and left undisturbed for centuries, with his help, would be lifted. They would be famous, and the find would hold eternal ramifications for them all.

Much to the relief of the youngest, they crawled, crouched, and ran from the cavern, their eyes narrowing in protest as they rushed back into the morning light. Excitement tightening their chests, shouts of triumph burst from their dusty throats. Marveling at the way the ornate metal caught the sun, the eldest hefted the artifact into a canvas bag he had tied to the handlebars of his bike. He knew his fingers were the first to grasp the object in ages, warming its shaft where they wrapped around it. With the bag tied tight, he paused, looking at his hands, wondering who had last held the prize—perhaps, he marveled, someone whose name he had read in the Torah.

Their trusty steeds of metal and rubber now beneath them, the children kicked off and pedaled hard, dust flying in their wake as they descended the slope. The town lay miles away.

In that town was one who had to be told, had to be shown—if he was still there.

◆ ◆ ◆

Dr. Sam Meridian sat beneath the shade of a table umbrella at Kibbutz Almog, sipping a cup of tea as he went over his notes. His early morning meeting with a representative of the

Israeli government had borne no fruit, yielding no extension of permission to excavate further at the temple mount in Jerusalem. The dig had ended abruptly, stopped by the political protests and threatened violence of a number of Palestinian activists, for whom any validation of the site's Jewish history was anathema.

It's got to be there somewhere …

Persistent belief among rabbinical scholars placed the long-vanished ark of the covenant in a deep chamber directly beneath the ancient Holy of Holies of the fallen temple, where King Josiah, who had feared the impending Babylonian conquest, had ordered it hidden. No one had seen the ark since—even in the time of Christ, its proper and sanctified place behind the temple veil had remained agonizingly empty.

As empty as the mount itself—in the eyes of the Jews—now was.

Meridian hadn't even gotten close. Less than ten feet of side tunnel had been excavated when officials ordered the dig to a halt. Sixty-three feet more, by Meridian's calculation, would have been necessary.

Might as well have been a thousand.

It was morning, but already the air was warm. Meridian unfastened the top button of his short-sleeved khaki twill shirt and fanned his chest with the loosened material. The arid climate was something Meridian never seemed to adjust to, no matter how often he came to the region. He fished around in a pocket of his cargo vest, seeking a throat lozenge as he looked out over the diminutive vacation retreat, its brilliant colors alive in the light of the climbing sun. Beneath a cloudless sky, roofing tiles of warm sienna topped walls of soft desert orange. Palms swayed in the gentle, salty breezes, their music further seasoning the air. The mountains beyond the rooftops formed a purple crown, and at their base, unseen from that vantage point, spread a Dead Sea as still as its name implied.

Meridian thought back over his life's work, his mind splashed with images of other more successful expeditions. He had led the group that had unearthed the tomb of Kharthunan—a previously unknown son of Merenptah—in the Valley of the Kings. He had also supervised the dig that found the first extrabiblical proof of the apostle John's imprisonment on the island of Patmos. He and his staff, using ground-scanning radar, had even discovered and excavated a forgotten wine cellar beneath the chapel of the world's most famous Spanish mission—the Alamo in Texas.

But the big one, he felt, had gotten away.

Perhaps, he mused, *it just isn't time yet.*

The thought provided little consolation, but it would have to be enough, at least for now.

Anna, he smiled, his mind turning to his wife of but three years. She had been the brightest part of his life, a treasure greater than any he had discovered hidden in the soil. While earning a doctorate in ancient history, she had also discovered a love for archaeology through her relationship with Meridian, prompting her to add a second degree to her résumé and to adopt his field as her own.

His smile widened as he remembered the first time she accompanied him on a dig, the expedition into Egypt. As he and his students dug down through the windblown sands, bringing to light the portal of Kharthunan's tomb, she had begun to speak of the king and his time as if she had been there. Hers was an exquisite, disciplined imagination, which, when fueled by known facts, could paint an uncanny and emotional portrayal of ancient days. While far from scientific, her musings had brought a new understanding to Meridian's work, making the past live again in a way he had never known.

This unique woman had brought color and meaning into a life once as dry and parched as desert earth.

I'm so glad you're here, baby.

His thoughts drifted to a dig in Mexico where he and his team—including Anna—had been victimized. As they slept following a long day inside the tomb of Pactalacata, their backs weary and their muscles aching, others had entered the site. Quietly, so quietly, the intruders had stolen a priceless stone calendar unearthed only that day, a beautifully chiseled circular artifact some three feet in diameter—a prize of the Aztecs.

In the years since, Meridian had kept a watchful eye on the black market and the Internet, following whatever tenuous lead presented itself.

And now, finally, he knew who had robbed him—and the world.

Meridian arranged the evidence before him—a handful of photos and scrawled notes—into a neat stack and placed them into a heavy protective envelope.

I've got you now!

◆ ◆ ◆

Authorities across the globe in Mexico City were already awaiting the information, and soon it would be delivered. As he slid the envelope into a leather satchel and closed the clasp, a sound caught his ear. Running feet, rapidly approaching.

"Professor!"

The word was shouted, the pronunciation flawed. Meridian turned to see three excited youths rounding the corner of the gated courtyard. In the hand of one of the boys—Ronen, he recalled—was a long canvas bag.

"We hoped you would still be here," panted the boy in Hebrew. "After you spoke to our science class yesterday, we went searching for scrolls. Instead, we found this."

He handed the bag to Meridian, who loosened the string tie and peeled away the fabric, exposing glinting metal.

How?

The object was now free and in his hands. His throat suddenly tightened, swollen with awe. He recognized the artifact at once.

A shovel.

No—*the* shovel.

It was ornate and ceremonial in design, its engraved contours splotched with far less tarnish than there should have been, given its age and the sulfurous pools that dotted the area. Its handle was almost five feet in length, its deep scoop wider than two spread hands.

It was an implement of the second temple, a vital part of the sacrificial process. The priests of ancient Israel had used it to carry ashes from the top of the *mizbeach ha'-ola,* the sacred altar of the burnt offering.

His mind ablaze, Meridian looked up and stared in the direction of a modern re-creation of the wilderness tabernacle, which stood nearby at the foot of the Judean Hills. Many times he had visited the site and had appreciated the carefully crafted replicas of the implements temple priests had used.

But this, he knew, was no mere reproduction. He could *feel* the ages in its metal, the antiquity in every contour.

"Where did you find this?" Meridian asked in the same language, amazement punctuating his words.

"There," the girl said, pointing toward the mountains. "In the caves."

Qumran!

"Which cave, Daphna?" the man asked, excitement tensing his throat. "Can you find it again?"

"Yes," she replied, smiling. "Easily."

"Is there more? Anything else in the cave?"

"There may be," Ronen said. "The ground was strange, as if the stones had been put there."

Meridian pulled a cell phone from his vest, fumbled with it for a moment, then punched in a number.

"Anna, it's me. There's been a find. A big one. Pack everything and meet me at the Qumran turnoff in half an hour."

"Qumran?" she asked, puzzled. "Why there? What did you find?"

"We may have been looking in the wrong place. You and Joe just meet me, and I'll explain when I see you. I have to go."

"All right," she said with a measure of audible frustration. "See you there. Love you."

"Love you, too," he returned softly. "So much."

He closed the phone, slipped it back into a vest pocket, and turned back to the boy.

"Show me." Meridian rose, grabbing his gear.

Running from the courtyard, they headed for the parking lot and the rough-terrain vehicle waiting there.

But their departure didn't go unnoticed.

◆ ◆ ◆

"Scooter, turn that down!"

The volume of the television slowly dropped as the frowning boy punched a button on the remote and cast a cutting glance toward his nanny. The seven-year-old, his brown eyes sparkling pools of liquid mischief, lay on his stomach on the king-size bed, his chin propped against his other hand.

"But I like this cartoon," he whined.

"You'll still like it if it isn't rattling the windows, dear."

"Not as well."

The room was modest but comfortable, one of the family rooms of Kibbutz Almog. The holiday hotel, nestled within an oasis at the northern end of the Dead Sea, was surrounded by deserts unchanged since the time of the exodus. A popular spot for local vacationers, researching historians, and those embarked upon globe-crossing pilgrimages to the Holy Land.

Anna Meridian emerged from the bathroom in a pastel green T-shirt and khaki shorts, still putting up her hair. With practiced precision, her fingers manipulated her chestnut tresses into an updo suited for the work she knew must lay ahead. A subtle smile played upon her full lips, crafted by the curiosity swirling behind it.

"We're supposed to meet Sam in fifteen minutes, Ruth," she told the nanny. "How's Joe coming?"

"He was almost ready to go," Ruth said, grabbing the remote and muting the television for a moment.

The much-chagrined boy kicked his legs against the pillows around him, knocking one to the floor, where the nanny retrieved it.

Anna, having seen too much such behavior from Scooter this trip, rolled her eyes and turned away.

"Joe?" she called out toward the adjoining room.

"Just a sec," came the response.

"Sam didn't say what he'd found?" asked the weary nanny.

"No, as usual. I could tell he thinks it's something important, though. He gets that sound in his voice … like a kid on Christmas morning."

"Think it's the ark?"

"Could be, but I'm trying not to get my hopes up."

A man dressed in a blue, short-sleeved shirt and khakis and toting a large metal equipment case entered through the door linking the two rooms. Joe Grant, a fellow professor and one of the brightest young archaeologists with whom Anna ever had worked, set the case on the floor and patted his breast pocket to verify that his sunglasses were there.

"You be good while I'm gone, sport," Grant said, reaching over to tousle the boy's hair. "Don't give Ruth any trouble."

"I won't," the boy said, never tearing his eyes from the television.

"I'll probably be gone most of the day, but we'll have supper tonight at that restaurant I was telling you about … The one with the game room."

"But you said we could go there for lunch," Scooter whined.

"Something came up," Grant replied. "This could be very important."

"But you promised!" Scooter exploded, grabbing the remote in his small, sticky hand and hurling it across the room. On impact, the back plate came off and batteries scattered everywhere.

"I said tonight."

Whatever the boy muttered in response, it was unintelligible.

"Everything in the Jeep?" Anna asked after an uncomfortable pause.

"So far as I know," Grant said. "If you've got what you need, we're all set."

Anna picked up her equipment bag and looked at the nanny, whose frustration with her charge was poorly hidden.

"We'll call when we get there," Anna said. "And then again around lunchtime."

"Fine," Ruth groaned, pulling a ragged, half-eaten sandwich from under the edge of the bed, where Scooter had left it. She glared at the boy. "Sure you don't want to take *this* one with you?"

Grant turned away, hoisting a backpack and the large case. "It's what you get paid for, Ruth."

"Not nearly enough," she muttered as he departed earshot, the door closing behind him.

Pausing to don their shades in the bright of day, the archaeologists crossed the newly striped parking lot where Grant's dusty, well-used vehicle waited.

"Gonna be a hot one," he said, glancing upward.

"It always is." Anna smiled, the glossy red of her lips catching the light. "Just once I'd like to do an excavation in Alaska. Or Antarctica."

"Not much to find in Antarctica," Grant laughed, lifting their equipment into the scarred rear bed of the Jeep.

"Well, if there ever is, I'm there. Who knows ... maybe an Atlantean parking garage will turn up."

They opened the doors and climbed into their seats. With everything secure, they clicked their safety belts into place.

"You say that now," Grant went on, "but even where there's no sheet ice to contend with, frozen ground gets mighty hard."

"Oh, that's right. You were on that dig up in Barrow. The prehistoric Inuit site. I remember your letter to Sam. 'Never again,' I think you said."

"And I've lived by those words," he laughed.

As Grant switched on the air-conditioning, Anna glimpsed herself in the visor mirror, played with a stray tress of chestnut hair, and closed the cover.

"I'll never understand why you keep your nails like that," Grant said, looking over his shoulder as he backed out of the space. "Or how, for that matter. You're just asking for it."

She waved the fingers of one hand briefly before her, enjoying the perfect polished nails she always carefully guarded. Almost half an inch beyond her fingertips they stretched, glistening red in the sunlight.

"Are those real?" he asked.

"One hundred percent homegrown," she said. "Sam loves having his back scratched. He says they're like steel."

"So when you're in the field, how can they not be in your way?"

"There are just some things I refuse to concede," she said, smiling. She picked up a pair of heavy work gloves from the seat beside her. "These protect them well enough. Plus, I'm careful. You learn how to manage. No big deal."

"'Refuse to concede,' huh?" Grant said. "Do you ever regret following Sam into this field?"

"Never," she said, her tone sharp. "It's like, I don't know … history with texture."

"And scorpions, and sand in your food, and blowing dust out of your nose for a week after every dig."

"Wouldn't have it any other way."

"You can't mean that."

Well, mostly, she thought.

"Okay," she confessed. "I could lose the scorpions. And the snakes."

"That's it?"

"That's it."

Anna had refused to let go of the vanities she had so easily maintained as a young classroom-bound history teacher, far different from the dramatic choices and changes her marriage had wrought. Her decision, however joyful, had not been an easy one, when in order to follow her new archaeologist husband around the world, she had pursued a new vocation, a new life.

And, as all who knew her had expected, she had excelled in it.

She had known Grant since their junior year of high school, when history had been her passion. She looked over at him as he drove, knowing that in those days he had made a point of noticing her whether across a crowded cafeteria or a busy street or a student-filled campus. He had confessed as much at her wedding, telling her even after she had walked the aisle that, though he had married someone else, Anna still haunted his thoughts from time to time, stirring creative imaginings as romantic as they were fleeting.

Had things been only slightly different, he might have loved her.

"But don't you miss the lectures?" he continued. "The lively hallways, the tutoring sessions …?"

She gazed at him as he adjusted a dashboard vent, her dark eyes hidden behind mirrored lenses.

"… and the air-conditioning?"

"Just drive, Joseph," she said, hiding a smile.

"Yes ma'am."

"Although," she went on, "I may not be doing this for too much longer, anyway."

"Why not?"

"Sam and I have been thinking of starting a family."

"Congratulations," Grant said, grinning. "You'll make great parents."

"Think so?"

"Know so."

Miles fell behind them. Mountains rose in the near distance, the rough terrain already wavering in the convective air.

"Witches' brew," Anna said, indicating the widespread, silvery phantoms hugging the ground far ahead. "That's what my grandmother used to call a mirage."

"My wife called it that too," Grant said, nodding. "Drew

many a desert traveler deeper into the desert, thinking water was waiting just ahead."

"I'm sorry I never really knew her … your wife, I mean."

"She was a lot like you," Grant said, a faint smile tugging at the corner of his lips. "But she wouldn't have been caught dead standing in a sand pit. City girl, through and through. Smart. Wonderful mother. I hope Scooter remembers her when he's older … She died when he was only three."

"I'm sure he will," Anna reassured him. "You've shown him pictures and videos and told him all those stories about her."

"Yeah, but I'm afraid *that's* what he'll remember. The pictures and the videos and the things I've told him, instead of his own memories. It's been four years now. He says he misses her, but who knows."

"I'm sure he does, Joe," she said. "The bond between mother and child is very strong."

"I know."

For a moment she thought of the child—a child she wasn't fond of, but who, she knew, had lost much in his short life.

"Scooter," she said. "How did he get that name?"

Grant chuckled, pausing to remember. Despite the shades he wore, Anna could tell that happier times were playing themselves out in his mind's eye. "Well, you know how most kids, when they start to move around, will get down on their hands and knees and crawl everywhere?"

She nodded.

"Well, he never did that. I'm not sure he ever crawled in his life. See, we had these polished hardwood floors and, well …"—the man stifled a quiet laugh—"instead, he'd just sit on that thick plastic diaper of his and scoot around the house, pushing himself backward with his feet. Everywhere he went you could hear that diaper sliding across the floor, and the patter of those little feet with his legs pumping away."

Anna laughed with him. "What a sight that must have been."

"It was. And how he kept from bumping into everything in the house, I'll never know. I used to tell Susan I hoped he would get over doing that before college rolled around."

"Looks like he did."

"Yeah, finally."

A silence followed, during which Anna decided not to bring up the child's obvious lack of discipline.

"Look," Grant told her, seeming to read her mind, "I know he's a handful. I know he's even a pain sometimes, but I'm sure he'll outgrow it."

"Don't apologize," she said. "He's got a lot to deal with. And he'll be okay … Once things settle down and you get into another place, he'll be fine."

"I sure hope so."

Anna turned her attention back to the way ahead and saw Sam's truck in the distance, well off the road. "There," she pointed.

They slowed, and Grant turned onto the rough dirt road that branched to the east. Meridian climbed out of his truck and waved as they approached. Anna rolled down her window. When they came to a stop, she noticed bicycles piled in the back of his truck and the faces of children through the tinted glass.

Looking into her husband's eyes, she saw the sparkle she had always adored. Seven years her senior, her husband had gained enough field experience to develop a sense of impending victory, and it had served him well.

"Hiya, stranger." She smiled, removing her shades. "Need a ride?"

He held up the shovel, and her eyes went wide.

"Time to put up the tree," he said. "It's Christmas in July."

◆ ◆ ◆

The children had been sent home on their bikes, sworn not to reveal what they had found. It was far too early, with far too much still to verify. In exchange for their silence, Meridian had promised them a share in the find, their names forever recorded in the annals of history.

Laden with the tools of discovery, the three archaeologists gently prepared to work the wide floor of the chamber. Nylon straps, ropes, and pulleys stood by, just in case. Simple torches atop tall metal stands threw conflicting shadows, their constant dance casting an amber glow onto ruddy stone.

Just such a grotto had surrendered the hidden Old Testament scrolls of the Essenes more than six decades earlier. Now, Meridian hoped, the caves would give up an even greater treasure.

The thick air crackled as, with pick against stone, trowel turning soil, and whisk broom sweeping away the dust, the work began in earnest. Grant, impatient to see what lay just beneath the surface, cast the earth aside little by little, his eyes reflecting the hope he gained with each passing moment.

"The underlying soil isn't packed as hard as it might be," he commented, ribbons of yellow light playing across his face as he flipped the trowel again and again. "I'd say it's been turned at some point."

"A couple thousand years ago?" Meridian hoped, flipping the latches on a large blue padded case. Lifting the lid, his eyes met the ground-penetrating radar unit that had become a mainstay. Even though it was an older model, it had still cost a fortune, but time and again it had proven itself worth every cent.

"Lots of loose stone," commented Anna, examining one of the flat shards layering the floor. "Small and irregular. I'd say these were *put* here. Good sign."

"Never expect the obvious," her husband said, smiling. "Keep all possibilities open. Don't narrow your options with too sharp a presumed focus."

"Jeremiah's cave," Anna speculated, referring to the apocryphal book of Second Maccabees. "What if the account is true after all? What if this is it? They bring the ark in here, with a pit already dug and waiting. They lower it, along with who knows how many temple implements, into the pit, then cover everything with some kind of protective layer. Fabrics, wood shavings, what have you. Then, atop this, they place carefully sifted soil and pieces of flat stone."

"What happens if we *do* find it?" Grant asked.

Anna shook her head in confusion. "What do you mean?"

Meridian's mind filled with images of the ark, all varied, all theoretical. It was *supposed* to have been hidden under the temple mount, according to the best information they had, but—

"Imagine the uproar," Grant went on. "We wouldn't dare breathe a word until it was safely locked away back in Tel Aviv. Lots of folks out there don't want it found, mostly of the Arab persuasion. Last thing they want to see is undeniable proof that the temples really existed—no temples, no legitimate Jewish claim to the mount."

"Amazing," Meridian said, fiddling with his digital camera. "Talk about denial."

"Politics," Anna added. "They know. They just won't *admit* they know."

"Even if we find the thing and get it secured," Grant went on, "the university will be swamped. Press from all over the world. Archaeologists. Religious scholars. Artists. Probably even Steven Spielberg, assuming he'd be up to coming to Oldefield."

"I'd settle for *any* of the temple implements," Anna said, smiling. "Doesn't have to be the ark itself. Just to know for sure what happened to them … to know they were safe and hadn't been melted down by the Romans …"

"The silver shovel survived," Meridian said. "And if *it* did, other things could have just as easily."

"What a find," Grant said triumphantly. "I'm holding my breath until I see some test results. But given its apparent authenticity, I'd say we have reason to hope for much more from this site."

"You could wait for the radar," Anna chided him as he continued turning his trowel. "No sense digging up the whole place."

"With any luck," Meridian said with a wink, "we might have to anyway."

"Hear, hear," Grant cheered.

"I sure hope something's down there," Anna said. "I could stand a good party, and this already feels like a perfect day for one."

Grant paused and checked the date on his watch.

"It's Susan's birthday," he said. "I can't believe I forgot until just now …"

The words faded and he went quiet. His wife's death had come far too soon, ended by the thoughtlessness of a drunk driver.

"What better way to celebrate her memory," Anna gently offered. "With the find of the century."

"Yeah," Grant agreed, returning to his work. "This one's for you, babe."

Meridian shook his head and frowned at the radar unit. It had seen a lot of use, its crannies caked with dried soil from around the world.

"Battery's dead," he sighed in frustration.

"Terrific," Grant moaned. "Where's the spare?"

"Where it always is," Meridian said. "Will you get it, Anna?"

She reached for the equipment bag and put her hand into the zippered side pocket. It was empty.

"Oh Sam …"

"What? What is it?"

"It was on the charger, in the corner over by the window," she remembered. "I meant to get it, but with all the commotion …"

Meridian considered the unit. Without that battery, it was only so much dead weight.

"Okay," he said, closing the radar case and turning to leave. "I'll be back as soon as I can."

"No," Anna said, rising to block his path. "It's my fault. I'll go get it. You two stay here and get some work done."

"You sure?" Meridian asked. "I don't mind."

"You and Joe just see what you can dig up in the next hour or two. I want to find a nice surprise waiting for me when I get back."

"We'll do our best," Grant saluted. "Hey, if you happen to pass that blintz place on the way back, maybe you could—"

"Don't push it," she replied, grinning.

"Fine," he joked. "If we find the ark while you're gone, it's ours."

"I think God might have something to say about that," Anna said, holding her hand out toward her husband. "Keys?"

He fished around in his vest pocket and handed them to her.

"Not a scratch, now."

"Honey, that ship has sailed." She tugged at the brim of his hat. "Love you."

"Love you more."

She gave him a kiss and was off, Grant's laugh echoing behind her. The sunlight ahead brightened as she carefully made her way along the ancient, water-carved passage.

"Could it really be in there?" Anna wondered aloud, awe in her voice.

Emerging from the tunnel, she quickly shielded her eyes.

The sun seemed much brighter than she remembered before they had entered the cave. Her eyes fought to adjust, even beneath her darkened sunglass lenses. She dropped the truck keys twice as she repeatedly lost her balance, her descent along the rocky, sandy slope a difficult one.

"Always easier going up," she moaned.

The ground leveled out, and she spotted the truck just ahead. She checked her watch and was amazed to find that three hours had already passed since she left the hotel.

As she opened the door of the truck, a scent on the dry wind caught her attention. Then, as quickly as she recognized it, it was gone. She looked around, but there was no sign of anyone. Only desert and mountains, for many miles.

Myrrh?

She climbed into the truck and started the ignition.

◆ ◆ ◆

Meridian knelt and began clearing away rock shards with a small shovel.

"I'm more than a foot deep, and still no soil or bedrock," he said. "This detritus was put here deliberately."

"Looks like it," Grant agreed. "I'm really trying not to get my hopes up, Sam, but …"

"Yeah, me, too."

Barely a minute passed while the men worked.

"There we go," Grant said, his tone cautiously triumphant. He lifted something from the tiny pit before him, wiped it with a thumb, and held it up to the light. "Pottery shard … Look at these markings. Etched in. Lines within circles."

He handed it to Meridian. They both knew.

Essene.

"Good sign," Meridian noted, smiling. "First century BC."

"There's a purpose to this place. The silver shovel wasn't just dropped here without a thought."

Faster, though still with care, the two men turned the earth. Metal implements against stone, man against time. The sound echoed and multiplied, filling the chamber as if a dozen men were digging.

"Wait," Meridian suddenly whispered, becoming still. "Quiet." He looked at Grant, who also froze.

"What is it?" Grant asked, his voice but a breath.

"Did you hear that?"

"No … what?"

Grant turned his head toward the chamber entrance, straining to listen.

And after a few tense moments, he heard it too.

Ruth slid a drawer closed, having just packed away some newly washed clothes. The television was still blaring despite her repeated demands for quiet.

"All right," she said, charging toward Scooter, who now lay on the floor. She reached down and tore the remote from his hand, shut off the television, and dropped the remote into her skirt pocket.

"That was my show!" Scooter cried out.

"They're *all* your shows," the nanny replied. "It stays off for a while. I told you three times to turn it down and you didn't, so go read one of your books or listen to your CD player with the earphones. I don't care what you do, as long as it's quiet."

"I'm telling Daddy."

"Not before *I* do." Shaking her head, she disappeared into the adjoining room.

Scooter rose to his feet, hurled himself onto the bed, and slammed a fist into a pillow. As he lay there, the sound of a key in a lock broke the momentary silence.

"Daddy!" he said, springing toward the door. Just as his hand touched the knob, the door swung open and Anna walked in.

"Where's my Daddy?" Scooter demanded.

"At the cave."

She crossed the room to where the battery charger sat, right where she had left it. Its green light indicated a completed charging cycle.

"Wish I'd remembered you a few hours ago," she scolded herself, pulling the battery from its cradle.

"When will he be back?" the boy asked expectantly. "We were going to go to the game room for lunch."

"I thought your father said that would be at suppertime," Anna reminded him.

"First, he said lunch. Before you dragged him to that stupid old cave."

She ignored the outburst and called into the next room. "Ruth? It's just me. I had to come back for something."

"Okay," Ruth's voice returned. "Get what you needed?"

"Yes …"

"It's *your* fault he isn't here," the child interrupted. "*You* took him away."

"I did not," Anna replied, trying to maintain calm. "He's a grown-up, and grown-ups have responsibilities."

The nanny's voice rang out again, and Anna was grateful. "How about you stay here where it's nice and cool, and I'll go dig in the hot, sweaty cave."

Anna chuckled. "No, thanks."

"Chicken."

Scooter circled behind Anna and plopped onto the bed.

"Anna," he asked, his tone suddenly sweet, "can I watch TV?"

"I don't care," she answered, her mind already beyond the door. "Bye, Ruth. I'm heading back out."

"Last chance," the nanny called.

"Bye …!" Anna repeated as the door closed behind her.

The boy rolled off the bed, went to the darkened television, and pressed the switch.

◆ ◆ ◆

The brakes squealed as Anna pulled to a stop.

She checked her watch. She had been gone barely an hour and a half, a good enough time considering a stop for gas.

And another for blintzes.

Taking the charged battery and the sack of pastries in hand, she considered for an instant calling her husband to ask if he needed anything else from the vehicle before she made the hike back up the mountainside. But there was no way a signal would reach him so deep inside the mass of stone. She made a cursory exploration of the passenger compartment and saw nothing he might need, so she shut off the engine and stepped out into the early afternoon heat.

Nothing like a desert in the summertime ...

She had only taken a few steps when she saw it. A plume of dust rising high into the still air rooted at the mouth of a cave.

Their cave.

She broke into a dead run.

No! Please!

The slope hadn't seemed so steep before. So agonizingly long.

"Sam!" she cried out, the name swallowed up by the stony colossus before her.

Her heart pounded with the exertion.

And fear.

Her legs grew heavy. She plodded on, slipping on sand and loose stone.

The phone, the blintzes, and the battery fell from her hands, thudding hard against the rough ground. She didn't care. They lay in the unforgiving sun, left behind.

Perspiration trickled from her brow, stinging her eyes.

"Sam!"

She ran the ascent and didn't stop—not until she rounded a protrusion in the rock face and saw the massive blocks of desert limestone sealing the cavern entrance, the lesser debris still settling.

"Sam!"

She hurled herself forward, into the fallen stone. Her bare hands dug into the smaller of the sharp-edged rocks, tearing them away, only to find others taking their place, as the quieting rumble of the cave-in filled her ears. Her polished nails glittered in the sun's glare as they snapped, tearing away, taking flight. Gashes opened in her fingers, the blood mingling with the parched, powdery soil. The heavy dust layered her, rendering her dark hair, her soft skin, her loose cotton clothes an ocher monotone.

"Sam!"

Unstable sand and lesser stones streamed around her. Sobs burst from her throat, choking her as much as the brutal dust. Tears streamed down her cheeks, leaving delicate rivulets of drying mud. A stifling cloud of debris swallowed her. She couldn't find air.

Forced back, her eyes caked with searing grit, she wept bitterly and gasped for breath.

And every time she found it, she screamed his name.

One

Fourteen years later—

A lovely spot for a garden, the woman mused.

Her name was Maria, as had been her grandmother's. For almost seven decades she had lived at the base of the southernmost of Rome's fabled Seven Hills, on land owned by her family for as long as anyone could remember. Long before, when the Roman influence had spread far and wide throughout the earth, the once celebrated Via Appia—the Appian Way—had passed nearby, a major thoroughfare of the once great empire. At that time, when senators and noblemen in chariots traversed the region, her family's land had been a prized location, along the primary trade route, the chief highway to Greece and points east.

Now, it was just—lovely.

Sun dappled the ground around her as it penetrated the overhanging forest of olive, sycamore, and lotus trees covering the two and a half acres of her inheritance. Mimosa brought a splash of yellow, and when the time was right, additional color dotted the trio of orange trees her grandfather had planted in celebration of her birth so many autumns ago.

Well within sight of her terra-cotta-roofed house, she

chose a spot, smiled, and brought her shovel down. The ground was soft, thanks to recent rains, and the grassy soil yielded easily.

Tomatoes here, she mused, smiling. *Nothing but the best for the recipes Mother taught me. And courgette and aubergine …*

Little by little, in the cool of the morning, she patiently turned the earth, casting it aside to reveal the rich, dark loam in which her well-chosen seeds would find a home. Her mind delighted in visions of sumptuous family meals yet to come.

Clunk.

Her blade hit something hard.

Oh no, she worried. *Stones to be moved.*

She scraped the steel edge of the shovel along the ground, trying to determine the size of her problem.

Whatever it was, it was flat on top.

For another hour she worked to clear away the soil, laying bare an unyielding thistle in her otherwise promising garden. When she had uncovered a straight length of more than eight feet and a width of two feet, her spade happened upon something immediately recognizable, a rounded fragment, its edges chipped and worn.

Sightless eyes looked up at her, the nose between them gone. What remained of a chiseled jaw displayed a resolve long since silenced, its polished marble contours discolored by unforgiving ages within the earth.

She stopped, dropped her shovel, and reached into a pocket for her phone.

"Il Museo di Archeologico di Roma," she told the operator.

It was an aging institution, its halls and corridors filled with erudite ghosts, the shadows of the hundreds of thousands who had walked there, played there, learned there. You could smell it in the air, feel it in the oiled wood trim, sense it in the plastered walls.

Knowledge.

Oldefield University was a rarity. Touched little by the advances of time and technology, it was a minor academe, nestled in a forest, hidden by the shade of towering oaks, maples, spruces, and pines, its campus more than a mile from the main road. The school was as beautiful as it was secluded, its buildings white-trimmed masterpieces of dark red stone separated by vivid, verdant lawns and precisely trimmed flowering shrubbery.

Tradition here had always been held in the highest regard, with change coming only grudgingly as necessity—and the school's continued existence—dictated. Its first parking lots, finally laid in the 1950s, came only after prolonged and heated debate. The campus had no air-conditioning, nor had it ever needed any. It did have a computer research lab connected to the rest of the world via small rooftop satellite dishes, but the facility had yet to supplant the books shelved within the university's vast library, home to bound volumes dating back to the early 1700s. A few professors, more each year, chose to bring personal computers into their classrooms, while others stayed with more conventional means of record keeping. Students, their class sizes small, were given direct and generous instruction with emphasis placed heavily on hands-on experience.

The school was timeless, ageless, and answered to no other educational or political entity.

And, as a result, it was impoverished.

Anna stood in the hallway outside the office of the dean of archaeology, looking into the reflective pane of a framed portrait as she tugged gently at her wispy bangs, unable to get them to stay just as she wanted.

Flexible hold, my eye!

Frustrated with her hair, she gave up and adjusted the bow collar of her white blouse. Her heart drummed within her.

You look fine, she told herself. *Oh, who am I kidding?*

She checked the delicate hands of her designer watch, a gift from the university several years earlier when she was awarded the Carl Fergusen chair.

That was such a lovely evening.

It was exactly noon. The moment had come.

It'll be okay … You'll get through this!

She smoothed her pale pink skirt and blazer, drew a deep breath, and walked into the office, her fingers subtly and fretfully kneading the strap of her purse. The smile she wore as she closed the door behind her and approached the secretary's desk was a mask.

"Good afternoon, Dr. Meridian," greeted the younger woman. "Dean Mercer is expecting you. You may go right in."

"Thank you, Amy."

The hinges of the heavy walnut door squealed a little as she opened it.

"Anna," said Albert Mercer, an elderly man sitting behind a massive, cluttered desk. He rose to his feet as she entered. "Please, come in."

The room spoke of treasured knowledge attained at great price. Heavy bookshelves of rich wood, filled to the limit with hardbound literary classics, research works, and meticulous histories, lined the walls.

Anna's heels met lush carpet, her steps silent as she entered. Unhurriedly approaching the desk, she felt like a child sent to the principal's office. She feared she knew why she was there. She prayed she would be proven wrong.

"You look lovely, my dear."

"Thank you."

"Have a seat," he said, gesturing toward a plush leather chair opposite his own. "There's a matter we must discuss."

Anna sat without a sound, clutching her purse in her lap, her fingers still rubbing the smooth, darkened strap. Mercer took his seat.

"How are things with your staff?" he asked. "Are the new grad assistants to your liking?"

"Yes, Albert," she said. "Everyone's quite eager to get out there and get their hands dirty. As usual, they all have visions of King Tut dancing in their heads."

"The idealism of youth." Mercer nodded with a slight smile. "I well remember. I must admit … I, too, fancied myself Howard Carter once."

"It does take a few years for reality to set in," she agreed. "Lots of work, very little glamour. And no Indiana Jones … at least not when you know what you're doing."

"Anna," the dean began with obvious reluctance, "reality *is* a harsh master. I would like very much not to have to tell you this, but …"—there was a long pause—"the board of regents met this morning. I'm sure you knew that."

"Yes," she said, crossing her legs. Her breath held fast.

"Know that we all hold your late husband and his accomplishments in the highest regard. Know also that those sentiments have also extended to you. However ..."

He was choosing his words carefully—too carefully. She looked down at her hands.

Please, just get it over with.

"It's no secret that there are those here who don't believe your carrying on of Samuel's work has brought the desired results, or that you are qualified to attempt as much. The past five expeditionary seasons have yielded nothing of consequence, and some on the board believe the expense of such fieldwork is no longer justified. And despite your degrees in both history and archaeology, it's no secret among those of us who know you that the former is your first love."

"I see."

"In Samuel's memory, we have gone beyond expectation and beyond what is justified in allotting the budgets within which you've worked, and this has caused, shall we say, *unrest* among some within the faculty. They see you as receiving favored treatment and have become increasingly dissatisfied with their own annual departmental budgets."

Watching his sharp gray eyes in silence, she nervously rubbed a couple of toes together within the confines of her tight pink pumps.

"In addition to this," Mercer continued, "the university's fund-raising efforts have proven less than stellar the past few years. The alumni have moved on with their lives, it would seem. While several very generous contributions have been made, some anonymously, we've still fallen well short of our goals. This past decade has seen a steady decline in operating funds, and we've reached a critical point."

For a moment he dropped his gaze.

"We've tried to do without new equipment for so long, due to the expense and many other reasons, but it has now become essential. While it means dropping other programs altogether, we have no choice but to implement a serious advancement of our … *technology* level." The word seemed distasteful to him. "For the fall semester, we will place at our students' disposal radically updated computer labs and such, and we will have to continue to modernize if we're to continue drawing new blood to Oldefield."

"I know," Anna said. Many, both faculty and students, had said it was time to bring the school into the twenty-first century, she recalled. Many others had said it was time to bring it into the twentieth.

He rose from his seat and stood beside a floor-mounted globe near the desk. "The tangible has become ineffectual, I'm afraid. Or at the very least, undesirable. Globes, wall maps, models—things you can touch and hold and sense—have fallen by the wayside. The scent of old, time-proven research volumes that have gone the way of the Pony Express."

"Progress," Anna said. "It's inevitable, if our students are to compete in the world."

"Indeed," replied the dean. "But it carries a great price. The purely experiential approach we've always cherished is a luxury we no longer can afford."

Anna lowered her head and closed her eyes, awaiting the blow.

"Effective immediately," Mercer said as gently as he could,

"it has been decided to restrict your teaching to the lecture hall. There will be no further archaeological expeditions. No more digs. I know that all these years you've carried on in honor of your husband's unfulfilled efforts. Fought to see his dream brought to fruition—"

"Not solely because of that," she interrupted.

He nodded. "In any case, the time has come to bring such ventures to a close. Perhaps you'd prefer to return to history at the end of the semester? Dr. Lowell is departing, as you know, which will leave us wanting in that department."

"I'd heard."

"Will you consider it?"

"Consider it," she repeated, "yes. But Albert ..."—he looked up from the slowly spinning globe into her golden brown eyes—"what about the dig already under way?"

"Ah, Rome," he recalled.

"What do I tell Roberto? Are they just supposed to drop their shovels and catch the next plane home?"

"Where do things stand?"

"A good bit of progress has been made since I was called back here," Anna said. "Much of the foundation has been cleared. Only this morning I was told that a series of descending stone steps had been uncovered. More than a dozen as of yesterday, and there may be many more."

"Leading down to who knows what," he said. "Could be nothing."

"Yes," she agreed, "but whatever's down there is highly unusual. The Romans didn't incorporate cellars into their common architecture, but the stone used, the location, and even a handful of coins we've come across ... every indicator says we're dealing with Nero's Rome. The fragment of a shattered marble bust found by Signora Verducci fits the era. We're dealing with a sizable foundation and whatever's under it, though we're not yet certain what the above-ground structure was. A villa most likely, or even a temple, as yet unknown. But we have every reason to believe there may be something of real significance at the bottom of those steps."

"Like what?"

She hesitated.

"A wine cellar?" he wryly proposed.

She smiled, appreciating his sense of humor. "No."

"So what reason do you have for such optimism?"

She was silent.

Mercer turned, swept a curtain aside, and peered through the tall, broad window behind his desk.

"Anna," he began, "for so long you've been like a daughter to me. I've watched you, seen your passion for your work, your love for your students and your profession."

She followed his gaze, looking out the window at the campus, the students, even the budding branches as they yielded to the gusty spring winds.

"And," he added, "I understand the sheer power of hope."

Her mind flashed back to that day in Qumran, to the faith she had clutched to her heart that somehow, against all odds, her husband would emerge alive. But her faith in miracles had been crushed as the hours, then the days, then the weeks had passed—as the rescue team, soon reclassified a mere *recovery* team, had laboriously cleared the cavern tunnel.

"If I were to allow the dig to continue," Mercer said, "even through the end of the month—"

"We could make history."

"I was going to say," he continued, "if I allow it to continue, it may jeopardize your very career at Oldefield. Unfortunately, there are those here who wouldn't be heartbroken to see you go, some who might not hesitate to use any wedge at their disposal to displace you. For many, archaeology is, as they say, a 'boys' club' … and for some, despite their respect for Samuel, you've never been welcome. No, it isn't lawful, or in the least, fair. And you could pursue legal action in return, were you to be released from your obligations here. But your case would be virtually impossible to prove, and they'd surely find other grounds for your dismissal."

"I understand."

He turned to face her.

"So, my dear … what is it to be?"

She rose to her feet and swallowed hard.

"The end of the month, then."

He nodded. "Very well. The end of the month. Your duties here shouldn't keep you beyond the end of the week, and then …" He took her hand and gave it a fatherly pat. "Give young Mr. Giordano my regards, will you?"

◆ ◆ ◆

The fire sizzled and popped, an eternal ballet, ever unchanging.

Anna's office was a storybook place built one hundred years earlier, when ornate trim in dark, polished wood had been the order of the day, and fixtures were as much works of art as they were functional. More than a dozen people had claimed the room as their own throughout the years, including her husband before her.

In the light of the hewn fireplace, her eyes shone—warm, dark, and expressive, deep russet flecked with gold. Her lashes fluttered like ravens' wings. Her hair was as spun cinnamon. Her lips were full and supple, her complexion pure and silken. A teacup in her hands, she sat staring into the flames in the darkness of the room, lost in their poetic motion. And as she watched, she found something appealing, even comforting there, amid the dancing light.

Fire, the same now as it had been when the first person saw it. The same sound, the same radiance, the same heat …

If she tried hard enough, she could almost allow it to transport her back through the ages, as if every fire ever set shared with its descendants a link through which she could travel to one and all. Back to ancient Egypt, where pharaohs ruled in luxury and slaves toiled under a merciless sun. Back to the height of Incan civilization, where ruthless blood sacrifices appeased gods of the worshippers' own making. Back to Stonehenge, where mystical Druids celebrated the changing seasons with fire, water, and blood.

Back to Qumran, five minutes before two good men died.

She took a deep breath. Usually, as daily life brought its challenges, she pushed the memory to the back of her mind, and there it lingered at the fringes like an ember refusing to be extinguished. But now and again it would rise, flaring to life, demanding from her something she refused to give herself.

Forgiveness.

I should have remembered the battery. Maybe if I'd stayed …

She closed her eyes. The self-imposed burden remained a heavy one.

Maybe I would have heard something. Maybe I could have warned them.

Logic found no place in her thoughts, not here.

I should have let Sam go back to the hotel, instead of me. He wanted to, but I stopped him.

Her guilt, so long entrenched on so many fronts, would not be buried.

I should have died instead of him. He should be the one sitting in this office now, not me.

Her scarred heart had refused to heal.

The ark wasn't even there. Nothing was there. Then, he died …

She took a sip from her cup, the warm tea a blessing.

And another good man with him.

She remembered a gentle face smiling from across a high-school campus.

And a little boy grew up an orphan, raised by an aunt with little patience, a woman he had barely known before that moment.

Another sip.

All for nothing!

Anna gazed into the quivering flames but didn't see them.

Oh, Sam …

After a moment she sensed another presence in the room.

"I knocked a few times," said a welcome voice. "The door was unlocked, and I saw the firelight under it, so …"

Anna turned from the light as a dark shape moved into the room. Her eyes would take a moment to adjust, but she knew the voice well.

"I'm sorry, Jack. The bell's not working."

John "Jack" Dyson, her fellow archaeology instructor and close friend, gently shut the door behind him. His collar was loosened, his tie gone. His hair the hue of harvest wheat.

"Getting late," he commented. "Long day."

No reply came.

He paused to set some papers on her desk and crossed to the stone-lined hearth, where he stood watching her. Standing next to her chair, his hand found her shoulder.

"You okay?" he asked.

"I will be."

In the interval since Qumran, the shaken professor had reassessed every aspect of her life. Every moment, every decision she could recall had endured her harsh scrutiny under an unforgiving magnifying glass. Only after she had finally determined herself worthy—and after many long talks with those closest to her—had she chosen to remain in the field.

Dyson was a brilliant man whose dedication to truth, and to discretion in the procurement of that truth, had won her trust. The prospect of working with him, though she might not admit it, had also played a part in her decision.

And as their friendship had blossomed, becoming something that transcended mere professionalism, she was grateful to have been swayed.

She glanced up at him, finding the sparkling eyes she had come to cherish. His presence had become for her a far greater comfort than she dared admit, whether to him or to herself. So often she had fed upon his strength, the many times her own had failed her, and he had always been there, day or night, anywhere she had needed him to be. But despite her reliance on him, she had kept her heart locked away, its passions reserved for one who never again could share in them.

Anything else, she told herself, would be unfaithfulness.

Several moments passed in silence as both watched the curling, writhing flames.

"Anna," Dyson finally ventured, the firelight splashing his rugged face, "I heard about the board's decision. I'm sorry."

"Thank you, Jack."

"It's a pity about Rome," he said.

"We're not giving up just yet."

His eyes widened. "We're not?"

"Dean Mercer allowed us through the end of the month. That's three more weeks, give or take. And in that time, something has to happen."

"Something has."

She brightened. "What?"

"I got a call from Roberto. He said he tried to call you …"

"I turned off my phone."

Dyson nodded subtly. "It's a villa. First century."

Anna set her cup aside, rose, and crossed the room, wringing her hands as she considered the news. She stood before a multipaned window, the moon beyond shining over the wooded landscape.

"He's sure?"

"He said he was," Dyson replied, his voice tight with excitement. "And the more they've dug, the more they've found the foundation intact."

"I've been away too long. Where do things stand?"

"It's going quickly. They've unearthed another ten steps, all inlaid with silver. That makes twenty-six. All in red travertine … exceedingly rare in the region, and surely expensive. Whoever had them made was a noble."

"Twenty-six steps so far," she repeated.

Twenty-six of thirty-three, she prayed.

"What exactly are you hoping to find?" Dyson asked. "You haven't told me."

She traced the pane with a long, burgundy-polished nail. She recalled vivid images, the essence of an unrelenting and recurring dream that had haunted her for weeks.

One she dared not share. Not yet.

She went to him and took his hand in hers. "Just … thank you for being here. It means a lot."

"Where else would I be?" he replied with a soft smile.

After a few moments he seemed to detect something recognizable in the air.

"Pizza?" he asked, puzzled. "Since when do you call out for pizza?"

"I … used to. Not so often anymore."

A glint shone in her eye, caught by the light of the fire. Her scent reached him, a harmony of soft perfume and …

"Ah," he noted. "Pepperoni."

"And sweet corn."

It had been Meridian's favorite. In his memory, with the extinguishing of his lifetime's desire now upon her, she had placed the order and had known the concert of its flavors for the first time in more than a dozen years.

Sam …

"I should get back to the dig," Anna said, moving to the desk.

"None too soon. They need you."

She pulled her purse from a drawer, which she locked afterward. "I'll call the airline. Care to come along?"

"Already taken care of." Dyson smiled, handing her a folded printout. "The red-eye to Rome. You leave in three days … Best I could do. Unfortunately, I can't go with you. Finals week."

"Right," she said, disappointment in her eyes. "I'll keep you updated."

"I'll be waiting for your call," he said, smiling.

Two

The traffic on the A91 had been a nightmare. Though rush hour had passed, construction had narrowed one section to a single lane, a situation made worse by a fender bender over which two men stood screaming at each other. And other motorists, passing by at a snail's crawl, screamed at them both.

Ah, I love the old country.

Anna's exit finally arrived, and none too soon. Still trying to adjust to the tight steering of her small rental car, she made her way off the highway, her mind filled with visions of what they might find at the dig.

Can it really be? I mean, what are the chances?

Pushing aside the shoulder of her unbuttoned, short-sleeved, pastel blue overshirt, she again tugged at the strap of her bra through her T-shirt. An irritant had been tormenting her for hours, a tiny bristly thing lodged there somewhere, sporadically digging into her soft flesh. Slipping her hand through the opening of her V-neck and under the strap helped only momentarily, for soon she again felt the minuscule jab against her upper shoulder blade.

But the annoyance, troublesome as it was, did little to divert her thoughts from the dig site, or from her students.

Her repeated calls to Roberto's cell phone since her arrival at Fiumicino Airport had gone unanswered, which meant he likely was up to his waist in dirt and must have left the phone in his backpack. But that was unlike him—that phone had been his constant companion since she had known him, going everywhere with him, no matter the situation. Over the past two years, Roberto Giordano had proved to be a bright and most ambitious graduate student, and she knew his extensive knowledge of his native Italy had served the team well in her absence. She had had no reservations about leaving him in charge of the dig until her return. *Thank heaven for worldwide phones,* she thought, recalling the days before the Internet had made all phone service global.

Again, she hit the redial key. And again his voice-mail greeting sounded in her ear. With a bit of unneeded force, she pressed the key to disconnect.

Where are you, Roberto?

She scrolled down through her phone list to find the number of another of her grad students, Neil Meyer. The young man had been with her only two semesters, having transferred from another school, but in that short time he had proven himself to her. He was a whiz with electronics, a handy skill to possess when excavating in the far reaches, miles from civilization's resources. Always the first to volunteer for the necessary but more unpleasant tasks presented by their efforts, Meyer often spent much of his day hauling the team's heavier equipment, fetching food or drink, or delivering paperwork.

Anna dialed Meyer's number. She scowled as his recorded voice greeted her as well.

Didn't anyone *take their phones down there?*

Then, in turn, she dialed Craig Dunn. He had a quirky and often cynical sense of humor, and his quips often brought both groans and smiles from his fellows. There was one ring, then two.

"Hello …?"

"Craig?" Anna almost shouted, overjoyed to have reached him.

"Yeah …?"

"It's Dr. Meridian. I'm on my way to the dig, and—"

"Ha!" the voice suddenly interrupted. "Fooled you! Just leave a message at the beep and—"

"Young man, I'm going to strangle you," Anna growled, driving a long thumbnail into the disconnect button with equal measures of worry and anger. "When I get ahold of you, Mr. Dunn …"

Finally, she tried Beth Whitney, the member of her class most like a daughter to her. A sweet girl, curious and bright, with an unquenchable need to learn what the world had forgotten. It was her first year with Anna, but she had already found a special place in the professor's heart.

Anna dialed. Again, no answer.

Okay, I'm officially worried.

As the miles fell behind, the sun neared the horizon. In less than two hours, it would set, and night would be upon her. Anna repeatedly fought to convince herself that everything was all right, that there was a simple reason for her inability to contact her students. She told herself that, over a nice dinner, they would update her on their most recent discoveries at the site, their wondrous triumphs.

Please!

And afterward, she knew, it would be a rough night—her internal clock was still set many hours behind theirs, which meant that sleep would come too late, and she would spend her morning hours fighting to stay awake.

Ah, jet lag …

Dense thickets now lined the road, shading the way, and finally the driveway of the Verducci estate appeared. Anna gently turned onto the elegant property, her eyes already scanning ahead for some sign of her team as the house came into view.

She followed the drive around the classically styled residence, enjoying its inherent antiquity, and found Roberto's van and a pair of rental cars parked in back, just where she expected them to be. Pulling alongside, she shut off the engine, gathered her keys and phone, and climbed out. Her gym bag, journal, a hand-cranked light, and maps remained on the passenger seat.

There was no sign of movement. No voices.

She walked up the slope of a low grassy hill toward the dig, a spot more than one hundred feet behind the house. Though she could see the team's equipment stacked and waiting as she approached, there was still no sign of anyone.

"Roberto?" she called. No response.

She drew near the site, stepping over the edge of the foundation. Much of it had been cleared of the overlying sod and soil, exposing a familiar masonry. Tools were scattered on the ground near the distinct rectangular hole that led to the ancient stairway.

And there, lying next to a shovel encrusted with red earth, was a blue-shelled phone she immediately recognized.

"Roberto!" she called again. But all she heard was the wind in the overhanging trees.

She picked up the phone and looked at the screen. It read "9 MISSED CALLS."

"Four of those were me," she whispered to herself.

From the top of the stairway, she called down into the darkness. Her voice carried an echo, but no answer came. Stone dust wafted within the tunnel.

No, not again!

She hurried down the steps, but the increasing gloom made the way treacherous, the visibility nil. With one hand on the stone wall of the passageway, she finally stopped and called out again.

"Roberto! Neil!" More echoes. No answers. "Beth! Craig!"

Oh, Lord! Please let them be all right.

She spun around and scurried back up the steps. When she emerged, the sunlight seemed brighter than it had before. Finding no flashlight on the ground around her, she took off in a dead run for her car and the hand-cranked light she had left on the seat.

Nearing the car, she glanced toward the house. It was dark.

Could they be there? Maybe Signora Verducci offered them a cool drink or a meal while they waited for the excavation dust to settle.

With a deep breath, she fought back the panic that had been trying to claim her. Quick steps carried her to the back door of the house.

She knocked. No response.

With a slight push, she found the door open.

"Signora Verducci? Anyone? It's Anna ..."

Please, Father!

She entered the kitchen and noticed several glasses on the table, and a pitcher of what appeared to be lemonade. Her mind ran through the more benign possibilities of where they might be, shoving the dire ones from her mind.

Maybe she's just showing them around ...

"Hello?" she called again, louder this time. "Signora Verducci? It's Anna Meridian."

She paused, her ears pricked by a sound.

Voices. Muffled.

"Hello?" she tried, louder now.

Again, voices. Followed by a single masculine voice uttering one word.

Her name.

"Roberto?"

"Down here." Faint but intelligible.

"Where's 'here'?"

"The wine cellar!"

Anna backtracked through the kitchen and down a narrow hallway. At the end stood a heavy wooden door, its sliding latch closed.

"Roberto?"

"Here," he replied, joy in his voice. Then came a pounding from the other side of the door. "We're locked in."

"Coming!" Anna said, rushing forward. Her hands flew to the large iron latch and slid it away with a *thunk*. Then she gripped the door handle, twisted, and pulled.

The door swung heavily aside.

"It was Raphael," Roberto said, in answer to the question on Anna's face.

"Is everyone all right?" she asked, looking past him at the others, who were hurrying up the stairs. Below, near the bottom, Maria Verducci smiled up at her.

"Are you all right, Signora?" Anna asked her.

"Yes," she replied, keeping her tone light. "A bit shaken, perhaps."

"We're fine," said Craig from just behind Roberto. "But I doubt the dig is."

"They had guns," Beth said, apparently still shaken.

"Who did?" Anna asked, alarmed.

"Six men altogether," Neil answered. "They surprised us about two hours ago. Took us at gunpoint into the house. Locked us up down there."

The professor, her eyes glistening, spread her arms and embraced each of her charges. She knew the stakes that dig-site looters played for—her students' very lives had been in great danger.

"I'm so glad you're all okay," she said, her voice breaking. *Thank you, dear Father.*

"It was Raphael," Roberto repeated. "He kept his distance, but I saw him. His hair was a little different than in the photo you showed us, but—"

Realization dawned, and Anna spun around, rushing back to the door. Roberto, Neil, and Craig were on her heels. Beth whispered something to the old woman, who smiled and pointed down a hallway.

"Thank you," Beth said, hurrying away. Maria went to the back door and watched the others as they headed for the dig.

"I will call the police," she called to them.

"No," Anna shouted back. "Not yet. Let us see what we're dealing with first."

"Very well, signora."

Anna broke into a run up the low hill. "I knew something was wrong," she said. "I tried to call several times …"

"They made us drop our phones," Roberto told her. "For all I know, they took them."

"I saw yours," Anna said. "On the ground up here. No others."

"Terrific."

"I started down the stairway you excavated," she went on, stepping back onto the foundation, "but there was so much dust, I couldn't see."

"There was no dust before."

Bad sign, Anna knew. *Really bad sign.* Dust meant force, and force usually meant …

Neil, trailing them, spoke up. "You don't suppose they're still down there, do you?"

"They're long gone, Neil," Anna assured him, frustration in her voice as she picked up a flashlight. "And we'll never know what they took with them."

"We excavated the entirety of the stairs. There's a door at the bottom … Looks like bronze covering wood. We decided to wait for you."

"I appreciate that," she replied, switching on the light as they started down the stairs. "I just hope that whatever was down there, still is."

Roberto drew a breath of relief. "I'm really glad you're back, *dottoressa*."

"Me, too," she said, smiling.

The stairway stretched below them. As they continued to make their way down the steps, Anna's beam cut a hard swath through the tawny cloud of dust. She noted the red stone beneath her feet, a gleam of silver tracing its surface. She counted each step she took.

Finally, Anna and her students found themselves on a lower landing. A floor. They had reached the bottom.

"Thirty-three," Anna said aloud, her heart pounding in her drying throat. "Thirty-three steps of red stone …"

"With silver inlay," Roberto added in amazement. "Is it possible?"

"Is *what* possible?" Neil asked, holding his shirt over his mouth as a crude dust filter.

"I'll tell you in a minute," Anna said, stepping forward, one hand extended and sweeping from side to side. After crossing a distance of ten feet, something glinted in the throw of her flashlight. She reached up.

Silver hinges.

And hanging from them were the shattered remains of a very heavy reinforced door.

"Explosives," she said. "The idiots! They're lucky they didn't bring down the whole tunnel."

"Are we safe?" asked Craig.

"I think so. But I'd rather not go any farther until this dust settles." She sniffed the air anew. "No scent of black powder or dynamite. Plastique, I'd guess."

"They blew it up?" Neil asked, anger in his tone. "Why? Who were they?"

"Looters," Anna said, barely maintaining a calm comportment. "I'm just glad you're all okay."

Roberto shook his head. "Let's hope they didn't destroy whatever was on the other side of that door."

"Did Beth bring that high-powered fan of hers?" she asked.

"As warm as it's been?" Roberto said. "I'm sure."

"Have her run power and bring it down here."

"Got it," Neil said, flying back up the stairs.

Craig followed. "I'll get the generator going." His footsteps faded, and he, too, was gone.

"It looks like you found it, *dottoressa,*" Roberto said, grinning. "The legend was true."

She nodded, the thrill swelling deep within her. "I dreamed of this more than once over the past several months. I saw this doorway, but it was closed. And every time I reached out to open it, I woke up."

"Really? It looked like this and everything?"

"Really."

Roberto studied the door frame. "They denied that such a place existed, even unto death in the arena. They protected their brethren. I wonder whether I'd have had the courage to do the same."

"When the time comes, you'll find out."

"Do you know something I don't?"

"Probably." She smiled, letting the statement hang in the particulate air. "But what I mean is, we all go through times of trial. And if our faith means anything to us, if it's genuine, it proves to be a source of strength."

Roberto fell silent for a moment, then said softly, "I hope so."

Anna coughed, the dust finally too much. She peered for

a moment into the darkness beyond the violated doorway, then turned. "Let's go back up."

◆ ◆ ◆

The blower motor roared halfway down the stairs, its work almost done as its focused tempest forced the impure air upward. Anna and Roberto stood at the top of the stairs, readying themselves for an exploration of the waiting chamber.

"Getting dark," Anna observed. "Looks pretty well clear now. We should go on down."

"Before we do," the student said, "let me show you something."

He led her to another part of the expansive foundation and pointed out a square depression in the floor, its bottom lined with shattered red and black mosaic tiles.

"The *impluvium,*" he noted, but Anna already knew. A feature common in the houses of ancient Rome, such reflecting pools were fed by equal-sized holes in the roof above, through which channeled rainwater would cascade.

"The crew from the university had cleared half the foundation when we came upon the stairway," he went on. "But when I saw that red stone, I paid them and let them go."

"I'm glad you did," Anna said. "You found no other artifacts?"

"We found there was nothing here to *be* found. Other than the coins I told you about, which turned up on the first day. The soil was like fill dirt, uniform and empty. And that's another thing …"

"Tell me," Anna calmly said.

"The coins. They were all identical, scattered in a tight cluster. Silver denarii, minted under Nero."

"And?"

"There were exactly thirty of them."

She looked into his eyes, and for a moment neither spoke.

"Interesting parallel," she finally commented.

"Isn't it."

The exposed part of the foundation, some sixty by ninety feet, stretched around them, warmed by the sun for the first time in almost two thousand years. Here and there, flooring tiles of vivid color remained, though none were fully intact.

"So this was the atrium." Anna nodded, playing a nail against the flat of her left thumb as she looked at the floor immediately around her. "And this"—she gave a broad sweep of her hand—"was a noble's villa. Given that the city limits were about half a mile north of here at the time, it would have been in the country … nicely secluded."

"No doubt." Roberto pointed to another section of the dig site. "There are definite signs of a peristyle over there, and an indoor well. Only the wealthy had gardens and direct water sources within their walls."

"A noble," she thought aloud. "Someone of importance. Someone beyond reproach, who wouldn't be suspect."

Anna walked slowly around the pool's perimeter, studying the broken tiles, thinking it through. "Suppose he is a man of power. Perhaps an *equite,* or even a senator. He has an impressive house in the country, surrounded by vineyards and groves of fruit trees. Dozens of slaves, servants. Beautiful wife, sons, daughters. Everything a man of the time could want. But inside him, something is missing.

"Then one day he hears of this 'Chrestus,' who had caused such a stir in Palestine. Quietly he seeks out those who follow him. As he listens to their witness, something happens. He changes."

Roberto watched her as she spoke, fascinated by her train of thought. "I love it when you do this."

With romance still afire in her heart, Anna couldn't help but speculate about the realms of the past as she so often did. Such speculation was grossly unscientific and greatly frowned upon in her profession—facts should be allowed to speak for themselves, with no emotional or personal biases—but Anna's love of the more quixotic aspects of ages gone by drove her to more colorfully imagine the lives of the dead, to try to see and taste and smell the worlds they lived in.

"And soon," she went on, "the noble finds himself a believer. But few of his station believe as he does. He must tread carefully. He avoids the subject whenever someone around him brings it up. He knows of the persecutions of Nero … knows what danger his fellow Christians face each and every day. They've secretly been gathering in one home after another … the homes of the poor, who are less comfortable and more likely to embrace Christ. But getting word out about each new location is dangerous, and he knows they take a risk every time they attempt to share the gospel or invite anyone to hear Paul."

"So," Roberto interjected, "he decides to give them a safe haven."

She nodded, a soft smile on her burgundy lips.

He gazed at the foundation around him with new eyes. "But something happened," he offered. "Something went wrong."

With a cant of her head, Anna scrutinized him. "What do you mean?"

"There are definite marks in the stone all throughout the foundation," he pointed out. "Not tooling marks but gashes … harsh, deliberate blows, as if chisels were taken to it. Chisels and far worse."

She had seen the many scars in the stone, brutally inflicted wounds endured by a once beautiful edifice. Their antiquity was apparent, though she seized upon the opportunity to tease her top pupil.

"I was *hoping* the university boys hadn't done that." She adjusted her collar. "So … what do you conclude?"

"This house didn't erode over the centuries," Roberto said. "The elements didn't do this. It didn't gradually fall into ruin. It was demolished, and I'd say in a big hurry. Nero must have finally found it."

"I don't think so," Anna said, considering the stone. "Demolished, yes. You're quite right about that. But by Nero? If he had, why are the steps still there at all? Why was the door down there intact, at least until these brutes got ahold of it today? And why isn't there a historical record of Nero finding and destroying this place? Surely he'd have boasted of that no end."

As they stood pondering, the powerful fan below went quiet.

"All clear." Beth emerged with the fan and set it on the top step. "Breathe away."

Anna pulled her ever-present work gloves from a cargo pocket in her vest and slipped them over her lovely, sculpted hands.

"Ready?" she asked.

"Lead on," Roberto gestured.

She gathered her students at the rectangular portal and made sure each of them had a flashlight. "Neil, bring one of the light stands and plug it into the cord Beth ran. Craig, make sure you have a good battery in the camera."

"Will do," said Neil, who sprang for the equipment van.

Craig silently showed Anna the digital camera hung around his neck, his smile a guarantee. His T-shirt, dirty and battle weary and bearing the forgotten legend *Vote for Pedro,* inspired less confidence.

In a moment Neil had returned with a folded tripod, atop which was mounted a quartz light. "All set."

They descended the stairway. For the first time, Anna was able to see its every detail as it wound gently counterclockwise before them. The stones lining the passage were precisely cut out of black marble, their faces contoured perfectly to follow the path of descent—those on the left hand slightly convex, and those on the right concave.

"Isn't it something?" Beth said, running a hand along the smooth stone. "We were so excited … we couldn't wait for you to see it."

"Something," Anna replied, her throat tight.

A delicate pattern in silver—Roman, yet not quite Roman in design—was set into each step beneath their feet. Its Judean influence spoke of a spirit beyond that of the Caesars, beyond that of Jupiter and Minerva and Apollo.

And in the pattern, Anna saw the heart of one man who had been shown the way.

She was grateful that the looters hadn't allowed themselves time to excavate the steps, though there was a sign of damage done—some of the silver on one of the steps had been dug away, crudely and with haste.

Again, the violated door loomed before them. Scorched and splintered, a portion of the once impressive barrier still hung from the upper hinge. Other fragments littered the floor, and the group cautiously stepped over them.

Anna raised a hand, signaling a halt. Fearing a weakened ceiling, she stood in the doorway, shining her light into the room. An upward look revealed heavy supports some ten feet above, broad beams of polished cedar apparently as intact as the day they were put into place. A spiderweb of cracks spread overhead where superficial fragments of plaster had fallen, shaken loose in the blast.

She was wary. She always was, after Qumran.

"Oh, man," said Neil, his eyes scanning as Anna's light swept from side to side.

"Okay," Anna began. "You all know the drill. I go first."

She stepped forward, ancient, sundered wood crunching beneath her feet. The still, cool air smelled of time contained. The chamber was the size of a two-car garage, its pale walls smooth, plastered, and oddly devoid of the murals or other decor so common in Roman design. Its dust-powdered floor bore a wall-to-wall mosaic of swirling patterns in blues and whites, its motif that of fish being gathered into wide, sweeping nets.

How wonderfully appropriate, Anna thought.

And ahead, at the focal point of the room, was an ornate altar of white stone, symbolically empty.

Anna moved forward, squeezing into the narrow space behind the altar so that she might examine the wall more closely. The plaster was mottled in a distinct pattern, a tinge of gray wrought by centuries of contact with something no longer there. A pair of jagged holes, spread wide within the irregular stain, spoke of mounts forced free.

"They used a crowbar," she said, indicating multiple points of damage to the wall. She knew what had been mounted there.

A cross.

Even in the harsh beam of her flashlight, which caught on every ripple of the ancient trowel work and cast rough shadows, it was obvious. And now it was in the hands of looters, for sale to the highest bidder.

"Get that light stand set up," she said, her eyes never leaving the wall as she invited her students to enter. "Over here … I need to see over here."

In a moment Neil deployed the tripod and switched on the lamp. Aimed upward, its quartz beam splashed the ceiling, revealing the entirety of the chamber to their curious eyes.

"Whatever was there," Roberto began, his gaze fixed on the painfully empty wall above the altar, "must have been a good three feet tall."

"And silver, I'd say," Anna noted, taking a scraping. "There's residual discoloration here, where metal leeched into the plaster over time. Could have been solid silver, or wooden with an overlay, or with an inlay like the stair steps."

"It must have been a genius," Neil proposed, referring to the representations of protective spirits common in Rome, usually crafted in bronze. "Or a Lar."

"A Lar wouldn't have been up there by itself," Beth said. "And neither one would have been silver."

"Could have been," Neil replied. "Ancestral spirits were important too."

"Not *silver* important."

"So what *was* this, then?" Craig asked, snapping a picture. "A shrine to Jupiter or something?"

"I don't think so," Anna said, her attention moving lower to a point just below the discoloration. A rotas square of white marble was set flush into the wall, some two feet on a side and as sharply defined as the day it was chiseled. She pulled the glove from her right hand and lightly ran her bare fingertips along its contours.

"Like new," she noted, reading the Latin words carved there, precisely arranged as they were in every such square ever found:

R O T A S
O P E R A
T E N E T
A R E P O
S A T O R

Rotas opera tenet arepo sator—"The Creator directs in secret the wheels of the world."

The words, configured so they read the same from top to bottom, left to right, and backward or forward, had been a subject of scholarly debate for more than a century. Many believed that the ancient wordplay, common in Rome, had been adopted by early Christians as a way of openly glorifying God in the face of persecution. Further, a simple rearrangement of its letters into a cruciform pattern produced the Latin words *Pater Noster,* which mean "Our Father." Others, less spiritually inclined, saw it merely as a good-luck symbol with no specific meaning, used by varied cultures and given whatever significance each chose to give it.

"No furniture," Roberto observed, looking around. "No statuary. No nothing. The room's empty, except for what's left of the door. But was it this way all along, or—"

"Or did the looters take everything?" Neil finished.

"There could have been anything in here," Roberto said, crestfallen. "And now we'll never know."

"They were in a hurry, as always," Anna said. "Crash and burn, plunder and pillage. Thank goodness the altar's fixed in place, or they'd have taken that, too."

"But who knows what was sitting on it."

Like the others, Anna had seen the ghosts of whatever had stood on the altar—the dust-free, dinner-plate-sized, roughly circular signatures of a pair of objects now gone.

"There just wasn't time for them to have taken much," she said, trying to bolster their spirits. "I doubt we lost anything really important."

"Except maybe the proof we were hoping for," Roberto added.

"Proof?" Beth asked. "Of what?"

"It doesn't matter now."

Burying her disappointment, Anna took a deep breath

and forced a smile for the sake of her students. "We've made a major find, and you can all be very proud. We have a first-century chamber here. Empty perhaps, but far from worthless. We have a pristine rotas square, which may well indicate that Christianity had taken hold within the Roman Empire only a few decades after Christ. Think about that."

"*May* indicate," Neil said. "It isn't proof. The proof of what this place was probably walked out the door."

"What's left of the door," Beth added.

Anna indicated the mosaic at their feet. "Look at this floor. Also pristine. A Christian theme of masses being gathered in by fishers of men."

"Or," Neil said, "this place was the meeting hall of the Rome Fisherman's Union, Local 502."

"Fair enough," Anna said. "Neil's right. Nothing we have here is definitive. So let's get to work and find something that *is*."

She thanked her students for their dedication, and the group set about documenting the find in detail. For more than an hour, they scrutinized every square inch of the room, photographing and sketching its meager features. While Beth and Roberto took pencil rubbings of the rotas square and Neil used a laser measure to record the room's precise dimensions, Craig put his camera to good use.

The hour grew late. Their initial examination complete, Anna called an end to the evening.

"We'll meet at the café for breakfast," she said, hugging each of her students as they passed by and headed back up the stairs. "Eight o'clock. Fine work, everyone. Get some sleep … Busy day tomorrow."

She turned off the work light and followed them out. Brilliant stars appeared overhead as the path wound upward, welcoming her back from the darkness. Emerging into the cool, perfumed breezes of the Italian night, she paused at the top of the stairs and watched as her team members made their way to their vehicles. Beth turned and waved a final time.

"She's so sweet," Anna said, returning the gesture as Roberto walked up, flashlight and sleeping bag in hand.

"I'm staying here tonight," he had decided. "There may be nothing left to steal, but that doesn't mean no one will try. At least I can get a warning out." He watched as the team's vehicles roared to life and began to depart.

"I'm so proud of all of you," Anna said.

"You know, you never did call the police."

She drew a deep breath. "I think you know why."

Roberto nodded. "Yeah. Because if that room down there really is what you think it is, we can't tell anyone. Not yet. The police will leak the story to the press, and the press will inform the Vatican, who'll immediately confiscate the site and order us away."

"And once that happens—"

"They'll build a church over it before the echo dies, and we'll have pilgrims lined up for miles."

She laughed a bit at the exaggeration, but she knew it wasn't too far from truth.

"What about you?" he asked. "Do you have a room?"

Anna patted his arm and peered into the blackness of the stairway. "Down there, I do."

"Signora Verducci said you could sleep in the house if you'd like."

"I'm still jet-lagged. I won't be able to close my eyes for hours yet. Why don't you go ahead and get some sleep up here while I look around downstairs a little more."

"Expecting a secret treasure room, Indy-Anna?"

"No." She smiled, hefting her purple gym bag. "But I *would* like to get a sense of the place. Just sit there and soak it in … and imagine the voices of two thousand years ago. Get to know the room and its builder a little better."

"Our friend, the wealthy noble."

"Something like that."

Roberto handed her his sleeping bag and flashlight. "Take these. I'll get others from the van."

"Thank you, Roberto."

"No problem, *dottoressa*. Be careful on the way down."

"Always."

In a moment the coolness of the room again surrounded her. She was struck by the quiet, the stillness. No echoed whispers of awed students, no questions spoken, no shuffles of movement.

She flipped the work lamp on and the flashlight off. Gentle brilliance bounced from the ceiling, bathing every corner of the room with soft light. She glanced around hoping to see something that hadn't been there before. Nothing became apparent. Nothing moved or lurked in the shadows of the stairway.

Anna dropped her gym bag and unrolled the sleeping bag in the center of the room. Her mind dancing with visions of what once had been, she sat on the down-filled pad and slipped out of her shoes and overshirt. After rubbing her feet for a few minutes, her fingers slid beneath the bra strap that had been troubling her all day, an irritant ultimately lost in the glare of bigger things.

Speak to me, she urged the chamber, scanning the walls. *Tell me who last stood in this place before the sun rose this day. Tell me whose voices you knew, whose words you heard.*

She reached into the gym bag for her hairbrush. With a few deep breaths, she closed her eyes and drew the bristles through her long chestnut tresses, recalling for a moment a time when Sam had done it for her after a hard day. Jumbled images came and went, memories of her husband, her friends, her parents, her students. Time, for that moment, seemed a cluttered singularity, a chaotic point rather than an eternal line.

Her eyes slowly opened as she drew the purple brush through her hair again. Her gaze was unfocused, her thoughts far away. Odd things flowed into her mind—snippets, flashes, disjointed fragments of her life. Her semiformal sixteenth birthday party, the flowing pink dress she had worn. Sam knocking over a storage shelf while cleaning out the garage. A phrase in Latin, penned originally by Virgil.

Equo ne credite, Teucri, flowed the words. *Quidquid id est, timeo Danaos et dona ferentis.*

"Do not trust the horse, Trojans!" she whispered, recalling the translation. "Whatever it is, I fear the Greeks even bringing gifts."

She smiled slightly, amused at the workings of her mind.

"Girl, you are all over the map," she told herself. "Relax. Try to wind down."

As she continued passing the brush through her hair, she became aware that she had been staring at the rotas square above the altar. She had seen a few in her day, in various places, on various digs, in museums here and there. None had been as well preserved as this.

R, she read, her eyes starting along the top line. *O-T-A-S.*

And then she paused.

Something was there, just barely. Dark. Shadowed in the throw of the lamp.

She set the brush aside, rose to her feet, and went to the wall. Her fingers delicately traced the upper edge of the two-foot marble square.

A crack in the plaster. And it was calling to her.

She pulled a penknife from a pocket of her shorts and lightly dug into the hairline split. The thin fillet of plaster fell away.

This is only cosmetic, she realized. *It isn't holding the square in.*

She drew the blade down, across the bottom, back up the other side, and across the top, completing the circuit.

Sam's words came back to her.

Never expect the obvious.

Anna closed the blade and set the knife on the altar, her eyes never leaving the seam she had just created.

Talk to me, she implored the wall.

Her fingers pressed against the center of the shoulder-high square, the ruby shade of her nails a striking contrast to the veined white of the stone. She pressed again, harder this time. Then again, in a different place. And again, and again, then in the lower right-hand corner.

Movement.

There's a pivot point.

She leaned in and pushed again in the same spot with the heel of her palm. The cold stone yielded half an inch. Harder. An inch more.

As the right side of the square slid inward, the left edge came forward.

A shadowed opening appeared, widening with every push. Finally she was able to slip her fingers inside and grip the rim of the stone.

The beautifully chiseled slab was loose. She pulled with both hands. It was free.

Suddenly, now apart from the wall, the stone began sliding downward. Its weight forced her arms to the floor, her small hands straining to maintain their grip.

And then, finally, unharmed, it came to rest on the floor, leaning against the wall. She looked at the hard lines etched into her palms, her fingers, and shook her overstressed hands.

She straightened and looked into the hole where the stone had been.

There—concealed since the moment of its creation—a darkened vault awaited discovery.

Three

For more than five decades the old church had stood, a landmark of the community, a pillar of strength in times both difficult and serene. Its stone walls had once withstood the direct hit of a tornado, a monster that had laid waste most of the surrounding neighborhood. Its new roof, a gift from members of the congregation to their spiritual home, shone in the afternoon sun. Its white steeple scraped blue sky and white cloud, reaching up expectantly toward heaven.

Though not so surely as once it had.

Pastor Jerry Orsen sat in his office, his desk piled with paperwork. The burden of leadership he had assumed following the death of the former pastor—his father—had been oppressive. The unaffiliated Church of God's Providence, under that universally beloved man, had amassed a crushing load of debt due to a withering combination of steadily decreasing attendance and mounting operating costs. On two separate occasions, the church had come perilously close to closing its doors for good, saved only by the last-minute heroics of an elderly donor whose love for the old church was surpassed only by her need for tax relief.

Sadly, less than three months before the former pastor

himself had succumbed, the old woman died, leaving her worldly possessions not to the church but to her two daughters, each of whom had then sued the other for the entire sum.

Orsen had been a salesman. He had left home at the young age of seventeen, bright-eyed and filled with ambition, and had found his calling in the enthusiastic distribution of superfluous goods. Hand-painted ties, porcelain animals, cheap jewelry, questionable electronics, and dozens of other such items—the silly, the tacky, the ridiculous and flashy had been his stock-in-trade, and as he spread his products far and wide, he had built a nest egg, moved from state to state, plied his trade, and spread his promotional fertilizer as thickly as the local laws allowed.

He picked up a framed photo of his father, which held an honored place near the corner of his desk. He recalled the day he had received word from his mother of the man's passing—a rainy Thursday, on which he had found himself on the outskirts of Tulsa, Oklahoma, selling home cleaning products from the trunk of his car. At once he had driven home, where he found not only a grieving widow but an entire community deep in mourning.

Never had he realized the depth of the bond between his father and the flock he had led. A spark of envy burned within him.

As he received repeated condolences from people known and unknown to him and spent day after day inside his father's church, Orsen had finally understood what they all had lost. Their unity, their anchor had been torn from them. That moment he had decided to put down the roots he long had denied, take care of his mother, and see to the immediate needs of the people. And as he came to know them all, the old and the young, the needy and the capable, the sick and the vigorous, they had come to know him.

And one fine Sunday afternoon, as Orsen sat at home watching the closing minutes of an overtime football game and valuing intrinsic family over earned credentials, the congregation had chosen him to be their new spiritual leader, their new shepherd.

Pastor Jerry, as he quickly came to be known, accepted the position. He had a working knowledge of the Scriptures—he had spent a great deal of time selling Bibles to motels and truckers throughout the Midwest—and saw the profession of religion as nothing more than a sales venture.

He used to sell goods; now he sold salvation. No difference, he felt, except the hours behind the pulpit were better, and a pastor enjoyed a respect no salesman ever could.

Facing the financial crisis his father had left behind, Orsen had quickly turned to what he knew best, the first rule of sales: *Give the people what they want.*

His father, shackled by the bonds of biblical truth and sound teaching, had almost destroyed the very church he supposedly wanted to save. Preaching of hellfire and sin and humanity's inborn need for salvation might have been a time-worn classic, but it wasn't going to bring the folks in, not anymore. The people needed to hear repeatedly that God loved them just as they were, just as he had created them. Their imperfections were what endeared them to their Creator, after all, just as one feels compassion for a limping puppy. There was no such thing as sin, save for any inability to love ourselves as much as God loves us and to be the happy creatures he wants us to be, free of such hellish encumbrances as guilt and want and fear.

There is no hell, they needed to be told, *but the hell we make for ourselves.*

So, with the mission redefined, the message echoing within the walls of the old church changed dramatically. The people left church each Sunday and Wednesday feeling better about their lives, knowing that God no longer expected them to lean so heavily upon him. *He helps those who help themselves,* they learned. *He loves you just as you are. Everyone goes to heaven, for God loves us all—so much that he sent his Son to show us that love.*

Attendance grew, and quickly. Some of the older members, disliking the new approach, voiced their objections and stopped coming, but their modest numbers were more than offset by those who embraced the message. Week after week the tills filled to overflowing. One by one, the creditors and the banks, their loans satisfied, stopped calling. The building fund swelled, and repairs too long neglected were made. Pay raises for church employees became commonplace. New recreational facilities opened, and frivolous events filled the calendar. Picnics, ball games, and carnivals—entertainment was the key. Everyone was happy.

With one notable exception.

Orsen, holding the old photo, looked into his father's eyes and saw past the gentle smile to the pain there, the burdens the man had shouldered for too long.

You handled it all wrong, Pop, he mused. *You gotta tell them what they want to hear. You gotta make them want more.*

He smiled and set the picture back down.

You gotta love them to death.

◆ ◆ ◆

Anna's heart pounded as her pupils dilated, soaking up the darkness. Beyond the deep breach a small, shallow vault, level with the bottom of the opening, extended beyond the reach of the light.

Something glittered from within.

She ran for her flashlight and shined it into the cavity.

Breathing became nearly impossible.

The tiny chamber was like a wall safe, its interior perhaps two feet wide, two feet high, and two feet deep. Several objects rested within, but her eyes fell first upon an inscription etched high into the rear of the vault, words in Latin she could discern as easily as the verse of Dr. Seuss. She read them once, then again.

She trembled. A deep thrill filled her.

A scream escaped her lips, not of fear but of joy. Her vision blurred.

It really is!

"It's true," she whispered, her voice breaking. "The legend is true!"

She heard a noise behind her and turned to find Roberto standing in the doorway, tensed and ready for anything.

"What is it?" he asked, watching her. "Are you okay?"

Words barely came.

"Oh, Roberto …"

"A vault?" he wondered aloud. "You found something?"

"Hand me my gloves."

He reached into her bag, then rushed to her side, noting the rotas square at her feet.

"A secret panel?"

After hurriedly slipping her hands into the gloves, she again brought the flashlight to bear.

"Just look!"

He peered inside. A gasp caught in his throat as his mind wrapped itself around three chiseled lines of Latin text spotlighted in her beam:

IN THIS PLACE WERE WE TAUGHT BY PAUL
BLESSED APOSTLE OF THE CHRIST
THE SON OF THE LIVING GOD

Roberto whispered something unintelligible, put a hand to his mouth, and turned away.

"You did it," he finally said, leaning against the wall, barely able to speak. "You found it!"

"The first church in Rome," Anna said knowingly. "The secret meeting place Nero worked so hard to find. To shut down." She drew a deep breath. "*Paul's* church."

"He must have taught here before his arrest," the student said, seeing the room as if for the first time. "Even if only once … he was here! In this very room!"

"Our noble friend hadn't simply heard the Christian message. He heard it from Paul directly. That's why he was so moved."

"Moved to build this room."

After Roberto snapped a series of photos, Anna reached inside the vault. Preserved there, just as they had been when last they had felt the light, stood three goblets, evenly spaced, each filled to the rim with something hard and granular.

"Myrrh," she said, pulling the first goblet free and turning with it to face Roberto. It gleamed in her hands, the lightly ornamented silver having suffered only a trace of tarnish. The pea-sized bits it bore were angled and jagged, gleaming amber and rosy tan in the soft illumination of the work lamp. She held the chalice gently by its stem.

"This looks Roman," she said. "The shape and scrollwork both." She set it on the altar.

The second goblet followed. It was bronze, dark and heavy.

"Frankincense," Roberto noted, as she held the goblet and its contents before him. Clear and golden, tinged with milky white, the irregular pieces of the ancient burial spice were as pure as any they had ever seen.

"The cup itself looks to have been made in Israel," Anna suggested. "It may even be Davidic, judging from the design." She handed it to him, and he studied it for a moment before placing it with the other.

As she reached back into the vault and began withdrawing the third goblet, Roberto could tell that it was much heavier than the first two treasures had been.

"Gold," Anna whispered, her breath stolen by awe. The polished nuggets shone, their color pure, their value incalculable. The cup that bore them was of a dark, glossy reddish brown.

"This wood is acacia," she said with a smile. "These three

vessels were made from the materials God designated for the Jewish tabernacle. Silver, bronze, and acacia wood—together they symbolize God's entire relationship with humankind."

"And their contents, same as the gifts of the magi," Roberto added. "That ties the earliest known Christian worship to the nativity."

"Burial spices and gold. Symbolic of the death, resurrection, and glory of the Lord."

"Maybe they used them in a celebration of his birth, even annually. The first observances of Christmas."

"I don't know," Anna said. "There was a fillet of plaster around the rotas square. The seam was hidden, as if the vault had been sealed for good. They may just have been icons that, even hidden away, played a role as if the tabernacle had been symbolically re-created here. But you're right about one thing. This proves that the story of the nativity was known to these people." She scowled. "Since they didn't yet have the Gospels, that means—"

"Maybe they *did,*" Roberto offered. "Maybe the Gospels were written sooner than anyone thought."

Anna grew excited. "What a verification this is! A detail as subtle as what gifts were presented, and the New Testament we know has it exactly right."

She placed the third goblet on the altar and turned back toward the vault.

"There's something else in here."

She reached in and removed an object much larger than the others, and heavier still. It was a box carved of red travertine that looked to be eighteen inches long, eight inches wide, and six inches high, polished to mirror smoothness. Its lid, also of the same stone, covered the top. The box had no carvings, decorations, or other features, save a small groove that ran around its edge at the point where the lid met the container.

She turned and set it on the altar next to the goblets.

"Any ideas?" Roberto asked, his eyes wide.

"Not a one," Anna said, examining it closely. "Odd. The lid is sealed with wax. That was common with amphorae and other containers of liquid, but I've not seen this before."

Roberto's brow furrowed. "You think something liquid's in there, then?"

"No, no," she said. "Doesn't seem heavy enough for that. But the stone may have been heated before it was sealed, so once it cooled, the air inside would have been less dense. With the wax, it would have stayed that way. Sort of an early hermetic seal."

"So, whatever's in there should be well preserved?"

"That's the theory."

It occurred to her that Christ's tomb had also been sealed with Roman wax—not in the same way, but the parallel was undeniable.

"Shall we open it?"

"Not here," Anna said, running a hand along its top. "Back in the lab. I want controlled conditions so that whatever we find inside can be properly documented and further preserved."

"Just promise me I'll be there when you do."

She smiled, her dark eyes sparkling. "Deal."

"Thank God the looters missed this."

"I have," Anna said, placing a hand against his cheek.

After they shared a moment of triumph, the vault and its liberated contents were further photographed, every feature documented, every aspect recorded in meticulous detail.

"I still can't believe this," Roberto said as the camera shutter clicked again and again. "Where we are …"

"Neither can I. I'm afraid I'll wake up and find myself still on the plane on the way here."

"Looks like our Roman noble was everything you said he was."

"He believed with all his heart. Just imagine the risk he took. He may even have ended up facing death in the Colosseum. Nero would have declared him a traitor to Rome."

"So, our noble friend, in the midst of all the persecution the Christians were suffering, built this."

"Or before, perhaps. Paul came to Rome several years before the fire that Nero blamed on the Christian sect. But in any case, to have been so inspired, the noble may have heard Paul himself speak. How powerful those words must have been."

"How'd he manage to keep it hidden? This place, I mean."

Anna resumed her conjecture. "Well, suppose he instructs a select few of his most trusted slaves to dig through the floor of his house, in an out-of-the-way place, perhaps in a storeroom or an unused bedroom. He tells them it's a hidden cellar where food and wine can be kept cool and safe from thieves. He designs and builds the congregation chamber as his heart leads him to, as he believes God leads him to. He brings in rare and expensive red azarshahr travertine from Persia, stone the color of blood. He incorporates silver as a symbol of redemption, just as it was in the Jewish tabernacle.

He gives his secret passageway thirty-three steps leading downward, one for each year of Christ's life.

"Once it's finished and concealed by a false floor, he contacts Paul."

Roberto closed his eyes. "The apostle was *here,*" he repeated, still in awe. "I can't get over it. Right here! Just think ..."

"And the Christians of Rome met safely here until the place was destroyed. It must have finally been discovered, but as I said, why is there no historical record of that? Nero would have reveled in his discovery."

"I guess we know now that there was a cross up there," Roberto said, indicating the wall above the altar.

"I'd say so." Then her expression changed to puzzlement.

"What is it?"

"Well," she began, "if Nero's soldiers found the place, why didn't they *destroy* this room and not just bury it? The chamber was untouched until today, as far as we can tell. It's as if the door was sealed and the stairway was just ... hidden."

"The whole house above was leveled."

"It doesn't make sense. Why destroy the house so savagely but not this room? Sentiment?"

Roberto lifted the heavy marble rotas square back into place, pressed it flush, and brushed it with his hand.

"Good as new," he quipped.

"Everything goes to Milan with me in the morning," Anna said. "I'm not risking another theft before we can do a full analysis."

"Do we still meet for breakfast in the morning? Do I need to call the others?"

"No, let them sleep. I'll tell them at the café. We'll head

up to the lab after breakfast and get a start on these tomorrow afternoon."

They ascended the stairs, with the objects from the vault carefully wrapped and packed in Anna's gym bag. Once outside, Roberto pulled a datapad from his pocket and slid the camera's memory card into it. "I'm uploading the pictures to a folder on my computer back home," he said, pressing a few buttons. "I'm not taking any chances."

"Excellent," she said. "I'll call and get a security team to guard this entrance while we're away. As far as I know, there's nothing left to be plundered except the stone steps themselves and that inscription in the vault, but someone's sure to try to chisel those up, given half a chance."

"The chancellor and the board of regents are going to be beside themselves when they hear about this. What a find, *dottoressa*. You'll go down in history, like Carter and Carnarvon."

She wondered, finally allowing herself the luxury of considering the more personal aspects of the discovery. *How* will *they take it? What will this do for my program? Will they finally see me as worthy of their trust, their backing?*

She smiled faintly. "I don't care about all that. I just want to bring forgotten truths back to the world."

Four

Anna and her team gathered in a basement lab of the Museo Archeologico Milano, an aging yet vibrant institution housed in the sprawling chambers of an ancient former monastery. Among its treasures were some of the oldest artifacts unearthed in the region, including Bronze Age tools and weapons, Roman art and statuary, and farm equipment more than four thousand years old.

The basement lab was as secluded a venue as Anna or her students had experienced, made available to them by special arrangement of the university. Anna and her husband had both made good use of the facility through the years, and the staff knew them well. The place was secure and well supplied, and it provided the privacy she desired, especially at that moment.

Until she knew exactly what they had found, the world would be told nothing.

She sat at a sprawling worktable, upon which skeletal remains, pottery, works of art, and all manner of relics and remnants had been studied over the years. Behind her rose tall shelves stacked with artifacts, all tagged and categorized, some awaiting display. Old storage units of dark wood and black iron lined the other walls. The scent of great age permeated the air.

To her left stood Carlo Laneri, the museum's director of antiquities, his silver hair and tailored dark suit the very image of sophistication. His anticipation was evident in the childlike gleam in his aged eyes, and as Anna's final preparations unfolded, he assisted in any way he could, however small.

"How wonderful, Anna," he said. "How wonderful."

"I hope so, Carlo."

Her students seated in two tiers before her, she slipped her hands into a pair of cotton analysis gloves, adjusted the table's three lamps, and cracked open one of two reinforced transport containers next to the table. Various implements—probes, scalpels, hemostats, seizing tools, and tweezers, all of varied configurations—were arrayed within easy reach. Safety goggles waited alongside, should the use of a high-speed rotary tool prove necessary.

Her hair was up, out of the way. Her pink poplin shirt with its three-quarter sleeves and her beige capri pants had been chosen not only for comfort but for practicality—she wanted no distractions during the examination, whether from her clothes, her hair, or anything else.

First on her agenda was the travertine box. She lifted it free, placed it before her, and picked up a surgical steel probe.

"We'll carry out our initial analysis here," she said, making a final adjustment to the stool on which she sat. "Then, once the proper arrangements have been made, we'll disseminate the various artifacts to other labs for more specific study. Beth, I know you were wondering when we'll be going home …"

The girl perked up, a smile crossing her face.

"I expect we'll be back at Oldefield and in our classrooms by the end of the week."

"Thank you, professor," Beth said.

"Don't thank me yet," Anna warned with a bit of amusement. "You all have theses waiting for you."

The students looked up from their notepads and exchanged glances, laughing softly.

Anna pressed a button atop a small digital recorder and saw its tiny, green telltale wink to life.

"As I mentioned earlier," she began as everyone watched in rapt fascination, "this box, like the other items, was contained within a wall of the underground chamber, in a vault hidden behind the rotas square above the altar. It is composed of red travertine and appears to be in two parts, the box proper and a separate lid. The container is sealed with wax, which is unusual except when liquid contents are involved."

She began to draw the probe around the seam, scraping the dark wax free as the point dug more deeply with each pass.

"The wax is more supple than I would have expected," Anna noted. "It's coming away relatively easily. However, its great age is apparent in its color and texture."

Roberto snapped a few pictures as she continued her analysis. The jagged, minute shards of her scraping littered the tabletop, dark speckles against pale gray. Around the seam she went, digging away the seal, the years.

The sanctuary a world had known for two millennia.

"I think that will do it," she said, setting the probe aside. She picked up a sturdy blade and began to pry, loosening the lid further. Little by little, more gently than the stone warranted, she worked the lid free.

There was a soft hiss as air separated by fifty generations began to mingle.

"Hermetically sealed." Roberto smiled. "You were right."

"I'm surprised," Anna remarked, fascinated. "I've never seen anything like this before."

The seam opened in full, yielding to a further twist of the wide blade.

"Okay," the professor said, drawing a breath as she set the tool aside. "Here we go."

The room was as silent as a crypt as she gripped each end of the lid and slowly lifted it. Roberto and Laneri leaned in, almost crowding her. As the travertine top came away, light spilled into the box for the first time since Paul himself breathed and walked and spoke.

Anna's eyes fell upon the contents.

Scrolls, a number of them, rolled together and tied with a single ribbon of red silk. Beneath these rested another smaller leaf, facedown in the bottom of the box.

"Oh my," she whispered, handing the lid to Laneri. Her fingers trembling almost imperceptibly, she reached inside and lifted the fragile roll from its resting place. Roberto's shutter clicked wildly.

"Papyrus," she said, measuring the roll with a transparent rule. "Fourteen and one-quarter inches wide. In amazing condition. Still pliable … Very little of the brittleness one would expect, though its age is evident in its scent and color. Perhaps half a dozen leaves here."

Taking tools in hand, she carefully loosened the ribbon, slipped it off and set it into the box.

"Silk," she stated for the record. "Also still supple.

Brilliant red, about an inch and a half wide. No leaching of color into the papyrus."

Slowly, gently, her gloved fingers tested the flexibility of the papyri. Finding it safe, she began to unroll them, exposing the first few lines of black writing on the top leaf.

"Greek," she said. "This is in Greek, not Latin. Interesting …"

She began to read. She had barely finished the first line when a gasp closed her throat. Her eyes darted from word to word.

"Oh my … Oh my …"

"What is it, *dottoressa?*" Roberto asked. "What does it say?"

Anna took a few deep breaths. She read aloud, excitement clipping her words.

"So that you may walk in truth, worthy of the Father, and increase in the knowledge of God; I, Paul … " She stopped, the words hanging in her throat.

A murmur swept the room. Delight shone on everyone's faces.

"Paul," Anna said, her pulse racing.

Laneri clasped his hands. "An unknown writing of the apostle!"

"What did he say?" Roberto implored her.

She swallowed and went on, her tongue strangely dry. *"I, Paul, according to that truth, hereby set forth these words; that our Teacher, Jesus, whom we follow as the Christ, having been put to death on a cross by the—"*

She halted again, more abruptly. Puzzlement swept her features. The others waited, their gaze dancing between her stilled lips and the papyrus she held. Though she had gone silent, all could see that she continued to read, her focus darting from side to side, tracing the words.

Her eyes glistened like wet diamonds. Sparkling more and more with each moment.

The faces of her students, as one, reflected a great worry. They all knew her, knew her well. But what they saw at that moment was something they had never seen before.

A hardness. A horror.

Anna quickly lowered the top of the scroll and looked away, trying very hard to contain herself. A single tear coursed down her cheek, carrying a faint streak of mascara with it.

"You're all dismissed," she said abruptly, in a tone verging on harshness. She spoke the words as if, at any moment, she would no longer have a voice.

Neil shook his head. "But, professor—"

"Later, Mr. Meyer."

"Where do we go?" he pressed.

"I'm sure you'll think of something."

Beth and Craig exchanged puzzled glances as they rose from their seats, then descended the few steps to floor level. Roberto stepped closer to Anna.

"*Dottoressa,*" he began, "I don't understand—"

"You, too," she said, not meeting his eyes. With a hastened glance, she caught the confusion on all their faces. "We'll discuss this later."

"Okay, professor," Beth said as they all moved toward the door.

"Roberto," Anna called after him. He paused and turned, anticipating something of an explanation. Instead, she held her hand out. "I need your camera, please."

He approached, holding it out to her. Without looking up, she took it from him. He paused for a moment, looking at her, then turned and followed the others.

"Anna," Laneri said, concerned about her sudden change of demeanor, "what is it? What does it say?"

She placed the scrolls back into the box and replaced the lid.

"Carlo," she said, removing the camera's memory card, "I'll tell you when I can. I promise. For now, I need some time."

"Shall we—"

"Alone," she emphasized. "Please."

"Very well," he said after a weighty pause, his brow furrowed. Then, with a subtle nod, he departed the lab, closing the door behind him. Anna tore away her gloves, placed both hands on the box, closed her eyes, and prayed.

Why? she demanded. *Why this? Why now?*

Why me?

She sat there for almost half an hour, almost unmoving, staring at the box. The red stone warmed beneath her hands. Gathering a sense of composure, she pulled her phone from a cargo pocket, scrolled through the directory, and selected a number.

She pressed the button.

No signal, the screen read.

I'm in the basement, she remembered, and headed for the door.

◆◆◆

Darkness lay beyond window glass as Dean Mercer drifted half in and half out of sleep, sporadically sliding his arms and legs within the soothing sheets of his bed. His vacation had arrived at last—weeks to spend with his wife, to visit the grandchildren, and to take care of things too long neglected—so he hadn't set his alarm clock. The time had finally come to work on the oak-and-walnut chess set he had begun in his workshop and laid aside the year before. Tending to the garden, painting the gazebo, and laying new stone for the fishpond—all these things would be seen to. Leisurely and enjoyably.

The phone rang, jarring him from a sound sleep, his heart racing. His wife prodded him, and he awoke just enough to reach out for the phone and find the receiver.

"Hello?" he said, the word a bit slurred.

"Dean Mercer," came a familiar voice, "it's Anna Meridian. I'm very sorry to be calling you so early."

Mercer's eyes found the bedside clock and focused just well enough.

"Four twenty," he said. "What's wrong, Anna?"

"The find I told you about … There's a complication. I need you to come to Milan. Right away."

"Milan? What is it? What's wrong?"

"I'd rather not tell you over the phone. You have to see this for yourself, and there's no way they'll ever let it out of the country. No one even knows but me."

Mercer sat up, switched on a small diffused lamp, and rubbed his face. "You can't just tell me?"

"No," she insisted. "I can't. You have to see this. I need you here. I don't know what to do."

"I've never heard those words from you, Anna."

There was a long pause. Too long.

"I've … never unearthed something that could destroy the world."

At that, Mercer woke to full awareness. "What?"

"You'll understand when you get here."

"The Museo Archeologico?" he asked. "Is Carlo not there?"

"He's here," she said, her voice unsure. "But this …"

Mercer waited. No other words came.

"All right, Anna," he said. "I'll arrange a flight, and see you as soon as I can."

As the call ended, Mercer turned to find his wife looking at him, her eyes sleepy, her head resting against her pillow.

"Milan, Albert?" she asked.

"Milan."

"Good." She smiled gently as she rolled over. "You promised me an Italian vacation seven years ago."

◆ ◆ ◆

Roberto, Beth, and the others sat in the museum cafeteria, trying to sort things out. They had seen their instructor joyous, angry, worried, overwrought, even playful at times. But they had never seen her like this. The woman they knew would never cast them out of the lab so abruptly.

"I don't get it," Craig said, his tone more of anger than concern. "What's the deal? What could have been on those scrolls that would have made her flip out like that? One second she was fine; the next … she's Ms. Hyde."

"I wouldn't go that far," Beth said. "But something sure upset her. She was crying."

"No, she wasn't," said Craig.

"Yes, she was. I saw her."

Roberto shook his head. "It couldn't have been simple disappointment. She wouldn't have reacted that way. Sure, when we discovered the vault in the wall, she was as excited as I've ever seen her. She got her hopes up. We all did. But whatever she read on that papyrus went way beyond disappointment."

"She said 'I, Paul' when she read it," Beth recalled. "Mr. Laneri even repeated it. Sure looked to me like she'd found something Paul wrote."

"So why did she react that way?" Craig asked. "She should have been dancing around the room."

"Maybe Paul wrote something she didn't like," Roberto offered.

Neil disagreed. "Like what? Anything he could have written would have thrilled her. I mean, we're talking *Paul* here. That doesn't make any sense."

His mind working the possibilities, Roberto rose and crossed to the coffeemaker, where he refilled his cup. "I don't know," he said.

"Could it have had something to do with her husband?" Beth wondered. "The only time I've ever seen her anywhere near that upset was on their anniversary last year. It would have been their sixteenth."

"Maybe," Roberto nodded. "But I can't imagine how it would have."

"Looked worse than that to me," Neil said, returning

from a trip to the restroom, twirling the straw in the soft drink he carried.

"What do you mean?" Beth asked.

"Didn't you see? She wasn't just upset. She was scared to death."

◆◆◆

Anna smiled politely at the guard as he led her into the small reinforced room. Its walls gleamed with brazen metal.

"This will be your unit," he said, pointing to a numbered metal door. He held out his hand. "And this is your key."

She took it from him. "Thank you."

"Ring the buzzer when you're done," the man said, "and we'll let you out."

He left, sealing the room behind him. She was alone and unobserved.

Why? she repeated for the hundredth time. The question haunted her.

She inserted the key and gave it a twist. The small square door opened. She reached in, withdrew a metal box with a hinged top, and placed it on a nearby table.

All my life, I've been dedicated to the truth.

Reaching into her gym bag, she took hold of the scrolls, now sealed inside a tube of tough white plastic. She checked again to make sure the end caps were screwed down tightly, then held it in her hand, staring at it, brooding over the consequences of its contents becoming known.

After lining the metal box with a suitable cushion of rumpled fabric, she gently lowered the tube into it, followed by the three goblets, their spices and gold sealed in ziplock bags. Then she slid the box back into the wall, closed the numbered door, and locked it. She dropped the key into a zippered inner pocket of her purse, sealed it, and hefted the strap of the much lighter bag back onto her shoulder.

She stood for a moment, her thoughts distant, her eyes sightlessly fixed on the room's single entrance.

Beyond it, the entire world had changed.

Five

Dean Mercer and his wife stepped through the portal of the airline boarding ramp and emerged into the passenger lounge of Milan's Linate International Airport. He scanned the crowd, looking at the faces of people reuniting after varied periods of separation.

"Was she meeting us here?" Mary Mercer asked, checking her watch. "Or out in the concourse?"

"Right here, I believe," the dean replied, his gaze still sweeping ahead. Then he saw the lovely face he had been seeking. She was standing at a distance, her lips red and full as ever, her eyes sparkling still, but they now betrayed an inner darkness, a bitterness, a pain.

"There she is," he said, leading his wife forward. As they met, he set his briefcase on the floor.

"Anna." He smiled as she reached out and hugged him. He held her as a parent would hold a child, easing, for that moment, her yet unrevealed burden.

"I'm so glad you're here," she said. "I trust no one else with this."

She turned to hug his wife, who smiled widely. "It's so nice to see you again, Anna. It's been so long."

"Lovely to see you again, Mary. Welcome to Italy."

"Come," the dean said, indicating the direction of the baggage pickup. "We'll get out of here and discuss things once we're on the road."

The night sky was filled with stars, though a few low clouds partly obscured the rising moon. Mercer carried a suitcase in one hand and his briefcase in the other as Anna led the couple across the loading zone to her waiting rental car.

"It wasn't as hard to find a parking place as I thought it would be," she said, pressing a button on her key fob. The car replied with a cheerful chirp, a flash of its lights, and a pop of the trunk. "I hope you had a good flight."

"It was," Mercer commented as he placed his bag next to Anna's purple gym bag and then closed the trunk. "Long, but the company was pleasant."

"Indeed it was," his wife agreed.

"But I will say I'm happy to finally be here," he admitted. "That's quite a stretch just to be sitting."

"I hope you'll still feel happy to be here an hour from now," Anna teased.

In minutes the car was pulling onto the A51, headed north. Traffic, as it always was in the late evening, was light.

"I told you of our initial find," Anna said, her eyes on the road ahead.

"Yes," Mercer called from the back seat. "But you gave precious few details."

"It's an underground chamber, beneath the foundation of a Roman villa. Accessed by steps of red travertine. I told you that much."

"Yes."

"Well," she went on, "we discovered conclusive proof that

the site was used by the apostle Paul during the time of Nero, during his first years in Rome. It was the first permanent church there, and the only one we're sure Paul himself preached in. The early Christians of Rome worshipped in their homes, especially predating Paul's arrival."

The dean placed a hand on his forehead. "Oh, my dear … what a discovery! This will change the history books. There has been no sign of whatever was looted?"

"None that I've seen," Anna said. "But it doesn't matter."

"Why not?"

"Because they missed the site's prime artifacts. There was a vault in the wall, behind the rotas square. Its contents were untouched and in remarkably good condition."

"*Too* good?" the dean wondered. "Do you suppose …?"

"What do you mean?"

"Could these things have been planted by the looters?"

Anna paused to consider the possibility. She was ashamed that she hadn't thought of it before, even though she had been rattled.

"I don't know. I don't think so. The plaster seal around the square was original, I'm sure of it. Fresh plaster less than a day old couldn't have cured that much. I'm certain I'd have noticed. It was brittle and very dry and carried the room's original paint."

"Very well," Mercer replied.

"I wish they *were* forgeries," she said. "In fact, I wish we could prove as much, even if we know it isn't true."

He was surprised by the statement. "Why, Anna?"

She paused for a moment, choosing her words carefully.

"You'll understand when you see them," she said. "Scrolls,

Albert. In Greek, on papyrus. And the situation … the place in which they were found argues very strongly for their authenticity."

The old man's eyes opened wide. He looked at his wife, who shared his astonishment. As he ran a hand through his snow-streaked hair, his mind flooded with images of lost gospels and exciting new histories.

"I didn't read more than the first few lines," Anna went on, "and there were half a dozen leaves altogether. But what he wrote just …"

She went silent, a prolonged cleansing breath her only utterance. Mercer could see the crushing weight pressing upon her and longed to relieve, to share, to remove the yoke she bore.

"Show me," he said gently. "*Then* we'll discuss it."

They entered Anna's darkened hotel room. Located a stone's throw from the museum, the colorful building dated to the late seventeenth century and had once housed, in different eras, a sanatorium, a fruit market, and the office of a city official ultimately convicted and executed for arranging the deaths of his political enemies.

She switched on a table lamp. Mercer, having dropped off his very tired wife and his luggage in another room on the same floor, took a seat at the end of the sofa and waited as Anna retrieved the mysterious menace that had brought him more than four thousand miles.

She set her gym bag on the bed and unzipped it.

"I've had these in a safe-deposit box since just after I called you," she said, "but I had to take them out before the bank closed for the day. I left the other artifacts there. These go back as soon as we've run our tests."

He was puzzled. "Why not just place them in the museum's storeroom? It's secure."

"Not secure enough," she said. "I gave them the stone box the items were in and watched as they locked it up. As far as they know, everything's still in it. But given the nature of … well, see for yourself."

She pulled the capped tube from the bag, unscrewed one end, and gently slid the scrolls out. She then brought them into the light and placed them, still heavily curled, on the table before him.

"These were tied with a red silk ribbon," she said. "All but one, which lay flat under them. It's here too."

"Greek, yes," he noted, adjusting his glasses. "Fine papyrus … amazing condition. Skillful penmanship. Whoever wrote this, wrote often."

He began to read.

"So that you may walk in truth, worthy of the Father, and increase in the knowledge of God; I, Paul, according to that truth, hereby set forth these words; that our Teacher, Jesus whom we follow as the Christ, having been put to death on a cross by the Romans, following the insistence of the Sanhedrin, was not the Messiah spoken of in the Scriptures—"

He stopped and looked up at her. Her expression spoke of the agonizing struggle she had faced alone since reading the words herself.

"Now I understand," he said gravely. Then he continued.

"—that we twelve knowingly falsified his emergence from the tomb, so that the hope that lived in the eyes of our brethren, his followers, would not be extinguished, that the love our Teacher spread among us would continue, kindled by faith in the Father—"

He paused, removing his glasses and bowing his head.

"I know," Anna said, placing her hand on his. "I can't believe it either. I had to stop reading too. But after a time I forced myself to finish. I looked over all six scrolls in the lab before I called you."

"Tell me what's here," Mercer said, his voice breaking slightly. "I'd really rather not …"

"Okay," she said, taking up the Pauline leaf. "They all say pretty much the same thing, with minor variations and differences in emphasis. I'll paraphrase. It says that James, before he became a follower himself, inadvertently told the original twelve apostles that he and his brother Jesus, as young men, had repeatedly stolen bread and wine while working as stone masons in Sepphoris. The apostles had a hard time believing such a story about the man they thought they knew, whom they believed was sinless, so they trusted their own experience with their Teacher and reserved judgment.

"Then, word reached them, through a man who had lived in Sepphoris and had known of Jesus' work there, that …" She paused, clearly hating her own words. "He said that Jesus, about ten years earlier, had been no stranger to a woman of the evening named Desida, whose favors this witness had also shared. He commented that he had seen Jesus in her company on a few occasions and that the visits were hardly innocent. The woman, he said, had even mentioned just after one such visit that she had a particular fondness for the prowess of youth.

"The apostles wanted to deny the claim completely, but given James's earlier account about the bread and the specifics of the witness's story, they found themselves doubting. Judas even paid the man for his silence, out of the apostles' treasury. They began to realize that they were following the *wrong* man … that Jesus *wasn't* in fact the Messiah they'd been waiting for."

"Inconceivable," Mercer said, shaking his head. "What did James have to say about the man's claim, I wonder?"

"Paul addressed that. He said that James wouldn't speak of it at all, not even to deny it."

"I can't blame him. What an accusation to make."

"It gets worse."

"It can't possibly, Anna."

"It does." She continued scanning the leaf as she spoke, her tone one of sorrow. "According to this, on the Sunday morning after the crucifixion, when the women left for the tomb, Philip, Simon, and someone Paul doesn't name went ahead of them. They found the body of Jesus right where Joseph had laid it. Following a plan a few of the apostles had devised, they hid the body in a second concealed chamber inside the tomb and quickly left, unseen. When the women arrived, they found the tomb open and Jesus apparently gone. In the confusion that followed, the men removed the body, took it to a secluded place, and buried it. Only later, once the wheels had been set in motion and a religion had been born, did the perpetrators tell their brothers the whole story. And at that point, the Twelve swore themselves to secrecy on pain of death."

"I can't believe it. I just can't. I won't."

"I know," Anna said, placing the papyri back on the table before him. "I can't either. It makes no sense. There are seemingly too many logical flaws I haven't worked through yet. But these documents were in that vault, Albert. They present themselves as confessions of almost half the apostles, and of Paul, all echoing the same basic story. They say they had dozens of meetings after the crucifixion, at which they planned their strategies. Paul was let in on the secret only after his missionary journeys had begun."

"But what about *his* conversion? Why would he suddenly go from persecuting Christians to becoming one of them if he hadn't seen the risen Christ, as the Bible says he did?"

"This says he didn't convert any more dramatically than anyone else. There was no vision on the road to Damascus, but somehow the story got started, and Paul just never denied it. The faith had swept like wildfire, and the apostles just couldn't bring themselves to let the dream die, so they continued this elaborate hoax … and they've fooled the world for two thousand years."

A distressed Mercer compared the leaves. "Wait a minute. The handwriting is identical on all of these."

"They're all signed by someone who refers to himself only as 'the scribe of the apostles,'" she noted. "Whoever that was. I doubt it was Paul himself, given the self-admitted poor quality of his own handwriting. Presumably, if they're genuine, they were dictated by others and written down by the same man. That wouldn't be all that unusual."

"So, we're to believe there was some clandestine meeting of the Twelve prior to Paul's going to Rome at which they unburdened themselves as this 'scribe' recorded their confessions?"

"Yes. According to these, yes."

"The smaller leaf," Mercer wondered aloud. "The one that wasn't rolled up with the others. What does it say?"

"That these aren't *all* the confessions. The other seven are still out there, buried in a separate location to ensure that at least some would survive."

"You mean there's *another* time bomb out there waiting to go off?"

"Yes."

"Buried where?"

"Pompeii," Anna said. "The papyrus gives the specific location, inside a specific house. And, if memory serves, that particular location is now easily accessible to anyone who knows where to dig."

"If they were so dedicated to perpetuating this lie, why in the world would they write this stuff down, then leave the scrolls where they could be found?"

"They unburdened themselves. Ritually, perhaps. Maybe they felt they could find forgiveness for the deception if they confessed, even if the confessions were hidden away. Who knows? I don't."

"You've always been good at such speculation, Anna. Despite my cautions."

"Not this time. I can't begin to get inside these men's heads."

"So they *died* for this massive lie?"

"Maybe. Guilt has driven many to suicide. Perhaps after years had passed and the guilt had compounded to a lethal point, they *wanted* to be captured and put to death. I don't know."

Mercer buried his face in his hands.

"This is a nightmare," he said.

Anna sat beside him on the sofa, visibly fighting tears. "So much of the world defines itself by its Christian faith, including me. It isn't just what we believe, it's *who we are*. If these confessions are true, then … who are we? Who am I?"

"Perhaps they're *not* true," Mercer said, drawing a deep breath, gathering his wits. "It's most reasonable that they not be. We mustn't panic. If these are forgeries, as they must be, then we reveal them as such, based on scientific data. They'll do no more damage than any of the Gnostic gospels ever did."

"I pray they're lies," she said with fearful determination. "I've been on my knees since I found them, begging God to prove these false. I pray they're just pieces of worthless, artificially aged ink and paper, or even ancient forgeries placed in that vault two thousand years ago. I don't know how such phony documents could have been planted there, but I pray they did."

"So do I, Anna. Even if they're old, they're just old. That doesn't make them true."

Staring across the room, she wrapped her arms around herself. "I feel cold," she said.

She leaned against him, and he placed his arm around her. He remembered another time, on another sofa, when he had comforted her in just such a manner, a time when her life had been wrenched from its foundation by falling rock.

"Have faith, my dear," he said. "We'll come to understand."

"It makes no sense," she said, her tone both miserable and angry. "You can't just yank a few threads out of a tapestry this way, not when there are so many proven elements in the whole. Christianity is the most intricate and tightly woven faith in the history of man. From the hundreds of fulfilled prophesies and ramifications, to the matching eyewitness accounts, to the sudden conversion of a dozen craven cowards into men willing to die horrible deaths for their faith ... This just can't be."

She covered her face, took a deep breath, and went on. "I don't know why this has shaken me so much. Maybe it's that room ... being there. I could *feel* Paul. Feel his presence, as if I'd only missed him by moments, not millennia. And for these to have been there, where no one but he and his most trusted should have known about them ... I'm trying to press my feelings down, to look at all this scientifically and with reason, but ..."

Mercer nodded. "A very powerful thing, such a presence. I can understand your struggle, my dear. But perhaps the documents indeed *are* fabrications. Their content suggests as much, despite the location where they were found. We can run initial tests at the museum and have some concrete facts before us fairly quickly. But one thing is sure ... No one gets wind of any of this until we know for certain whether the apostles authored these. Only *then* do we tell the world."

"If they prove authentic," Anna worried, "should we? Why should we tell anyone? What would it accomplish? Hundreds of millions of lives worldwide would be destroyed, Albert."

"If it's the truth," he replied softly, "the truth must live."

"And two days ago, I'd have agreed with you. All my professional life I've been dedicated to the truth. I've fought those who try to twist history to suit their own purposes. But this is *personal.* Jesus isn't just some long-dead historical figure. He's *alive.* Now. And he's more dear to us than any husband or wife or child. If you found evidence that your own mother had walked the streets and had picked up sailors on liberty nights, would you tell the world, just for the sake of truth?"

Mercer nodded, appreciating her point. "An ethical challenge, yes. But if these confessions are verified … if we prove to our own satisfaction that they *are* true, *then* we'll worry about whether to release them. We must trust God and remember that he is in control, even through such trials."

"Is he?" she wondered. "If these confessions are true, it will change everything. If we can't trust the Bible, how do we know God's even up there?"

"Holy Scripture far predates the New Testament, Anna," Mercer reminded her. "Archaeological evidence has confirmed so much of the Old Testament that very little of its history remains in doubt, however extraordinary. You know that. You unearthed some of it. So did Samuel."

"History is so much easier," she said in soft breaths. "It's done. It's over. You pick up a book long after the fact and learn from the mistakes of others. You don't go out with a shovel and risk exposing the world to something better left buried."

"Would you really have preferred never to have picked up that shovel?" he asked.

She remembered her husband and the passion he had, the

passion for a living, tangible past that had drawn her to him and to his vocation, irresistibly and forever.

"No."

"There is purpose in all things. We're too close to see it, but with distance comes clarity."

"So, God is in control … even if it doesn't seem that way."

"He is indeed," Mercer said. "One need only look as far as the modern rebirth of Israel to see proof of that. It was nothing short of miraculous. The entire history of her people, even through their periods of exile, speaks loudly of his dominion, and his love."

He felt the sheer exhaustion in her.

"Have you slept since you got to Italy?"

A single burst of quiet laughter escaped her lips.

"Not enough," she confessed. "Between the find and the adrenaline …"

"No wonder you're overwrought," the man comforted her. "It's well after two, my dear. Get some sleep. Trust that all will be well. Mary and I will be right down the hall. The documents aren't going anywhere … We can begin the tests tomorrow afternoon, after you've had time to rest and get your legs back under you."

"I'm so glad you came."

"You are so very like my daughter," the elderly man said, smiling. "And just as I am of her, I'm so very proud of you." He kissed her on the forehead.

Anna sat up, took a cleansing breath, and looked over at the scrolls.

"I wish I'd never found them."

"All things happen for a purpose," Mercer said. "Where

these writings are concerned, we just have to sort out what that purpose is."

◆ ◆ ◆

Anna awoke to find the sunlight streaming through the curtains and into her face. The sun was high, much higher than her groggy mind thought it should be.

What? How late did I sleep?

She looked over at the clock, forcing her eyes into focus. Slowly, stubbornly, the red, glowing blur took form. *Eleven fifteen.*

Mercer hadn't called. No one had called.

She fought to shake off her confusion, to awaken.

Didn't I set the alarm? I was sure I did!

She sat up and ran her fingers through her sleep-mussed chestnut mane, letting life and consciousness take hold once more.

The confessions.

It all came flooding back in a rush.

Please let me have dreamed that.

But no, she knew. It was real.

She glanced over at the closet, where the scrolls rested inside her purple bag.

The door was open.

I thought I closed that!

She flipped the covers away and swung her legs over the side of the bed. The wood plank floor was cold against her bare feet. She hurried to the closet, her long nightgown flowing behind her, and looked down at the inside floor.

Her shoes were there, untouched.

Her bag was not.

No!

With no thought of her intimate attire, Anna rushed barefoot from the room and down the hall to the Mercers' room. She pounded on the door, trying very hard not to panic.

"Albert!" she cried.

The door opened. Mrs. Mercer stood before her, a puzzled expression on her face.

"What is it, dear?" she asked. "Is something wrong?"

Anna pushed into the room. "Where's the dean? Is he—?"

Dean Mercer emerged from the bathroom, his face half covered in shaving cream.

"I'm here, Anna," he said, concern on his face.

"The scrolls," she said breathlessly. "My bag … They're gone!"

"Oh," Mercer said, his demeanor relaxing. "I'm sorry. It's here, my dear."

"Why? How? My door was locked."

"This morning, very early, I became concerned about the safety of the artifacts. If anyone had learned of them, I was afraid they might easily track them to your room. Since our friend Raphael had already made an appearance at the dig site, I feared he might be keeping tabs on you. So, when I went out for the morning paper, I saw the maid had opened your door and was exchanging the toiletries in your bathroom. I began to wake you, but you were sleeping so soundly, you didn't stir. I checked to make sure the scrolls were still there, then I thought it might be wise to put a little distance between you and them. I took your bag and brought it here, where it's more securely hidden."

Anna breathed easier. "Oh."

"Would you like to get dressed, dear?" Mrs. Mercer asked.

"Yes," Anna said, realizing her present state of dress and folding her arms across her chest. "I was upset, and ..."

Mrs. Mercer smiled at her, as did the dean.

"You get dressed, and we'll find a nice lunch somewhere," he said. "Then we'll go to the museum and start our analysis."

"Okay," Anna agreed. "Give me about twenty minutes."

She walked briskly back to her room and heard the Mercers' door close behind her.

I guess that makes sense, protecting the scrolls ...

Still, she felt a nagging doubt and scolded herself for not trusting this man who, time and again, had proven himself to her. A man with whom she had felt safe sharing such a crucial confidence.

And then she grew angry with herself for allowing the wretched scrolls to influence her confidence, her judgment, her faith.

Let's just get this over with!

Anna stood at the dresser mirror, her mind racing as she finished getting ready. Her hands were on autopilot as they pulled her thick hair back, fixing it into a ponytail with a red scrunchie.

Suppose they are *true. What happens then?*

She dreaded the very thought, more determined than ever to proceed as if the documents were hoaxes.

If you're real, you're gonna have to prove it to me—and it won't be easy.

The mascara wand tickled along and between her lashes, leaving behind a dark and feathery trail, a dramatic amplification of her natural beauty.

How can they be genuine? There are a thousand logical and historical proofs supporting the Christian faith!

A few rapid strokes of a wide, soft brush across her cheeks left shimmering, ruddy traces of color, further defining her already striking contours.

Based on statistics alone, the odds of any one man fulfilling so many established prophecies in a single lifetime are beyond astronomical.

She twisted a tube of lipstick, bringing its deep shade out of hiding. In a few smooth motions she glided the rich, scented color down and across, coating her full lips. They glistened in the light.

What about all the prophecies fulfilled beyond Jesus' control, incontestably written hundreds of years before his birth?

She closed the tube, dropped it into her purse, and reached for a small jewelry box. She raised the velvet lid. A sparkle shone inside.

What about the prophecies of his death by a form of execution still to be invented? The specific piercing of his hands and feet? The guards casting lots for his garments? His death alongside two other men, whose legs were broken as they hung there, while his weren't?

She slipped a fragile silver chain around her neck, from

which dangled a little gleaming cross of silver, reminiscent of the cross at the dig site. Her fingers, reaching behind her neck, worked the tiny clasp with practiced precision.

Even the place of his birth, his lineage, and his betrayal for thirty pieces of silver?

She slipped the posts of a pair of small, delicate hoop earrings through the piercings in her lobes and fixed them in place. They had been her mother's.

All this is to be rendered meaningless by a few leaves of papyrus?

A dab of perfume, a final tug at her bangs. Then, meeting her own gaze in the mirror, a flash struck as she recalled Mercer's question of the night before.

"You mean there's another *time bomb out there waiting to go off?"*

Anna reached into her purse for her phone. Pressing a speed-dial button she had pressed many times before, she heard only one ring, followed by a welcome voice.

"Anna?" asked Jack Dyson. "Hey, how's Italy?"

"Jack, I need you."

"Be still, my heart. You want to clarify that a little?"

She smiled, seeing in her mind his mischievous grin. "Behave, now. What have you heard about the dig at Rome?"

"Only that you made the find of the century. Paul's church. Outstanding! It's all anyone at the university's talking about. No way they'll pull the plug now. Schools everywhere are going to want you. Good going, girl."

"Nothing else?"

"Like what?"

"You tell me."

"No," he said. "That's all I've heard."

"Okay. Well, to fill you in a little, Dean Mercer's here with me now. We've got to run tests on some artifacts unearthed at the site, and that's got me tied up. But I need a favor from you. I need you to go to Pompeii."

"When?"

"As soon as possible. You can get a connecting flight here in Milan … I'll need to fill you in, in person."

"I can be there in a couple of days or so," Jack said. "I have business to wrap up on this end. What's in Pompeii?"

"Let's just say you're my personal bomb squad."

"Come again?"

She gave him the barest basics, telling him only that a further relic was indicated as having been buried there. As the call ended, she looked into the mirror and found herself looking back, lovely and ready to face the world.

"Huh," she whispered.

She had no memory of putting on her makeup.

The museum lab had been sealed. A disgruntled Laneri stood outside, complaining to a museum staffer and taking occasional peeks through the door's small rectangular window.

For two days Anna, Dean Mercer, and Roberto had carried out a battery of tests on one of the scrolls, doing all the museum's equipment would allow so as not to reveal to the outside world the focus of their analysis. Anna, after careful consideration, had decided to take the grad student into her confidence and had invited him to join her and the Mercers for lunch before the tests began. His acceptance of the issue at hand had been as professional as she could have hoped for, though the young man's concern about the implications for his own faith, and that of others, had been evident.

"The Raman spectroscopy results are in," Mercer said, studying a computer display. Not far across the room stood the analyzer itself, mounted atop a mobile stand.

"What's the verdict?" Anna asked, studying a sample of papyrus under a microscope.

"The ink is carbon based. Soot, as was common with ancient inks, bound with a gum adhesive. No metal-gallic constituent. That dates it prior to medieval times."

"It also possibly dates it to the first century," Anna said, her displeasure evident in her sarcastic tone. "Why couldn't it have been India ink? Or even ballpoint?"

"Several tests yet to go," Mercer reminded her. "The transmission electron microscopy data won't be back until Friday."

Anna focused the microscope and continued studying the structure of the paper. "No visual sign of pigments. The chemical tests gave no indication of sodium hydroxide or any other substance having been used to age the material artificially. Looks for all the world like genuine papyrus from the era."

"I think it is," said Roberto, entering from another room and holding a printout. "The MSI results match those of confirmed ancient papyrus samples. I checked through the museum's catalog and found a Roman sample from the first century that matches exactly. They could even have been made at the same time, in the same place."

Under normal circumstances, Anna would have considered multispectral imaging almost conclusive. But not now.

You're gonna have to prove it to me.

"You ran every wavelength?" she asked.

"Yes, as you asked," he said. "Even those that didn't strictly apply."

With every result they got, the evidence for authenticity mounted. Anna and Mercer did little to hide their disappointment, holding out hope that, ultimately, the documents would be proven false. Anna prayed continually, fearing for the first time in her career that she might have unearthed a genuine article.

Please, Lord …

"When do we get the AMS results?" she asked. Another lab, possessing carbon-dating equipment the museum lacked, had been sent a small piece of the papyrus. The lab hadn't been told of its origin, or of the nature of the writings in question.

Mercer checked his watch. "The radiocarbon dating lab promised they'd have something for us by six. That's just over half an hour from now."

The minutes ticked past slowly. Too slowly. Anna and the others knew the carbon dating might be their last hope of proving the papyri too recent to be genuine, though hopes of that weren't flaring as brightly as they had the day before.

It can't be true … please!

"What if it's real?" Roberto asked as they sat together, still sealed within the lab. "What do we do? How do we tell the world that Jesus was a fake?"

"He wasn't a fake," Anna insisted. "Lies have been written for as long as men have walked the earth."

"It may not matter if they're lies," Roberto pointed out. "The world wants to believe that Christ was just a man, if he existed at all. Look at the staggering popularity of *The Da Vinci Code.* And all the attention the Gospel of Judas got back when it was released. The world loves this stuff. If you want to make money, slam Christ."

"Sadly, he's right," Mercer said. "Every year newspapers run stories questioning the Christian faith, and they usually do it on Easter, when believers are most focused on the resurrection. They never write such things regarding Islam or Buddhism. Science is always trying to explain away the miracles of the Bible, claiming that the Red Sea was parted by natural winds or that the plagues of Egypt were caused by fungus in the grain storehouses. Even something as absurd as claiming that Jesus walked on ice, not water."

"Stands to reason they'd say as much," Anna sighed. "All the faithful were promised was that the world would hate them, because it hated him first."

"True enough. The unbelieving will embrace these confessions like nothing that came before them. It won't matter if reams of historical and statistical evidence support the assertion that Christ was who he said he was. If they can point to supposed confessions from the apostles stating they made the whole thing up—"

"They'll use it as a battering ram," she said, completing the thought. "How will the believers maintain their faith in the face of that? Can they?"

"Faith is far more than fact," Mercer said. "It is also

embodied in things *not* seen. In things one cannot catalog or quantify."

"I understand that, Albert. But knowing that and *believing* it are two different things."

"If the documents are true, we must share them with the world," Mercer emphasized. "It isn't our place to conceal such truth. All our lives we've devoted ourselves to the dissemination of genuine knowledge, however painful or inconvenient doing so might be."

"Inconvenient?" Anna asked. "This would go *way* beyond inconvenient! I say again, do we have the right to take it upon ourselves to destroy so many lives? Can the Christian church stand up to a seeming overwhelming amount of contradicting evidence? Even if some question remains, will we be dealing a blow that ultimately will be fatal? How will *my* faith fare? Or yours? Or Roberto's?"

The phone rang. Mercer looked at his watch.

"I guess we're about to find out."

He walked over and picked up the receiver. Whatever was said was brief and to the point. He thanked the lab for their effort, hung up, and returned to where the professor and the grad student breathlessly waited.

"They got a solid date range," Mercer said austerely. "AD thirty to ninety."

Anna closed her eyes. Roberto rose from his stool and walked into the other room, from which soon came the loud crash of something forcefully striking the floor.

Mercer picked up the papyrus Anna had been examining under the microscope and considered it for a long moment before setting it down.

The phone rang again. And rang. And rang. Roberto emerged from the side room and apathetically crossed to the phone.

"Laboratorio," he answered. He listened. A look of surprise and alarm crossed his face.

Anna looked up.

"What is it?" she asked. "Who is it?"

"It's the press," he said, stunned. "*Il Giorno*. They want your comment on the confession of the apostle Peter."

Anna's heart stopped. In a panic she hurled herself at her purple gym bag resting on the worktable, almost knocking Mercer off his feet as she swept past him. Roughly pulling the papyri out of the bag and free of their protective tube, she rifled through them.

"Paul," she read aloud. "Philip. Matthew. Thomas. James …"

Her eyes went wide.

The leaf bearing Peter's name was missing.

Dyson again looked at his watch. His layover at Kennedy International was well into its second hour, with the promise of two more to come. The trip from his arrival gate at Terminal 7 to Terminal 1, where he now waited, had been an endurance test, thanks to a temporarily inoperative interterminal travel system. What should have been a comfortable ten-minute ride had become a tiring forty-five-minute walk, and his feet had made their protest known.

He sipped coffee in a small café, passing the time by reading a paper, watching a news channel on one of several wall-mounted televisions in the terminal, and glancing at the arrivals-and-departures board. His Alitalia flight would be on time, it still said, though delays had a knack for prying their way into the schedule even at the last minute.

I wouldn't do this for anyone but you, Anna.

Finishing that section of the paper, Dyson considered doing the crossword puzzle. It had been a while since he had worked on one, and as he scanned the clues, sizing up its relative difficulty, he figured he would give it a shot.

As he opened his briefcase and fished for a pen, words spilling from the television speaker caught his ear.

"Shocking news out of Rome—"

He looked up. As the woman on the screen read from a teleprompter, a level of astonishment became woven into her voice while she herself became aware of news for the first time.

"An ancient document verified as having been written by the scribe of the apostle Peter, unearthed in what may have been the first church in Rome, is purportedly a confession that the resurrection of Jesus was a hoax carried out by the apostles themselves—"

So what else is new? Dyson scoffed, not surprised in the least. *No wonder you didn't tell me, Anna.*

Not even he had ever believed. Out of respect for her faith, he had remained silent on the issue, changing the subject whenever religion came up, as it often did. He didn't want to see her hurt, ever, in any way, and wanted even less to be the cause of that pain. He knew what her faith meant to her, and at times he wished he could share in it.

He loved her. He had from the moment he had laid eyes on her.

"Initial tests, conducted in Switzerland, have verified the document as authentic. The archaeologist who made the discovery, Dr. Anna Meridian, an American, is at Milan's Museum of Archaeology, working to further verify the papyrus. If these tests all confirm its authenticity, the ramifications of the find, for Christians worldwide, could be catastrophic. Our Roger Stine is standing by at the Vatican …"

An image of St. Peter's Square appeared, filled to capacity with frightened Catholics hoping for assurance from the pope. It was a sea of turmoil and wailing, agony and fear, with uncounted hands and rosaries raised to the heavens.

"This is Roger Stine, reporting from Rome. The shocking news became public less than an hour ago, but already hundreds of thousands have come here to St. Peter's Square, seeking guidance and comfort that their long-held faith is not in vain. As of yet, the pope has not made an appearance, but we are told that he is on his way and that arrangements have been made for an address like none other in the history of the Catholic Church—"

Dyson looked away, knowing that in that hour the world had changed.

"Bomb squad," he whispered.

Anna's students sat transfixed, huddling around a small radio in a small restaurant near the museum, where they had gathered for an early dinner. Their professor had told them to meet her in the museum's lab that evening at which time she would inform them of the exact nature of the find at Rome.

But to their surprise, the English-speaking station they had tuned in while seeking the *American Top 40* had stolen her thunder instead.

"No wonder she freaked out," Beth said, visibly shaken. "A confession by an apostle ..."

"Peter," Neil clarified.

"I know that," Beth said, slapping at him. "Declaring the whole thing a fake ... the whole resurrection ... This can't really be happening. I mean, we found evidence for Paul's church! That was supposed to *confirm* Christian history, not destroy it! How did we get from that to this?"

"The stone box," Craig said. "The stupid scroll must have been put inside to hide it. No one was ever supposed to find it at all."

"There were several scrolls in there," Neil recalled, "all rolled together. Teach said so. Remember? One was written by Paul. We know that. But it must have been something harmless, since the press is focusing on this one."

"She didn't react like it was harmless," Beth said.

"Maybe not, then. I'm just saying it's weird that no one's mentioning the others."

"So why did Peter write the thing in the first place?" Beth wondered. "Why leave something like that lying around if you never want it to come out?"

"Why did Nixon tape all his meetings?" Craig offered. "Important people do stupid things all the time."

"Poor Dr. Meridian," Beth said, looking out the window in the direction of the museum. "Imagine what she must be going through. We have to get over there."

◆ ◆ ◆

Anna glared at Mercer, who stood facing her.

"How could you?" she said icily. "It wasn't your decision! You had no right to leak that to the press!"

"I didn't," Mercer said, maintaining calm. "I'm as surprised as you are."

"You're the only one besides me to have the papyri in your possession since they were found," she accused. "The other morning, when you came into my hotel room and took them while I was sleeping—"

"What?" Roberto inadvertently said aloud.

"I only took the bag back to my room for safekeeping," Mercer insisted. "I told you that. Mary will tell you the same thing. I never even took them out of the bag."

"You didn't show them to her? You didn't take Peter's leaf and keep it for yourself before giving the rest back to me?"

"No, Anna," Mercer said, meeting her livid stare. "I did not."

She desperately wanted to believe him.

"How else could they have gotten out?" she puzzled.

"Were the scrolls ever left in this room unguarded?"

"No," she replied flatly. "Wait … yes. For just a few minutes, when I left the lab to make a call. I couldn't get a signal down here. But I locked the door behind me, and it was still locked when I got back. Except for Dr. Laneri, only you and I have the new code. And there's no other way in."

"Laneri?"

"He'd never have given up exclusivity," she insisted. "And I've known him for fifteen years. He'd never have taken the leaf. He's an honorable man."

"And I'm not," Mercer added.

"I didn't mean that," Anna said. "I never meant that. I'm sorry, Albert … I was upset."

He nodded, placing his hand on hers. "I know, my dear. It's all right."

"No, it isn't. I should never have said that."

"All is forgiven," he smiled. "Now … no one else had access to your safe deposit box?"

"No."

"You're sure?"

"Yes."

"And the scrolls were never otherwise out of your possession?"

"No."

"Well, Anna," Mercer said, sitting down, "I'm at a loss. I don't know what to tell you."

Roberto had slipped on a pair of earphones and was listening to a radio broadcast.

"They're saying an analysis was done in Switzerland," he said. "Both of the paper and the ink. They reached the same conclusions we did … that the document is authentic."

"It's just *old,*" Anna corrected him. "That's all we know. We have no definite proof that the apostles wrote them."

"Dictated them," Mercer corrected her, without thinking.

"Dictated them, then," Anna snapped.

"I'm sorry," he said. "This isn't a time for petty corrections."

"It was you who kept saying the world had a right to know," Anna pointed out.

"Yes," he agreed. "And I also said that no one should be told until we were absolutely certain of their true authorship. If I were going to leak the papyri, why would I have sent one of the leaves out before I was certain it was legitimate? Why would I have risked the ridicule had it proven to be a forgery?"

"Maybe you had an arrangement with a friend in Switzerland," she proposed. "Maybe he ran your tests for you and was told to leak the story if they came back positive."

"Do you really believe that, Anna?"

She looked into his gray eyes, finding the gentleness there she had always known. She then searched herself for an answer.

"No," she said. "I don't." She walked to him, put her arms out, and hugged him. "I'm sorry, Albert."

He patted her on the back and smiled as he returned the embrace. "It's all right, my dear," he said soothingly. "I can't blame you."

"Raphael," Anna said, as they broke the hug. "Somehow, it had to be him. He was there in Rome … Roberto saw him at the dig."

"I recall Samuel speaking of the man," Mercer reflected, nodding. "He's been a plague on archaeology for a long time and surely has built up a sizable clientele. Such a pirate, no doubt, would have many buyers lined up waiting for such an antiquity."

"Then why not take them all when he had the chance? Every sheet? It doesn't make any sense to steal only one, when each sheet could bring millions."

"Perhaps, in a gamble that we'd not notice right away, giving him time to run his tests and release the findings. First word is everything … Perception usually overrides truth. Now, anything we say will sound defensive, not scientific … and the black-market value of the papyrus will be much higher."

"I don't buy that," Anna said, shaking her head. "I see what you mean, but all Raphael sees are dollar signs."

"Then maybe it *wasn't* him."

Roberto spoke again. "Now they're saying the Vatican's gone crazy. A million people, or better, crowding the square."

Anna and Mercer looked into each other's eyes, more gently now. There was a shared pain, an anxiety that was rapidly building.

"It's started," Anna said.

"Yes," Mercer agreed. "We must now speak to the press. Tell them all we know. Perhaps, despite our delay, we can still ease the suffering. Minimize the damage. Convince a few through reason that the stolen scroll is a fluke … a forgery."

She glanced at the phone, turned off since the moment Roberto had hung up on the reporter, then she rushed to her purse and got her own.

"One document can still be a fluke," she said. "A dozen, likely not."

She positioned one of the scrolls under the lamp and snapped a close-up picture with her phone, then dialed.

"Who are you calling?" Roberto asked.

"Texting," she said, flipping the phone open and pointing it in different directions. "If the signal down here will let me."

Receiving a weak but present indicator, she began punching buttons, her long nail moving swiftly and decisively.

"When they stole Peter's leaf," she said, "they may have paused to read the one telling where the other seven are buried. And if they get their hands on those, we'll *never* quiet the storm."

◆ ◆ ◆

Dyson's phone beeped three times as it skittered across the table. He had already tried phoning Anna but had been unable to reach her and had resorted to voice mail.

Picking it up, he read the legend that filled the screen: *Text Message Received.* Pressing a few buttons, he called up the display and recognized Anna's number across the top.

"Hi, professor," he said. "I was expecting you."

The message, following on the heels of the reports he had seen, wasn't altogether unexpected: *Do not come to milan. go directly to pompeii. will call with specifics.*

"That's my girl," he said.

With a subtle smile, he gulped down the last of his coffee, gathered his things, and went to the Alitalia counter, where a pretty uniformed agent greeted him.

"Yes sir. How may I help you?"

"Change of plans," he said, pulling his ticket from an inner jacket pocket. "I need to switch for the next flight to Naples."

◆◆◆

The Bologna Room in the apostolic palace was as hidden away as it was magnificent. Few outside the hierarchy ever saw its walls, covered with ancient frescoes of geographical maps of the city and surrounding territory, or its vaulted ceiling, bedecked with murals of the apostles amid arches and columns of architectural splendor. Built for Pope Gregory XIII in 1575, it had served as the site of some of the most vital gatherings of the leaders of the Roman Catholic Church.

Now, another meeting was about to take place.

Cardinal Theodor Sefala and Cardinal William Burke of the College of Cardinals stood at the center of the room, their faces grim, their duty clear. Another, Cardinal Bishop Antonio Vicoro, entered through the room's double doors, and as they shut behind him, he crossed the black-and-white-tiled floor to where the others waited.

"We have considered the matter," he said. "The Roman Curia have made their concerns known, and his Holiness has decided upon a course of action."

"These documents cannot be allowed to gain in importance," said Burke, one hand gripping the bridge of his nose. "I do not believe them true. They cannot be."

"His Holiness shares that belief," said Vicoro.

"The question is," Sefala said, "how do we extinguish this flame before it grows any larger and spreads out of control?"

"His Holiness will make a full condemnation," Vicoro said. "The faithful will listen."

"Indeed," said Sefala, "those who remain. But what concerns me are the sheep who will be lost to us, who will scatter before the storm. They will depart the flock before we are able to get the situation under control. Already there is much dissent."

"Those whose faith is shallow quickly fall away," Vicoro observed. "It has always been so."

"We must give them a reason to doubt the scrolls," Burke suggested. "Despite their age and apparent authenticity. We cannot lose souls over such a disclosure."

"What if they *are* true?" Sefala pondered. "Do we serve God by denouncing truth?"

"They are not," Burke insisted. "Our heavenly Father would never unleash such a thing as this upon the world."

"It is not sufficient merely to decry the scrolls themselves," Vicoro said. "Their source must also be discredited. From wickedness comes wickedness ... We cannot allow *any* measure of credibility to stand behind them. It has been decided. In an hour his Holiness will speak to those in the square."

Cardinal Vicoro turned to leave, his footsteps echoing off the walls.

"By 'source,'" Sefala called after him, "do we mean the woman who discovered them, who made them public? We would train this condemnation upon her directly?"

Vicoro replied, the words laced with regret. "For the sake of the church, we do what we must."

◆ ◆ ◆

"Pastor Jerry, have you heard?"

The church secretary stood in the doorway of Orsen's office, clutching her Bible to her chest, shaken by the morning's events. He was reading a fishing magazine, his glasses turned up on his forehead.

"Yes, my dear," Orsen replied, absently nodding and pointing to his radio, seemingly unconcerned. "I heard." The news broadcast had ended; oldies from the sixties now wafted from the speaker.

"What if it's true? What if Jesus wasn't really who we all thought he was?"

"It doesn't change a thing, Tiffany," Orsen said. "Jesus taught us about kindness and generosity and loving our neighbor, and those things are all true no matter where they come from."

"But, doesn't it make a difference if—"

"Now, listen," the pastor interrupted, lowering the magazine. "Don't get yourself worked up. God works in mysterious ways. Always has, always will. Besides, they're pulling old stuff out of the ground all the time. Doesn't mean a thing to the here and now. Life goes on."

Orsen returned to his reading. The young woman still was anxious and stood in silence for a few moments, staring out a window. She had come to the man in search of reassurance but had received only trite, insubstantial sayings. Seeing that no real comfort was to be found, she turned and slowly walked away.

"How about another coffee, darlin'?" Orsen shouted after her. "Four sugars this time."

◆ ◆ ◆

Beth, Craig, and Neil entered the museum grounds on foot, having walked from the restaurant. As they approached the entrance, they realized the commotion that lay ahead.

"Oh no," Beth moaned.

Television news crews and other members of the press had surrounded the building, running to and fro as they hurried to set up their chosen shots. Dozens of camera trucks crowded the narrow driveway; others had already congested the modest parking lot. Technicians ran wires and erected transmitting equipment, which gleamed white against the dark stone of the edifice behind them. Boom microphones swayed, finding their targets. A news helicopter swept low overhead, slowly moving as its cameras captured the throng below.

"Smile, guys," Craig said.

The students dashed forward, hoping to run the gauntlet of reporters without resistance. As they neared the museum doors, they saw Laneri to one side, dealing with the hungry press as best he could. Italian was being shouted, loudly and quickly, both questions and answers.

"I wish Roberto was here," Beth said. "He could tell us what they're saying."

"You don't need to know Italian for that," Craig replied. "They must want to know where the professor is, and the old guy in the suit is stalling for time, keeping them away."

They had started up the steps, when suddenly a security guard confronted them, commanding them to halt.

"We're Dr. Meridian's students," Beth said, showing her student ID. "We have to get in to see her. You know us ... You've seen us before."

"Ah, Meridian." The guard nodded, gleaning their meaning though his English was poor. "Oldefield. *Si, potete entrare.*" He motioned them all inside, opening the door and closing it behind them just as several reporters made a rush to follow. Denied admittance, they pressed against the windows, their camera strobes lighting up the hallway.

"Wow," Craig said, waving to the crowd as the trio walked away. "I feel like Elvis."

"Just shut up," Neil snapped. "This is serious."

They rounded a corner and found Anna on her phone in the elevator lobby. She looked up, saw her students, said good-bye to the person on the other end of the line, and hung up just in time to hug Beth, who had run to her.

"We heard," Beth said, holding her tight. "It's terrible. No wonder you were so upset."

"Why did you tell the press before *we* even knew?" Craig asked.

"I didn't," Anna said in frustration. She pressed the elevator call button. "Someone leaked it. One of the papyri was stolen and sent to an outside lab."

"How?" Neil asked. "Someone broke into the museum storeroom?"

"No," Anna said. "The documents weren't in the storeroom."

The bell dinged and the door opened. They got into the elevator.

"You look nice," Beth told her professor during the descent, trying to cheer her up a bit. Anna smiled and gently ran a hand along the back of the girl's head.

"Thanks, sweetie," she said. "So do you."

At the basement level, it was a short walk from the elevator to the lab. With Anna in the lead, they entered to find Mercer and Roberto still scrutinizing the papyri leaves.

"Roberto!" Beth said, hugging him.

"Hello, Dean Mercer," Craig said, suddenly and noticeably on his best behavior. "When did you get here? I hope you had a good flight."

"It was fine, Mr. Dunn," he said, smiling. "You may relax." He then nodded at the others. "Ms. Whitney … Mr. Meyer."

"Hello, Dean."

"Anything happen while I was upstairs?" Anna asked him. "I was gone ten whole minutes."

"Well, Mr. Giordano and I began to scrutinize the writing on the other leaves, hoping to perhaps find a contradiction or linguistic error that might still call them into question."

"Nothing so far?"

"Not as yet, no."

"You should see outside," Beth said. "It's crazy. The press is all over the place."

"I'd like to get my hands on whoever told them I found these, and that I'm in here," Anna said. "I'll never get past that mob, short of an armored car."

"You're going to have to talk to them sooner or later, Anna," Mercer said. "They need to hear something definitive, and they need to hear it from you."

"I'd prefer later."

He smiled, nodding. "As would I, were I you."

Anna sat down, kicked off her shoes, and rubbed her neck.

"At least I got ahold of Jack," she said. "Gave him the particulars on Pompeii. He should be in Naples"—she checked her watch—"at about five in the morning. Puts him at Pompeii around sunrise, if he goes straight there."

"Pompeii?" Craig asked. "What's down there? Besides a bunch of rude frescoes, I mean."

"One of the scrolls I found sealed in the box gave the location of another stone box hidden in Pompeii, the other seven supposed confessions. I sent Professor Dyson a shot of the little map doodled at the bottom of one of the leaves."

"Wait a minute," Beth said. "The other seven? How many were in the box?"

"Six," Anna replied. "Paul's, and those of five of the twelve apostles. Plus the note leading to the others."

"There are confessions from all twelve apostles?" the girl asked, incredulous. "They *all* say they faked the whole thing?"

"Pretty much, yeah," Roberto replied.

Beth plopped down hard on a stool and just stared, trying to come to grips with it all.

"I know it's a lot to deal with," Anna said, trying to be strong for them despite her own nagging doubts. "But it just can't be that Christianity is a hoax."

"Tell *them* that," Craig said, jerking a thumb upward. "It's like fresh meat night at the piranha house, and we're all in sirloin underwear."

"Even if they date right, they *have* to be fakes," Anna said. "They have to be! But if they are, why were they hidden in that wall?"

The room went silent. No one had an answer.

"How can something make so much sense," she added, "and yet at the same time, make no sense at all?"

Mercer shook his head.

"Well," Anna said, "we've come to a parting of the ways. There's nothing more to be done here."

"What do you mean?" Beth asked, no longer so anxious to return home.

"I want you all headed home tomorrow afternoon. I contacted the airline, and the arrangements have been made."

"But what about the site?" Beth asked, hopefully, wanting the woman she so admired to tell her she needed her. "The foundation hasn't been completely cleared, and we could—"

"I'm turning the dig over to the museum. You were going back to the States anyway, remember? Your enthusiasm and support have been invaluable, and I love you all, but you have other responsibilities waiting. I've kept you away from your theses and your families long enough."

The students' heads hung low.

"Well," Roberto said, "we sure can't say we didn't learn anything."

Seven

News of the find had crossed land and ocean with lightning speed. The North American continent, with the world's highest per capita Christian population, had received word just after noon on the day of the leak. Immediately sensing blood and unprecedented vulnerability in the water, atheists and long-time critics of the Christian church's every facet filled the domestic airwaves, crowding talk shows and news broadcasts, crowing proudly that they had been right all along, that their minds had been the rational and reasoned ones.

And in the span of that first hour after the news broke, two hundred fifty million people who had professed themselves as followers of Christ no longer knew who he was. A church body largely weakened by decades of political correctness and social pressure, having embraced carrying a lighter load rather than gaining a stronger back, found itself unable to cope with an adversity their forefathers would easily have weathered.

As the report was repeated throughout the day, stating that the "confession of Peter" had been verified as authentic, many believers stood steadfast. They knew what they knew and clung to the hope that somehow, in some way, the document would yet be proven false. Others went into complete denial, as if the news had never broken and there was no crisis with which to deal. Still others went into mourning, crying hysterically or locking themselves away, unable to deal with what they were hearing.

And some simply went to the phone book and picked out a religion not too dissimilar from that they had known, based largely on geographical proximity.

Pastor Jerry Orsen left his office for the day and crossed the freshly paved parking lot, headed for the new Mercedes waiting for him in his reserved space, its bronze and chrome gleaming. The pavement was uniformly black, its new striping standing out sharply in vivid white. The new landscaping surrounding the lot was awash in color, with blooms of red and yellow and blue nestled amid vivid green. So many such improvements had been made since Orsen had taken the helm, with many others to follow.

As he neared his car, he noticed an elderly man sitting on one of the concrete benches installed alongside the beautiful new flower garden. The man was dressed in a gray suit that showed its age but wasn't tattered. His hat, too—a fedora—had seen better days since leaving the milliners,which, judging from the wear around its edges, had been well before the Second World War. He held a small paper bag of peanuts, from which he had been feeding squirrels.

"Afternoon," Orsen said, uncomfortable with the man's presence and never breaking stride.

The gnarled stranger stared at him, his face shadowed by the brim of his hat, his fingers curled as if by arthritis, and gave a subtle nod of acknowledgment.

Orsen turned toward his car and pressed the button to deactivate its alarm system. As the expected chirp sounded and he opened the door, he caught an odd flurry of motion at the corner of his eye, a swirl of light and dark. He glanced over at the man again.

He was sitting there as before. Still staring.

"Lovely day," the pastor added.

And then, never blinking, the man spoke in a voice bolder than Orsen would have expected.

"He will tear down what you have covered in whitewash," he said, "and will level it to the ground, and when it falls, you will be destroyed in it."

Orsen, taken aback, paused before speaking. Though he was shaken, his tone as always remained jovial. "I look forward to seeing you Sunday morning, friend."

He climbed into the car, started it up, and headed home. As he sat at the edge of the lot, waiting to pull out onto the street, he looked into his rearview mirror, which framed the now-distant bench.

It was empty.

◆ ◆ ◆

Jack Dyson drove south, hoping his was not a race against anything—or anyone—but purely against time. Not knowing who might have seen the papyri, Anna had warned him that he might not be alone in his quest for the second trove.

He found himself pressing a little harder on the accelerator.

With him were two Italian archaeologists with whom he had worked before, both men of solid reputation, whose credentials were impeccable. Gianni Valerio and Stefano di Meo worked their notebook computers as he drove, calling up reference data on the excavations at Pompeii and reacquainting themselves with the ancient city's layout. Dyson had given them the file Anna had provided—a simple description of the specific location accompanied by an even simpler map.

"She really said it was in the Villa of Juliae Felicis?" Stefano asked. "That should make it easy. It's one of the few places in the city where we have the actual name of the ancient owner."

"And it's one of the more impressive houses in town," Dyson observed. "A big place. As I recall, the owner rented upstairs rooms with a five-year lease. Had its own public baths and gardens, and art to die for. It wouldn't be an unusual choice for hiding something, especially if you wanted someone to be able to find it later without too much trouble."

"Who?" Gianni asked. "Who hid the scrolls there?"

"Supposedly the 'scribe of the apostles,'" Dyson said. "Whoever that was. If not the apostles themselves."

Mount Vesuvius rose ominously to Dyson's left, its formidable shoulders tinged with the golden light of the sun rising behind it.

"Don't blow up, baby," he joked. "Not while we're here."

The miles swept by. The peace of the road, largely empty at that early hour, was welcome. The beauty of the surrounding countryside, more visible with each passing moment, briefly wiped away the urgency of the excursion, and the possible risks involved.

"So," Gianni wondered, "where exactly in the house do we dig?"

"Sorry," Dyson said. "It's 'need to know,' guys. I'll tell you when we get there. Anna's really nervous about this. She doesn't know who she can trust and who she can't."

"So she's taking a chance on *you,*" Stefano laughed.

"And don't think I don't appreciate it."

"You don't trust us?" Gianni kidded. "After all the times we've made you look good?"

"A promise is a promise."

"Especially one made to such a *bella ragazza,*" Stefano said, kissing the back of his own hand.

"That may have a little something to do with it," Dyson admitted with a grin.

Soon their exit presented itself, and they left the highway, finding themselves on a narrow, paved road. The fields and groves around them looked especially green and lush in the early-morning light, reflecting the fertility of the region's volcanic soil. That richness came at a price, however, as those of the area well knew.

Dyson slowed. Not wanting to risk detection by those who made it their job to protect the excavated town, he parked in the lot of a nearby business. From there, they would walk to their target.

"We're about a quarter of a mile from the Julia Felix villa," he said, killing the engine. "We should be able to get there from here without being seen. If we're spotted, we're legit archaeologists, remember. Don't panic. Just tell them we're checking something out for the Museo Archeologico Milano."

"I'd feel better if we had a few security men with us," Stefano said. "Just in case."

"I've always hated when people do what we're about to do," Gianni said.

"Yeah," Dyson replied, grabbing a canvas gym bag, "but it's for a good cause. We're trying to keep something out of the hands of looters so it won't wind up for auction and sold to a private bidder. If it's here, it belongs in a museum."

"Right," Stefano agreed, nodding.

As they climbed out of the car, a chilled breeze swept past. Dyson zipped up his jacket halfway and adjusted his collar, then the three left the car behind. The villa they sought lay at the very edge of town, making access and their mission easier than it otherwise might have been.

They made their way across field, road, and trail, finally entering the city proper. Once there, they crept along the Via del Abbondanza—the "Road of Plenty"—hugging the ancient walls of the buildings along its south side, trying to attract as little attention as possible. Across the narrow thoroughfare, still unexcavated, rose a twelve-foot wall of compacted volcanic soil, the face of a large area within which lay buildings, artifacts, and no doubt, human remains as yet unknown.

When Vesuvius erupted in AD 79, the city had at first been buried in pumice and volcanic ash to a depth of ten feet. Hours later, in the latter stages of the cataclysm, a pyroclastic surge had rushed down from the mountain, its scorching violence slicing away almost everything standing above that point. Few buildings had retained their upper floors, and none had survived unscathed.

Dyson had been here many times. They all had. As they moved along, once more they felt the magic that permeated the place—there, time did not exist. Dyson always felt that, had he arrived but a day sooner, he might have captured the city in its vivacious prime.

And then, it stood before them—the Villa of Julia Felix.

Following the destructive earthquake of AD 62, the owner of the once resplendent building, the daughter of a wealthy man named Spurius Felix, had decided to offset the cost of rebuilding by renting out some of its upper rooms as apartments and shops and by making its generous baths public. Signage chiseled into stone at one north entrance, which specified the name of the owner, the rooms offered, and the five-year duration of the lease, had inadvertently preserved her name forever.

The men approached the villa cautiously, looking around to make sure they hadn't been noticed. "I'll handle the chisel work," Dyson said. "You two stay out of plain sight, but watch for any sign that we've attracted attention. Digging the thing out of the wall is going to make some noise … Nothing I can do about that."

"Right," Gianni said. "Good luck."

Dyson flipped open his phone and called up the photo Anna had sent him. Zooming in on the crude map, he determined that the artifact in question rested inside a wall of the atrium north of the main portico. He paused, inhaled the cool sea air, and made his way into the room, where he hurriedly located the correct point in the specified wall.

Two cubits above the floor, he had been told. Estimating with palm widths, he chose his spot.

Man, I hate doing this!

He pulled the chisel and hammer from his bag and started to work, intensely conscious of the distinctive sound his tools were making. He tried muffling the noise by wrapping the chisel in a rag, but still the toll of metal into stone rang out.

He repeatedly looked back over his shoulder and scanned the courtyard, finding no one each time.

We might just get away with this.

The chisel dug at the mortar, freeing a few of the stones from their home of thousands of years. Since the day Julia's workmen had set them in the shadow of Vesuvius, they had remained unmoved.

Until now.

He pulled the stones away, carefully setting them one by one on the floor, trying to minimize the damage. When an area of almost two square feet had been opened, he pulled a small flashlight from his pocket and shined it into the hole.

Something red glinted low and to the left.

Again, the chisel freed the stone. Sundered mortar coated the floor at his feet. Finally, he set his tools aside and reached into the opening. His hands found cold, smooth stone.

A box. Of red travertine.

Twisting his body to create leverage, he freed the box from its dark tomb and pulled it clear, into the light. For a few moments he couldn't help but study it. Polished smooth, it was featureless save for a seam running around the sides, a groove filled with dark, hardened wax.

Bull's-eye, Anna.

"Thank you, Dr. Dyson," a voice sounded, echoing in the room. "You've saved us a bit of effort."

He spun around to see a face he knew—and dreaded.

Raphael.

Unblinking blue eyes were fixed on him, piercing, set amid angled features. Framing the eyes was a crop of short, perfectly arranged blonde hair. Below them, a chiseled jaw.

His clothing was impeccable, his heavy cotton shirt tucked into pleated gray slacks. But Dyson's eyes registered none of this. They were locked upon the dark open barrel of the automatic pistol being leveled at him.

Three other men emerged and entered the atrium. All carried guns equipped with silencers, every weapon trained on Dyson.

"I'll be taking that," Raphael said, indicating the box. "I have a very interested party waiting. Interested … and generous."

"You don't even know what's in it," Dyson said.

"But I do," Raphael replied, smiling. "And soon, so will the whole world."

Dyson detected movement to his right, beyond the portico door. A loud report rang out and stone exploded near Raphael's head. The bullet dug deep into the wall, shattering ancient plaster and limestone. The looters fell back, seeking cover outside the doorway in which they had been standing. Dyson ran for the portico, only to be cut off halfway along the covered walk as another man emerged at its far end, his gun raised. The professor, weighed down by the travertine box in his hands, dove sideways through an opening in the wall to his right and found himself in the triclinium of the house—the dining room.

Unfortunately, like many triclinia, it was enclosed on three sides. There was only one way in—or out.

He looked around and up, desperate for an exit. The ceiling, coated with shards of stone from the river Sarnus, looked for all the world like that of a cave. A small opening on the back wall admitted light but was too narrow for a man to pass through. Dyson reached into his jacket pocket and withdrew the small pistol he had brought with him, just in case. Rarely did he carry one. But today, knowing the possibilities, he had. He knelt low, hugging one end of the U-shaped stone couch on which diners once reclined, and tried to get out of sight, away from the door. Looking out across the way, he saw Gianni taking cover across the courtyard, his gun also drawn.

With the box tucked under his arm, Dyson slowly approached the doorway. The only doorway. He took position at its side but no longer saw Gianni across the way.

"Come now, Doctor," Raphael called out, the direction of his voice disguised by echoes. "I only want the box. I have no interest in killing you."

Dyson didn't reply.

Do they know where I am? Did they see me come in here?

He took another cautious look around the edge of the doorway, his pistol primed and ready.

A searing impact struck his shoulder and jarred him, spinning him and knocking the gun from his hand. He fell backward, the box crashing to the floor as he landed hard against the stone couches. His head slammed into the wall, but he didn't lose consciousness.

Raphael entered and approached the box, his gun leveled at Dyson, who could do little to stop him. One of his men stood just outside, scanning the courtyard. Dyson's hand, clamped to his shoulder, was covered in something warm and wet.

"You might want to get that shoulder looked at," Raphael mocked. "Bullet wounds can be rather nasty. Ask your friends outside … though I'm afraid one of them is no longer capable of answering you."

Bending down, he took the box. Then he was gone.

After a moment Dyson struggled to his feet. Retrieving his gun with his bloodied left hand, he staggered outside and across the square, almost losing his balance as he crossed one of the ancient reflecting pool's three bridges. There was no further sign of the looters.

Gianni lay still, his body sprawled in the cool grass, his face raised toward the sky. Dyson tried to find a pulse, but his own hands were shaking, his grip weak. Stefano, blood soaking the side of his gray sweatshirt, was on his hands and knees. Dyson went to him, trying to lend what help he could.

"Take it easy," Dyson said, helping him into a sitting position. "Looks like you took one."

"So did you."

"Just a scratch."

"Gianni …"

"I don't know," Dyson said. "Looks bad."

He winced, burying the urge to cry out in pain. The bullet buried deep in his shoulder was agonizing. He was losing blood. His right arm was going numb. With his left hand, he struggled to pull his phone from his pocket and dial for help.

A man appeared at the edge of the courtyard, a security guard. He had heard the unsilenced shot fired by Gianni.

"Chiami un' ambulanza!" Dyson shouted, trying to recall his seldom-used Italian. *"Questi uomini sono gravemente feriti … ci serve aiuto!"*

"Presto!" Stefano weakly added.

The guard waved an acknowledgment and ran for help.

Dyson felt his balance slipping away. "They'd better … better … hurry …"

He dropped to his knees, wobbled, and fell to the lawn. The world spun madly as everything around him broke into bright orange sparkles. A loud whine flooded his ears.

Then, everything went completely black.

◆ ◆ ◆

It had been a rough night. When sleep finally came, it hadn't been without a struggle.

Her mind ensnared in a maelstrom of anxiety and guilt, Anna had fought to shut it all away, to find a haven, however momentary, in denial. She had struggled to convince herself that Mercer had been right, that God was in control and that all things happened for a reason, but she couldn't escape the one truth that haunted her.

I found the confessions. I shattered the faith.

And worse.

I destroyed Jesus Christ.

For hours she had lain awake, her body and mind weary to the point of exhaustion, her consciousness unwilling to yield.

If only I could go back. If only I could have stopped myself from breaking into that wall.

If only.

Finally, with the nocturnal hours slipping away, she had found sleep. Not a restful one, devoid of nightmares of pursuit, but sleep nonetheless.

An hour. Two.

The sun had risen. Anna tossed, tangling her lithe form in the covers, sometimes rising to partial wakefulness before drifting off again. Constantly, the anguish was there, awaiting its moments, seeking the chinks in her armor, reaching in to torment her.

She was being chased through a city somewhere. Her feet were like lead, her heart pounding as she tried to get away. Her pursuer was unseen but almost upon her, surrounded by a cloud of shadow, a zone of bitter cold.

Music erupted, wedging its way into her dream, jarring her. It came from everywhere. The city melted away. The music grew louder, more distinct.

Her phone.

Lifting her head, she found her hair draped over her face, obscuring her view. She swept it aside, trying to focus on the bedside table and the clock atop it.

Six forty, she read. *No—nine forty. Nine forty-one.*

Still, the ring tone sounded, the refrain from "Everybody Wants to Rule the World." She reached out with an unsteady hand, fumbled for the phone, and managed to get it open.

Jack's number was on the screen.

"Hey, Jack," she began, trying but failing to sound awake. "Did you find them?"

"Dr. Meridian?" came a woman's voice she didn't recognize. It carried a mild accent.

"Yes?" a puzzled Anna said, trying to force herself awake. "Speaking."

"This is Dr. DiRisio at the Rehabilitation Institute in Telese …"

"A hospital …?"

"Dr. Jack Dyson was airlifted here this morning with a gunshot wound to his shoulder," the doctor said. "You were the emergency contact programmed into his phone."

The stubborn veil of bleariness began to fall away. "Jack? Is he all right?"

"He is resting comfortably. The bullet was removed, but we're watching him now for signs of nerve damage. Two of his associates have similar wounds and are also being treated."

Anna reached for her purse, grabbing a pad and pen from it and knocking the bag to the floor in the process. "Tell me again where you are … where Dr. Dyson is." She listened, scrawling the address on the paper. "Via Bagni Vecchi … Got it. Does he have a room number?"

"He's still in ICU, but we're hoping to move him this afternoon."

"Okay," Anna said, sitting up. "I'll be there as soon as I can. Thank you, Doctor."

She closed her phone, kicked herself free of the tangled covers, and threw them aside. Rising to her feet, she stepped on the spilled contents of her purse, snapping the handle of her brush as she staggered toward the closet.

"Ow!" she moaned, hopping before brushing away her nightgown and checking the bottom of her foot for a cut. None there. Then she reached into the closet for the first neutral blouse and skirt she saw.

Hurriedly she dressed, slipping the wrong shoe onto the wrong foot and scolding herself for that wasted moment.

Shot—he was shot! And I put him in the bullet's path. Oh, Jack!

She grabbed her phone and took a quick glance in the mirror.

No makeup, not now … later, in the car.

She knelt for her purse, scooped everything back inside, then ran the broken brush through her hair as she made for the door.

◆ ◆ ◆

The sea was calm, the sky clear.

The cargo ship *Arctic Breeze,* a small vessel with a deadweight tonnage approaching thirty thousand, broke for open water, having passed through the Suez Canal. Her broad, white superstructure and red-painted side contrasted dramatically with the gentle waves surrounding her, waves easily cast aside by the white churn of her wake. The Mediterranean now lay before her, its calm expanse of blue promising an uneventful journey.

The ship had last docked at the Port of Sudan, where more cargo had been offloaded than taken aboard. She sat high in the water now, carrying a lighter load than most ships making for open sea. She had always been an unimportant vessel in the scheme of international commerce, barely a blip on the sonar of maritime history. She was common, run-of-the-mill, often forgotten.

And yet hers would be a special destiny few ships come to know.

A man in dark, heavy clothing stood at her rail, his eyes not on the sparkling sea all around him but on the wide, rust-flecked cargo hatch near his feet.

He simply stared, squinting slightly against the salty ocean gusts, as if to see through the metal to something beyond.

That something, crated and headed for a distant shore, was known to a very few. Those who knew had sworn their willingness to give their lives in its cause.

And the man at the rail—when the time came—indeed would.

◆ ◆ ◆

The late-afternoon sun cast long shadows as Anna rushed into the emergency center of the hospital. The room was not as crowded as she had feared it might be, so she went straight to the admissions desk and got the immediate attention of a nurse.

"Mi scusi," she said, reaching into her purse for her identification.

"Sono la dottoressa Anna Meridian—"

"Ah," the uniformed woman said in well-practiced English. "Yes, Dr. Meridian. Dr. DiRisio told me you would be arriving this afternoon."

"Oh," Anna said, opening her wallet to show the nurse her ID. "I got here as fast as I could. How is Dr. Dyson? How are the others?"

"Your fiancé is doing well," she said. "The other gentlemen are still in critical condition, in intensive care. Dr. Dyson has been moved upstairs to room"—she checked her computer, then pointed down a corridor—"room 422. It's private. The lift lobby is right down there, just past the newsstand."

"Thank you," Anna said as she slipped her wallet back into her purse, smiling through her puzzlement.

Fiancé?

Upon reaching the fourth floor, she followed a green painted stripe as a sign near the elevator instructed. In moments she found herself standing in front of room 422. She paused to identify herself to the nurse at the nearby station, then went to the door and pushed it open.

Dyson lay in bed, eyes closed. He was shirtless, his right shoulder heavily bandaged. An intravenous drip next to the bed fed the crook of his left elbow, while monitoring equipment silently kept watch over his vital signs. A television mounted high in the corner was set on a news channel, its sound muted.

Anna quietly stepped up to his bedside. For a moment she just stood and looked at him, her hands on the safety rail.

Oh, Jack …

A thousand thoughts ran through her mind in that instant—the way he had taken to calling her "And the Rest," insisting she was "the perfect combination of the Professor and Mary Ann, rolled into one." The way he had once given her his slice of coconut-cream pie—her favorite—in the university cafeteria when she realized too late that they had run out.

The way his hand felt in hers.

She leaned over him, reaching out to push his sandy hair lightly aside.

"Hi," she said, gently stroking his forehead. "How do you feel?"

He opened his eyes, looked over, and found her.

"Top notch." He smiled softly, his voice weak and wrought with discomfort. "Just resting my eyes."

She set her purse in a chair beside the bed.

"They're determined to immobilize me," he said. "My shoulder's wrapped up like Ramses' cat. Other arm has this needle stuck in it. I can barely work the remote."

"For a guy," she teased, "that's rough."

"Heaven help me if I get an itch."

She studied him. "What did the doctors say?"

"Lost some blood," he said dismissively. "They put it back and plugged the hole. Good as new."

"Your color's good."

"Same as it ever was."

Her smile was forced and faint.

"You look great," he said.

"I don't feel great."

"Rough night," he guessed. "Not much sleep."

"No. Not much."

He nodded toward the television. "It's all over the news."

She recognized the on-screen graphics, all in English. "American TV?"

"Satellite. Little piece of home nestled among the Italian channels. Every fifteen minutes they show your picture. Your find is all they want to talk about."

"Don't say that," she said. "Don't call it 'my' find."

"I'm sorry," he apologized. "But I think you should know if you don't already ... The Catholic Church has completely censured the scroll. They say there's no way Saint Peter would have made such an admission."

"No way it's true, or no way he'd have admitted it? There's a difference."

"They didn't get that specific. They just—" Dyson tried to shrug, cutting the action short with a wince. "Owww!"

"If it's the former, I'd agree wholeheartedly," she said. "Peter wouldn't have. *None* of them would have. This whole thing's a fraud. It *has* to be."

"That wasn't all they said, Anna," he added reluctantly. "I don't guess you heard."

"What else?"

He remained silent.

"Jack, tell me."

"I know you aren't Catholic, but they … uh … they denounced you, too. Personally. They branded you a heretic."

She dropped into the chair. Shaking her head, she stared with wet eyes out the window across the room. Dyson said nothing, letting her work the moment through.

"God must hate me," she said.

"God doesn't hate you."

"How would you know?" Anna said. "You don't even believe in him."

"Yeah, well …"

"I wanted nothing to do with any of this."

"I know."

"Everyone seems to think I gladly forced these papyri on the world, as if I were set on destroying the faith."

"Yeah," he said, shaking his head. "That's pretty much what they said on the news. Looks like whoever leaked word out of Switzerland made sure to attach your name to the scrolls and told the press you stood behind their authenticity."

"It's a lie!"

"I know."

"Why would anyone say that?" Anna wondered, rising from the chair and beginning to pace. "Why attack me personally?"

"Maybe to make you a scapegoat," Dyson offered. "Maybe to take the pressure off themselves."

"I didn't want these to get out. I understood the consequences of that happening. I told Albert that repeatedly."

"What did he say?"

"He said we had a duty to the truth."

Dyson scowled. "Anna, you don't suppose he—"

"No," she was quick to say. "Not Albert. Anyway, it doesn't matter. It's too late. I sat there in that lab and opened Pandora's box, and somehow it got out and it's too late." Her head dropped back. "First I destroy the greatest source of hope in the world, then I send you out and get you shot. I'm a walking disaster."

"This wasn't your fault," he said, indicating his shoulder. "None of it."

"I wish I could believe that. At least the second box is …"

It dawned on her that she had no idea what he had found at Pompeii. She whirled to find his blue gray eyes, the question written on her face.

After a beat he told her, his tone grave. "I lost it, Anna."

"What?" A whisper, shallow and desperate.

"The box," he went on. "I lost it. I had it in my hands, and I lost it. It was right where you said it would be, in Julia's place. I dug it out of the wall. And then Raphael showed up …"

Anna dropped back into the chair.

"They're on the market by now," she said with resignation. "They'll be made public."

"He said he had a buyer."

"How does he do it?" she cried in frustration. "He's always

right there with me, or one step ahead. It was the same with Sam … Raphael was always right there. How?"

"We were armed, but they had numbers. Maybe half a dozen … I don't know. I ran with the box, but … he cut me off, and …"

"They shot you." She reached out and took his hand. "I'm so sorry. What kind of horrible person am I? You're lying in that bed, and I'm sitting here feeling sorry for myself."

"I'll be fine," he insisted. "I promise."

"There were others, you said. With Raphael."

"Yeah. They hit Gianni and Stefano first … They're both here too. Downstairs."

"I know," Anna said, her eyes tearing up again. "The nurse told me."

"Last I heard, they were stable, but none of us will be doing any digging for a while. They say I'll be out of here in a week, give or take."

"You just rest. All of you." She tried to smile. "Get better."

"You bet."

"The police … What did you tell them?"

"I said we interrupted some looters in the midst of their dastardly deed," he told her, a pain-driven grimace crossing his rugged features.

She nodded with an empathetic wince. "I'm sorry. I was wrong to have put you in that position."

"It was for a good cause, Anna. You were afraid someone else might try to grab the papyri for the wrong reasons, and you were right."

"I don't feel very right."

She was clearly suffering. He saw it and changed the

subject. "What about Mercer? When's he going back? To Oldefield."

"Monday, I think. They're going to see Rome first. I told him what happened. That you were here."

"You told him I'd be a little late getting home?"

"Yeah. They're giving you whatever leave you need. Paid."

Dyson cleared his throat. "So, you have a place to stay? A hotel room?"

"I just drove six hours," she confessed. "I came straight here."

"You didn't fly?"

"They didn't have an open flight until tonight, and I didn't want to wait."

"You drove four hundred miles?"

She smiled faintly, wiping under her eyes. "Maybe ..."

"Be glad you didn't have to go through Naples," he said. "The people there can't drive for squat. Worst drivers on the planet."

"I've heard the stories ..."

She trailed off, her attention seized by the television. He followed her gaze to find a still image of her face, framed in an upper corner as the newscaster spoke.

"There you are again," he said.

"Turn it up."

With some reluctance, he pressed a button.

"—in Milan, where Dr. Anna Meridian performed preliminary tests on what we now understand were several manuscripts she unearthed in Rome."

The picture shifted to video of Anna outside the museum, microphones shoved at her face as she tried to navigate the herd.

"Yes," Anna was saying in the interview, "the papyri do appear to be first century, but that doesn't lend them complete veracity. We know only that they aren't recent forgeries."

"But Dr. Meridian, how many are there? Is it true you discovered such confessions from all twelve of the apostles?"

"I do not have such as that in my possession, no."

"Dr. Klein in Switzerland has declared the 'confession of Peter' authentic … Did the tests you ran here reach the same conclusion?"

"I told you, we know only that they date correctly for the period indicated by the text written on them."

"Them?" one reporter caught. "So there are more than one?"

"I'm not going to discuss that at this time."

Dyson turned to see Anna with her head down, her face in her hands.

"Please, turn it off," she said softly.

He pressed the button. The screen went black.

Seeing her anguish tore into him like a dull blade. "Hey, you were great. Bunch of vultures … You did a good job there."

"Hardly," she said, sinking back into the chair, sliding her purse to one side. She didn't look at him.

For several minutes no one spoke. Dyson closed his eyes, feigning rest, but he could think of nothing but her.

Anna rose and went to the window. He watched as she traced the birds in their flight, the cars as they passed by, and maintenance personnel as they went about their jobs.

"So," Anna finally said, "what's this about me being your fiancé?"

Dyson smiled broadly.

"Oh, that."

She turned to face him, her eyes moist but a faint smile played on her lips. "Yes, that."

"Well, when you're in the ICU instead of a normal room, they only let family in to see you. I thought it would, I don't know, simplify things."

"I see."

"Besides," he grinned, "you take a bullet, you get the girl."

"What?" She playfully slapped at him, striking only air.

"Hey, I don't make the rules. But I've seen enough movies to know what they are."

Anna rolled her eyes, chuckling despite herself.

"You've had a very positive effect on me," Dyson said.

"It doesn't look like it."

"No, really," he went on. "What you said before, about me not believing in God. I don't know what it is, and I don't know why it's happening now, but I'm really giving the whole thing a lot of serious thought."

"Oh, sure," she said, surprised. "*Now* you get spiritual. Now that I've assassinated the character of Jesus and the apostles."

"Enough of that," he said with gentle sternness. "You didn't write those scrolls. You didn't bury them, and you aren't out there hawking them to the highest bidder. You didn't pull a trigger. None of this is your fault."

"Yeah, well …"

"I mean it. Stop blaming yourself, Anna. You aren't responsible."

"Then who is?"

"Whoever wrote those words two thousand years ago.

Whoever put them in those walls. Whoever leaked them to the press before all the facts were in."

"I think the facts *are* in, Jack."

"You're being defeatist. This isn't like you."

She was silent.

"It *wasn't* your fault, Anna," he stressed. "I *mean* it."

She took his hand again.

"Thank you," she said, smiling. "It helps to hear it."

"It's the gospel truth," he replied, looking into her eyes.

"Okay."

"Besides," he added, "I think you should keep running your tests. Something's fishy here."

"You really are serious about this. About God."

"Yup," he said. "I don't know. On the plane ride over, I just got to thinking. Maybe being up that high got me close enough to heaven that I could hear a whisper or two."

She smiled. "Maybe so."

He relaxed his neck and lay back, watching as she once again took a seat in the bedside chair.

"I think I get the Italian version of *Wheel of Fortune* in twenty minutes or so," he said. "Wanna stick around?"

"I don't really have anywhere else to go," she said, amused. For a few moments she just watched him.

He noticed.

"What?" he asked, teasing her.

"Nothing."

"You know," he said, "since you're my fiancé and all, you can stay here for the night if you want. Save the cost of a room. They'll bring in a roll-away bed. Nurse told me so."

Anna looked at her hands, smiling anew. "I might do that."

She rose, picked up her purse, and dug for change. "But first, I'm going to find a coffee machine."

"I'll be right here."

Anna went out into the hallway, took a quick look in both directions, and walked to the nurses' station. She smiled at a nun in a flowing black habit, who sat watching television in an adjoining waiting area, and received an odd look in return.

"Dove trovo una macchina del caffè?" Anna asked the nurse.

In reply, the woman pointed down the hallway.

"In fondo al corridoio, dottoressa Meridian."

"Mille grazie."

As Anna began to turn, the nun rose and called out to her.

"'Meridian?'" she asked, her accent heavy. "*Anna* Meridian?"

"Si," Anna said.

The sister approached. She was elderly, her gait hobbled and assisted by a cane. Her stature was small, her steps slow and deliberate. As she drew near, her gaze remained fixed on the woman before her.

Anna was silent, smiling pleasantly, trying to place the old woman.

Do I know you?

They stood opposite each other, Anna a full head taller. The nun, anger suddenly flaring in her aged eyes, reached out with a paper-skinned hand and struck her hard across the face. Shocked, Anna brought a hand to her stinging cheek and could only watch as the nun, without a word, turned and walked away.

Eight

The initial effect of the confessions was staggering.

In the United States, many churches opened their doors the following Sunday only to find attendance cut by more than half. Across all denominations, all divisions, all creeds, many had elected to reevaluate their faith, to take time away, to try to decide whether their time was being wisely or properly spent with the institutions they had chosen. A question had been raised, one for which no one seemed to have a definitive answer: *What is faith?*

For many, the sudden undermining of what they claimed to have believed was disastrous. Like houses without foundations, the storm of uncertainty came upon them brutally, uprooting the realities they had woven about themselves. Many had never been sure of their faith in the first place, and thus had never been able to give a reasoned answer for their convictions.

Others had never really believed, using the faith and their church ties purely for social purposes. And not knowing what they believed, or why exactly they believed it, they feared appearing as fools in the eyes of those around them. In the face of a few scraps of papyri, they fled.

Others asked deeper questions. *Is faith real if proven false?*

If faith is based not in evidence but in the invisible, can it be proven false in the first place? Does physical evidence matter?

Thomas, one of the original Twelve, had insisted on physical proof of Christ's resurrection only days after it supposedly had occurred. Unwilling to take anyone's word that the impossible had taken place—this despite the raising of Lazarus before many witnesses—he had demanded evidence to satisfy his intellect. Those who wrote the biblical accounts had recorded that Jesus then appeared to him, among his followers, and having passed through a sealed door, Jesus told the man to satisfy his need for proof by touching with his own hands the wounds of Christ's crucifixion.

"Blessed are they who did not see, and yet believed."

But now, could anything those once-revered men had written down be trusted? If they later denied their previous claims, what was one to think?

Fool me once, shame on you …

If the one book Christians looked to more than any other for moral guidance was indeed just a pack of lies, where then could one turn?

Fool me twice …

But so much of the Bible had been proven true down through the ages by so many, and through so many methods! The physical, logical, and historical evidences had steadily mounted over the centuries. Was all that just to be thrown away? Looking back, what part of it, if any, had been hard fact? What part had been surmise based on a house of cards?

Can there be faith without underlying fact?

Or, to take the issue to the opposite extreme, as many often had done, *Isn't faith genuine only if it flies in the face of apparent evidence to the contrary? Isn't its very essence that of things unseen?*

Never had Christianity been a blind faith! Rather, it alone had been declared a gift from God, recognizable to fallen men only after the Father had *opened* one's eyes!

"Do not fear their intimidation, and do not be troubled, but sanctify Christ as Lord in your hearts, always being ready to make a defense to everyone who asks you to give an account for the hope that is in you, yet with gentleness and reverence.... 'Blessed are you, Simon Barjona, because flesh and blood did not reveal [the truth of My identity] to you, but My Father who is in heaven.'"

Religious pundits of every stripe tossed their views into the arena, adding greatly to the confusion that had seized so many. Authors and scholars who for so long had denounced the crucifixion as a hoax wasted no time shouting "I told you so!" to all who would listen—and to many who would not. Jewish and Muslim religious leaders also claimed that they had been right all along, that Jesus had never been more than a prophet, a great religious teacher, a revolutionary. They stepped forward, mounting whatever platform presented itself, inviting their long-deluded Christian brothers and sisters to finally embrace the truth, to approach God through laws and works and acts of self-sacrifice—all of which they claimed Jesus had taught in the first place. Many listened and converted, abandoning Christ, no longer believing him to be God.

"And yet Jesus *forgave* sins committed against God," declared a few vocal Christian leaders who clung to their faith, and to the gospels they yet treasured. "He accepted and encouraged the worship of himself! He claimed, standing in the temple, that in him and him alone were messianic prophecies fulfilled, that day, in the hearing of those present!

"He claimed himself to be fully God, one with the Father!"

But if these assertions were falsehoods, could any man who told such monstrous, blasphemous lies be a prophet or a great teacher?

His only credentials lay in those things all being true. There was no gray area, no middle ground—otherwise, he was a deception, a devil, a wicked liar *worthy* of death, falsely leading others to place their eternal destinies in his impotent, outstretched, nail-pierced hands.

But left to the devices of men ...

◆ ◆ ◆

"It's bad, Pastor Jerry."

The morning's first service had been a disaster. Attendance had dropped to the levels Orsen had found when he first arrived at the church, numbers his father's arcane policies had brought about. The collection plates had come back nearly empty, the take barely a third of the previous Sunday's showing.

"Yes, Marty," the pastor said, placing a large, warm hand on the shoulder of one of his ushers. "It is."

"What will we do?"

"God is like a conductor on that big heavenly train," Orsen said, "punching tickets and checking the passenger list. The important thing is to get folks in those seats. What they hear once they get there is secondary. Numbers, Marty … numbers."

"But how? How do we get the people back?"

"We go with the flow, my boy. Plain and simple. We adapt. It doesn't matter how you worship God, so long as you do. All roads lead to the Big Man, Marty."

"I suppose so." The man's face knotted in thought. "Adapt how?"

"However we have to."

Orsen turned away, grabbed a jelly donut from a box atop a desk, and went into his office, checking his watch along the way.

Raspberry—excellent.

It was an hour until the next service, the primary gathering of the day. Between now and then, he would think of something.

You gotta give the people what they want. You gotta tell them what they want to hear.

No matter the crisis, he always had.

◆ ◆ ◆

Bonnie Henson straightened the magazines atop her coffee table, the third time she had done so that afternoon. Within the last hour the family knickknacks on the mantel had been dusted, the couch cushions and chair had been fluffed, and the carpet had been vacuumed. All these were tasks she did with a measure of regularity anyway, but when expecting company, she figured, one may as well do them again. Just in case.

Her doorbell rang. Running to the mirror over the fireplace, she quickly primped, adjusting the feathering of her layered hair and straightening her top.

Much better.

She opened the door with a big smile.

"Well, hello stranger," she said through the glass of the storm door as her eyes met those of her two visitors. She twisted the handle and pushed the door open for them. "Come on in."

Anna and a handsome man walked past her into the house, pausing just inside. The man moved a bit stiffly, Bonnie noted. No sooner had she closed the door than she turned and shared a huge, heartfelt hug with her sister.

"It's so good to have you here," she said. "I've missed you. We all have."

"Good to be here," Anna said, eyes closed. "Missed you, too. You don't know how much."

As they broke the embrace, Bonnie turned to the man just beyond her sister and extended a hand.

"Bonnie," she said, introducing herself. "So you're the Jack I've heard so much about."

"I swear," he said with a smile, removing his shades and taking her hand, "none of it was true."

"You were right," she whispered to Anna, before turning again to Dyson. "Are you being good to my baby sister?"

"Um … yes?" he replied, not sure how to answer.

"Bonnieee," Anna softly said. "Please."

"Oh, you know what I mean," she said lightly. "Come on in. Make yourselves at home."

She led them into the living room, where they took a seat on the plush, blue floral sofa.

"You must be thirsty," Bonnie said. "Can I get you anything?"

"Tea would be nice," Anna said.

"I'm fine," Dyson waved. "Maybe later."

Bonnie walked into the adjoining kitchen and poured tea from a pitcher into a tall glass sandblasted in a pattern of birds in flight, wings spread. "It's been what, four months since you were here last?" she asked.

"About that," Anna replied.

"Ellie graduated from elementary school two weeks ago," Bonnie said. "You should have seen her at the ceremony … She was just darling."

"I'm so sorry I missed it."

"Ben got it on disc. I'll have him make you a copy."

"That would be nice. Thank you."

"Ben's my husband," Bonnie explained to Dyson as she emerged from the kitchen and handed a glass to her sister.

"I figured," he replied.

"And Ellie's my daughter," she went on as she took a seat kitty-corner.

Dyson nodded, having gathered that as well.

"She's at a friend's birthday party right now. She'll be home soon."

"Sounds fun."

"So, how was Italy?" she asked the two. "I'd love to go there sometime. I mean, how romantic is that? Looks like such a lovely place."

"It is," Anna said.

"Did you ever see *Come September*? That Rock Hudson movie with that Italian actress whose name I can never remember? Anyway, he was a wealthy businessman with a big seaside villa there in Italy, but he was away in America most of the year. And whenever he was gone, his valet turned the place into a hotel without his knowing about it. Really funny. Beautiful scenery."

"I guess I never saw that one."

"You should. You'd love it. I know you like those kinds of movies."

"Well, I'm kind of 'Italy-ed' out for a while," Anna said. "I don't think I'll be wanting to have anything else to do with the place anytime soon."

"Oh, sweetie," Bonnie said, leaning over to place a hand on Anna's knee. "I know. I couldn't believe all that stuff they were saying on the news. Is it really true? Everything?"

"Afraid so," Anna said. "Mostly, anyway. I wish it weren't."

"I can't imagine what you went through. Finding that room, then those awful papers."

"We're not certain they're authentic," Anna explained. "I mean, they're old. We know that. But we don't know for sure the apostles authored them."

"When will you know?"

Anna let a silence descend. Dyson gave a subtle shake of the head.

"Oh," Bonnie realized.

"There's really no way for us to get one-hundred-percent verification," Dyson added. "Not without a further find of some kind. And to be honest, I don't even know what that would be."

"But everyone's talking about them like they're a done deal … like there's no question."

"I know," Anna said. "It seems those who want to believe in them do, and those who don't, well, don't."

"'A man hears what he wants to hear and disregards the rest,'" Bonnie quoted.

"Yes," Anna said, nodding.

"I keep hearing interviews with people who've been told there's no doubt. I've been surprised by how many people just packed up their faith and moved on, as if their country club had burned down, and they needed to find another one."

"I think that's exactly what church is for a lot of folks," Anna said. "Just something to do on Sundays. A way to be seen in the expensive dresses and suits they don't get to wear all that often."

"You know, that is so true," Bonnie agreed. "That's all it ever was for Margie Hancock. Did you ever meet her? Anyway, to hear her talk, I don't think she's ever cracked open a Bible in her life. Doesn't know Jesus from a jelly bean … Always thought being a good little girl got you to heaven, and that was that."

"Was she?" Anna asked. "Good, I mean."

"Define *good*."

The women exchanged a look and softly laughed.

"Shame on me," Bonnie said, with a mimed slap of her hand.

"Shame on both of us."

"How about you, Jack?" Bonnie asked. "You in town long?"

When Dyson heard his name, his attention snapped back to the conversation at hand. He had apparently been paying little attention, letting his eyes and his mind wander around the room, jumping from framed family photos to the mantelpiece clock to an iron wall sconce opposite him.

"Uh, no," he said.

"He just gave me a ride here from the airport," Anna said.

"I heard about your arm," Bonnie said. "Hurt it in an accident, right? How is it?"

"A lot better, thanks," Dyson said with a smile. "A little stiff, but not too bad. I can drive okay."

"He's going back to the university tomorrow," Anna announced. "He's meeting with the dean of archaeology to discuss … things. My leave lasts a couple more weeks, so Jack's going to be there for my students, in case they need anything."

"I'm so glad you're going to be staying with us," Bonnie told her sister. "We've got so much catching up to do."

"I'm so glad you asked me," Anna said. "I'm just not up to that empty apartment right now. I need to get my mind off everything … get back on track. Reassess where my life is headed. My heart just isn't in a lot of things right now."

"Bless your heart," her sister frowned. "If there's anything you want to talk about, you just tell me. That's what I'm here for."

"I will."

"Well, I'd better run," Dyson said, rising. "I've really enjoyed meeting you, Bonnie."

"So soon?" she said, reaching out to hug him as she whispered to her sister, "Don't you dare let him get away."

Anna rolled her eyes, clearly embarrassed. Dyson pretended he hadn't heard.

"You're welcome here anytime, Jack," Bonnie said, then she whispered in his ear.

"We'll see," he replied with a smile.

"What?" Anna asked. "Bonnie, stop it."

"You hush," her sister teased.

Suddenly the front door opened. In walked a pretty girl of eleven, her blonde hair long and swept back. She wore a sunny spring dress and carried a glittering party bag.

"Whose car is that …?" Ellie began to ask, but the words fell away when she saw Anna. A huge smile appeared on her face, and she rushed forward, her arms spread for a hug. "Aunt Anna!"

"Well, hi there!" Anna said, holding her tightly. "How's my big girl?"

"We missed you so much," Ellie said.

"And I missed you, too."

The girl looked at Dyson. "Hello."

"Hi," he replied, smiling.

"This is Dr. Dyson," Bonnie told her. "He's a friend of Aunt Anna's from the college. He's a professor too."

"It's very nice to meet you," the girl told him.

"And you, too, Ellie."

"I was at Christy's birthday party," she told Anna, holding up her bag. "We got all kinds of neat stuff. Can I show you?"

"Sure, sweetheart. In a few minutes. Dr. Dyson is just leaving."

"Can *you* stay? Will you be here for a while?"

"Yes," Anna said. "For a while."

The girl smiled anew and hugged her aunt again, then she hurried down the hallway toward her room.

"She's lovely," Dyson said.

"Thank you," Bonnie beamed. "She's a good girl. She gets so easily distracted, though."

"She's a kid," he reassured her. "Goes with the territory. She'll be fine."

Anna followed Dyson to the door and out onto the front porch. Standing one step above him, she gave him a farewell hug. "Be careful. You sure your arm's still okay for driving?"

"Rock solid."

"Hey … what did she say to you just then, right before Ellie came in?"

"Bonnie?" he teased. "Oh, just that she wants me to keep my Thanksgiving open."

Anna looked away for a moment, her hand to her mouth, hiding an uncomfortable grin.

"You'll have to forgive her," she began. "She gets kind of carried away, but she means the world to me. She's been trying to fix me up since high school. Except for when I was married, of course."

"It's okay," he said, slipping his sunglasses back on as he walked to the car. "She's a doll."

"I'm glad you think so."

"And so's her sister."

He smiled, opened the door, and slid onto the seat.

Anna was smiling too.

"And tell her … in that movie, it was Gina Lollobrigida," he called with a wink through the open window as he backed out of the driveway.

◆ ◆ ◆

"We have no choice, now," Mercer remarked aloud.

He spread the week's copy of *Archaeology Journal International* on his desk, the sight almost too grim for him to bear. There, in full color on the center spread, were reproduced in their entirety, though in somewhat reduced form, the seven papyri stolen from Pompeii. The weave and texture of the paper was visible in extreme detail in the high-resolution images, aiding any who might wish to run a comparative analysis. The text, written in the exact ink he had seen before, was clear to anyone with a working knowledge of ancient Greek. And for those without one, translations in English, Spanish, and Italian ran alongside, all boldly declaring not only their content but their authors.

Andrew. John. Bartholomew. James. Thaddaeus. Simon. Matthias.

Do you have any idea what you've done?

Other publications had simultaneously run the story as well. The covers of *Time, Newsweek,* and *U.S. News and World Report* had all declared the scrolls' likely authenticity. More than a dozen authorities worldwide had also been quoted, their words damning to the faith. Yet nowhere was the name of the person in current possession of the leaves revealed, nor was the present location of the documents. They could be anywhere in the world now, on any continent, surely in the hands of a private collector. No museum would claim them outside of Italy's borders—none would dare to. But despite the uncertainties, the lack of provenance in their presentation, Mercer knew immediately that they were authentic.

The papyrus matched, to the very weave.

The handwriting matched, to the letter.

It's out of my hands, Anna. I know what I said, but if I could stop this now, I swear to you I would.

The reproductions even included a smaller leaf similar to the one in the first box, giving the location of the vault found in Rome. Each box, Mercer now knew, had contained instructions for finding the other.

Anna, I'm so sorry …

His phone rang. He answered to find the chairman of the board of regents on the other end.

"Yes, Mr. Chairman," Mercer said. "I saw. I have it in front of me."

He glanced over the texts as he listened to the man speak. The words he heard were not pleasant ones. The words he read were even worse.

"I don't think that's necessary, sir," he said. "Yes, I'm aware of the response. Yes, I … I know, sir. I …" He listened. There was little else he could do. "All right. Do what you have to. So shall I."

He dropped the phone onto its cradle for a moment, took a breath in frustration, then picked the handset back up and pressed a button.

"Amy, please get me Dr. Meridian."

◆ ◆ ◆

The water was warm and soft, its embrace melding with that of the music and soft light into a soothing, healing tranquillity.

Oh, how I've longed for this.

Anna lay back in the bubble bath, her eyes closed, trying

to lose herself, to be cast adrift upon the serenity of the room. Scented candles flickered, casting a vanilla glow upon the air. Every muscle relaxed, she lolled in the warmth of the perfumed water, letting it buoy her as if gravity no longer took hold. Even the most subtle motion brought the same response from the heavenly liquid, an all-too-brief rocking like that of a cradle, gentle and soothing. She slid one leg along the other, losing herself in the honeyed piano concerto caressing the tile walls around her, trying to let the warmth and the melody draw the pain from her soul.

Let me just stay here for a while—maybe a month or two.

She opened her eyes, her mind far away, and gazed absently at the pastel swirl of wallpaper in the candlelight. Her body was at peace, drifting on a quiet sea, but her mind retained at its core, like a pit amid a fruit, a question that refused to let it rest.

"Who do you say that I am?"

That question had lived at the heart of her being for so long, shaping her every thought, her every decision. Like no other before it, it was the very essence of a reality she could never have fathomed otherwise, a truth closed to her until the coming of a moment set aside at the birth of time itself.

"Who do you say that I am?"

Seven words—the most important ever asked, in any language, in any era. Seven words—the answer to which carried the very destiny of a human soul.

She drew a heavy breath, torn by the question. Its answer still lay within her heart. But its surety had been tarnished by the finds in Rome and Pompeii.

A foundation once solid was crumbling from beneath her, and she was powerless to stop it.

Please, she struggled, *tell me something—anything…*

Only silence echoed from the tile walls.

It just doesn't make any sense. They couldn't have been wrong about him. They couldn't have led such false lives, promising salvation where none lay!

Her hands formed fists, her long nails digging into her water-softened palms.

But forgeries wouldn't have been in that wall!

She cast her eyes upward.

Would they? Christ had been unique in too many ways, both in life and in death. His brief span on earth was the pivot point of all history, the crossroads at which the eternal path of all humankind would be determined.

The culmination of all things, before or after.

Even discounting the gospel accounts, Anna knew through Josephus that Jesus had been tried before Pilate. Yet Jesus had been convicted and executed not for what he had done but for *who he was.* And just as that question had determined his own earthy fate, so has it determined the destiny of *all* people.

"Who do you say that I am?"

"Why, Lord?" Anna whispered. "Why now? Why *me?* Why bring this upon the world? Why inflict such a devastating blow? I love you. You know that. I'd never have hurt you! But because of what I've done, your Son has been branded a fraud. Why did you put me in that room? Why did you let me open that wall? *Why?*"

She lifted a leg from the water, watching the wetness

glisten on her skin and the suds slide away. Her toes, accented with wine red–polished nails, found the front lip of the tub, her calf tightening to keep them there.

So fearfully and wonderfully made …

Her thoughts traveled down a new path.

How could an all-knowing God who's powerful enough to bring into being something as intricate and wonderful as the human body be defeated by the deceitful actions of mere humans? How could he allow false Scriptures declaring a false Messiah to linger and mislead the entire world for two thousand years? How could he create a universe from utter nothingness, yet be so impotent as to be unable to make himself known—as he wishes to be known—for century upon century?

She lowered her leg back into the water, finding it warmer than before, and sat up, her mind racing, her thoughts afire.

What do you want me to do? Please, give me a sign … anything.

A knock broke the stillness.

"Anna?" came Bonnie's voice. "There's a call on your phone. I hope you don't mind, but I answered for you."

"Who is it?"

"Dean Mercer at the college."

"Just a sec."

Anna rose from the water, grabbing a large pink towel from the rack as she stepped onto the plush bath rug that lay against the tile. With mincing steps she wrapped the towel tightly around herself, warding off the cold, then reached out and unlocked the door.

"He's waiting," Bonnie said, handing her the phone

through the gap. "Oh, and Ellie's home now, so be careful coming out."

"I will. Thanks."

Anna turned away, closing the door again as she brought the phone to her ear.

"Hello?"

"Anna," came the dean's voice. "This is Albert."

"Hi," she said, happy to hear his voice. "How's Mary? How's Oldefield?"

"Both are fine. I trust you had a pleasant flight back?"

"Very nice. Yes."

"My dear," he said, assuming a tone she had learned to dread, "I need to talk to you."

Clik clik clik.

Anna tapped a high heel against the polished, speckled flooring of the hallway, knowing at any moment the vote would come. She sat on one of three benches spaced against the wall, each bearing the name of a past benefactor whose generosity had allowed many passersby throughout the years a moment or two off their weary feet.

She glanced over at the sealed double door again, hearing nothing from beyond it.

This isn't going to be good.

She pulled a tube from her purse and freshened her lipstick, more from nervousness than need. It soothed the butterflies a little just to do something normal, something she did so often. A small thing, but it helped.

As the minutes crawled by, she studied the hallway around her, finding in every element echoes of almost two centuries of learning. The dark wood-paneled walls, lovingly maintained just as they had been since long before her birth, bore framed photographs of past faculty and staff. A succession of presidents, provosts, trustees, and deans—almost all men, with a very few recent exceptions—watched her from behind decades-old glass, their clothing and eyewear telling the era of their service. Some of the faces, she imagined, bore looks of disapproval.

Why did I have to look behind that rotas square? Why couldn't I have left well enough alone?

She momentarily closed her eyes, shutting out the faces, then diverted her gaze to the rest of the history surrounding her. A row of display cases held the remnants of a long-discarded football tradition, its last season having been played in 1949. Trophies, their tarnish and style betraying their age, stood right where proud coaches and players once had placed them. Awards of merit, decorations, prizes, and other tributes, some in frames, some not, stood right alongside, declaring the all-but-forgotten achievements of honorees past.

And in one case she recognized a small photo of herself being awarded the Fergusen chair.

My kingdom for a time machine.

She glanced down, tugging at the hem of her black suit dress, her purse close beside her. She looked at her watch.

They've been in there an hour.

She dropped her head.

Oh, Lord, please tell me you'll open a window.

Mercer had warned her what to expect. She knew the

nature of the meeting. He had hoped to spare her at least some of what was to come, if at all possible.

A sound. She looked up to see the door opening. Rising at once to her feet, she picked up her purse and smoothed her dress as the board of regents, all men at the top of the local business community and dressed accordingly, began to emerge.

Here we go …

One regent kicked a doorstop into place with his toe as the others filed into the hallway and came in her direction. One after another, in something not unlike a funeral procession, the almost two-dozen men walked past her. Some never broke stride and didn't meet her eyes. A few paused and reached out to take her hands in theirs, as if to show deep regret.

As the last of them passed, Anna looked over at the door. Mercer stood there, his face set, beckoning her approach. She took a deep breath and went to him. He motioned her into the university's grand meeting room.

Only one man remained inside. His eyes were hard, his woolen hair raven black. He was Carl Broden, the chairman of the board of regents and president of the largest bank within a seven-county area. Clad in a dark suit and navy tie, he stood opposite Anna at the head of the long, dark conference table. He was tall and well built for his age, his imposing bulk apparent even in business dress. His angular face was stern, his demeanor intimidating.

"Dr. Meridian," he said flatly.

"Mr. Chairman."

"No need to take a seat. This won't take long. Dean Mercer has been asked to wait outside."

Anna glanced over her shoulder to find Mercer gone and the door closed.

"Why am I here?" Anna asked.

"Dr. Meridian," he began, "you are aware that for some time this institution has considered and reconsidered the wisdom of maintaining your archaeology program. Out of the university's appreciation for the achievements of your late husband, we continued to fund you in your efforts. Unfortunately, those efforts bore few results."

She remained silent.

"That is, until this past month," he went on. "The events in Italy initially but all too briefly focused a positive spotlight on Oldefield. The prospects for increased enrollment in the fall seemed promising. Your discovery of a legendary and long-sought-after site was the fulfillment of every university's dream. I commend you on the find."

"Thank you, sir."

"Don't thank me. Since the discovery and the subsequent release of the documents you uncovered, a great deal of new attention has fallen on this institution. *Unwanted* attention, Dr. Meridian. Our phones have rung off the hook with calls from angry parents and parishioners the world over, with threats of every stripe … and with the publication of the other texts, the threats have only increased. Financial threats. Bomb threats. Even death threats and threats of violence against specific members of the faculty, including Dean Mercer."

She was surprised at that. "He didn't tell me."

"He wouldn't. I also doubt he told you that our physics professor awoke this morning to find his home vandalized and his tires slashed. This stops, Dr. Meridian, and it stops now."

What have I done?

"The board has reached a decision, and the duty of informing you of that judgment has fallen to me."

"And what has the board decided?"

"That it would be better for all concerned if you immediately tendered your resignation, word of which will be released at once to as many outlets as possible. Any affiliation you have with Oldefield will be severed. You will receive the standard separation package, but no longer are you to have anything to do with this university, in any capacity."

Broden picked up his briefcase and walked around the table. Stopping before Anna, he looked down at her.

"Your husband would have known better," he said. "He'd have burned those texts the moment he uncovered them. He would have understood the ramifications of their existence becoming known."

He shook his head.

"Look what you've done to his good name. What would he think of you now? Archaeology is a man's game, not a place for feminine sentiment or delicate egos … It's for those who can make the hard decisions, those who know what to reveal and what to keep buried in the past in order to protect the present."

She glared, hating him. Hating herself.

Oh, Sam—I'm so, so sorry …

Anna was crumbling inside, feeling the tears rushing to the surface, the breath catching in her lungs. Her fleeting composure was all but gone. But she refused to give the horrid man before her the satisfaction of seeing the toll his verbal assault had taken.

As if sensing her wounds, he stepped up, leaning over her, pushing into her space. His professionalism fell away like a skin, revealing a long-held resentment for her, for the special treatment he felt she had received for too long.

"Go home, little girl," he said coldly. "You've done enough damage."

Then he spun around, pushed his way through the door, and was gone.

Now alone, Anna dropped into a chair, grabbing for its arm. With Broden's words like daggers in her mind, she lost all restraint. Her purse fell to the floor. Sobbing bitterly, she dropped her head and could not stop shaking, could no longer contain the despair and anger and self-doubt that had been building for weeks. It spilled forth, a torrent of misery, obliterating the fragile barrier behind which she had kept it at bay.

After what seemed an eternity, she felt hands upon her shoulders. Becoming aware of her surroundings again, she looked up to find Mercer standing beside her, trying in silence and in vain to lend a comfort that no one, at that moment, could give. She leaned into him, shuddering as she wept, clinging to the sleeve of his suit jacket.

He gently cradled her head, his heart breaking as, he knew, her own had.

Nine

The sun had dropped low in the Italian sky, rays of orange-gold bathing the countryside. Gentle breezes, sweeping inland, brought with them the scent of adventure, of distant lands beyond the curvature of the world.

An older white-panel van, moving somewhat slower than the surrounding traffic, headed northward on the A3 Autostrada. Its suspension was strained, its engine taxed by its cargo, a crate nursed from moment to moment by the three men who had brought it to Italy's shores. They drove past one sleepy village after another, ignoring the colorful, centuries-old structures and long-celebrated vineyards, having no appreciation for the living history all around them.

There was a job to be done. A mission to be carried out.

Theirs was a holy charge, demanded of them by a god of brutal vengeance.

The traffic slowed, a sea of red taillights igniting ahead. Road construction, the bane of every motorist, claimed the next five miles of highway for itself, forcing the traffic into a narrower flow. The driver of the van studied the scene before him, scanning the heavy equipment, the cranes, the helmeted workmen, and the surrounding stockpiles of steel and concrete. He checked his watch.

Their planning had been thorough. Unless the situation worsened, their time line would remain intact.

Their cargo had suffered a fall aboard ship. A rope had slipped, allowing the crate to slam hard onto the hold's deck. An inspection once the crate had been placed into the truck indicated that its precious contents had suffered no damage, so they had chosen to proceed.

And yet they worried.

A flagman on the shoulder waved them by, his attentions primarily absorbed by an animated conversation he was having via walkie-talkie with another unseen member of the road crew. A radio-controlled loader stood just off road, waiting for commands, its arms filled with structural bracing. Men in varied locations all communicated, working as one to carry out their assigned tasks.

Suddenly the driver of the van was seeing radios everywhere, all around him.

◆ ◆ ◆

"I just sat there," Anna said. "I sat there and cried like a baby."

"You had every right to," Bonnie told her, taking her hand at a table in Rose's Coffee Shop, a warm, comforting place they had cherished since their teenage years. "I would have too. What an awful man."

"I know, but …" She paused, hating the words she was about to say. "I couldn't say anything to him. He was right. He may be a compassionless jerk, but he was right."

"He was *not* right."

"Yes, he was," Anna insisted. "Everything he said was true. I've done more damage than I'll ever know. The lives of millions of people I'll never even meet have been destroyed. And I've disgraced Sam and everything he stood for—"

"You have *not,* Anna," Bonnie said firmly. "That isn't true. None of it."

"Yes, it is. All those poor people. I've given atheists worldwide exactly the opportunity they've been waiting for—"

"Anna ..."

"Because of me, the body of Christ has a gaping, open wound, and those who hate him are standing there pouring salt into it and dancing on his no-longer-empty grave. Well, I've done enough harm ... and God took my job away so I couldn't do any more. He wants me to sit down and shut up and just disappear."

"Sweetie, don't you think—"

"I got Jack hurt," she interrupted. "And because of me, Albert and a lot of other good people have been threatened."

Bonnie just held her sister's hand, hurting along with her.

"If only Sam had lived," Anna mourned. "We were going to have a family. Did I ever tell you that? We were finally going to settle down, and we'd have had beautiful babies, and I'd have stayed at home and raised them, and ... we'd have been happy." She looked at a couple across the room, new parents blissful and aglow with youth, sitting at a table with a toddler in a high chair. Anna's hand went to her abdomen and lightly stroked it as she watched the blonde, curly-haired child, a girl.

"I have these dreams, Bonnie. Still. Different dreams, different nights. Not always, but often enough. Sometimes I'm teaching my class in maternity clothes, and I'm out to here, and I feel the baby kick. Or I'm at a shower you and Mom are giving me. Or I'm giving birth with Sam standing there … holding my hand …"

"Oh, sweetie …"

Anna felt agonizingly empty. Her life, her flesh, her soul. Bonnie, watching her sister eye the toddler, knew hers was a pain not easily allayed.

"The chairman was right," Anna said. "I should never have gone into archaeology in the first place. Look at me. I'm not cut out for digging in caves. I hate the dust, and the snakes, and the desert, and the jungle, and the isolation of being a jillion miles from nowhere. I'm no Lara Croft."

"Well, *no one* is, Anna."

"I'm Vyse and Belzoni, that's who I am. Destroying whatever I touch …"

Bonnie subtly waved a hand. "Laywoman here …"

"Sorry. It was back in the nineteenth century. Howard Vyse used dynamite and gunpowder to clear Egyptian tombs, then picked through the rubble for artifacts. Giovanni Belzoni wasn't much better, using hydraulics to crack apart statues and chamber walls. They ruined so much in their misguided search for quick treasure."

"You're nothing like them. You're a trained archaeologist."

"The board of regents would disagree with you," Anna sighed. "I don't belong out there. I mean, what kind of archaeologist ever worries about breaking a nail?"

"Most of us would kill to have nails like yours."

"Just my point," she said, wiggling the long, wine red gems at her fingertips. "Who am I kidding? The closest I should ever have gotten to fieldwork was exploring the makeup counter at Creighton's."

"Anna Dawn Meridian," Bonnie insisted, "you stop that right now. You're a wonderful professor. You hate the dust and the snakes and the desert … fine. But you love a mystery, and you love uncovering the answers to questions the world forgot thousands of years ago. You love your students and they love you, and you love knowing you've made a real difference in their lives. You have a talent for making a subject come alive that any teacher would envy. So what if you enjoy the softer things? So what if you're beautiful?"

"Beautiful? Have you *seen* these hips?"

"Beautiful!" Bonnie repeated. "Who says you can't embrace being a woman while doing what you do? Who says you have to throw away who you are in order to be an archaeologist?"

"I know," Anna said, "but—"

"But nothing. You're one of the smartest people I know. Girl, you hold two degrees! You're kind and loving, and you've been given the gift of being able to share your knowledge and compassion in ways that are meaningful. What a blessing that is."

Anna sat quietly for a few moments, sipping from her cup as she considered her sister's words.

"I wish Mama and Daddy were here," she said. "I miss them so much."

"I know, sweetie. Me, too."

"They always knew just what to say. And there wasn't a problem in the world that could stand up to Mama's hot cocoa and Bing Crosby."

Bonnie smiled. "Yeah. Mama loved those old records of hers."

"I just wish I could have had kids before she and Daddy …" She stopped, letting the thought hang there. "I hope Ellie remembers them."

"She does." After a moment Bonnie steered the subject in a more cheerful direction. "You know, speaking of settling down and starting a family, that Jack of yours is something special. He'd make a wonderful father."

"Jack isn't *mine*."

"He *could* be. Maybe he already is, and you just don't want to see it."

"Why would I do that?"

"Because you think loving another man somehow makes you disloyal to Sam. It doesn't. It's been more than fourteen years. It's time to be happy again. You *need* to be happy. Sam's happy … I promise you."

Anna clinked her spoon as she stirred more cream into her cup.

"It's just so hard, Bonnie. You don't know. You can't imagine how it was."

Bonnie took her sister's hand again. "*Was,* honey. No, I haven't been through a loss like that. But I can see how things are *now*. I've seen you two together, you and Jack. You light up when you're around him, and he can't take his eyes off you. Sweetie, that man is in love."

"You really think so?"

"Trust me. And he's *gorgeous*."

"I know," Anna said, smiling. "I have eyes."

"Sometimes I wonder. You say how much you want to

have a baby, and yet here you are at your age, still putting off a relationship. We aren't teenagers anymore."

"I know, I know. 'The clock is ticking,'" she said, repeating a phrase she had heard too often from Bonnie.

"You'll make such a wonderful mom. I've always known it. I've seen how you are with Ellie. But I'm afraid you're going to let something that happened about fourteen years ago rob you of it all."

Anna was silent.

"Sweetie," Bonnie said gently, "I love you so much. I just want you happy."

"I know," Anna replied, squeezing her hand. "I love you, too."

"If you do … if you *really* do … please stop beating up my only sister."

Anna nodded, seeing things, if only darkly, through someone else's eyes.

They sat quietly for a few minutes, watching the people around them. Some they had known for most of their lives—the town was not a huge one, and no one remained a stranger for long.

It was then Anna realized that she, too, was being watched. And the faces turned her way weren't happy ones. One man in particular concerned her. He was staring, unblinking.

"Not again," she whispered.

"What?"

"Maybe we should go," Anna worried.

"Why?"

The man rose and approached her, an older gentleman in well-worn coveralls. The sisters knew him only as Luke, a longtime handyman who, years before, had been hired by their parents on occasion for work around their house.

"Hello, Luke," Anna said, hoping for a pleasantness she knew would not be forthcoming.

"Why did you do it?" Luke asked, his pain evident. "Why did you have to go and do it?"

No words came to her. Bonnie tried to intervene.

"Luke, Anna didn't mean anything—"

"Tell that to my wife," he said, almost breaking down. "She's been in tears ever since. That church was her whole life, and you took it away from her."

"I didn't …"

A waitress came over and took the man gently by the shoulders. "Luke, please come and sit down. How about if lunch is on the house today? Okay, honey? Anna wasn't trying to—"

"Some things are better left buried!" Luke barked as he allowed the waitress to turn him back toward his table.

"They aren't true," Anna said boldly. "The confessions aren't true."

"How do you know?" he asked, as if responding to a sudden ray of light in a sea of darkness. "You have to tell me so I can tell *her*. How do you know?"

"They *can't* be," she insisted. "It's impossible."

"Then why did you pull 'em out of the ground in the first place?"

She had no answer. The coffee shop was deathly silent.

"I want to know too," a woman spoke up, rising to her feet. "What did it serve to tell the world that Jesus was a lie? We didn't want to hear it!"

"It wasn't like that," Anna began. "I didn't release them … *we* didn't. One of them was stolen—"

"But you're the one who found them," another man said.

"Well, I'm *glad* she found them," said a young man seated near the door. "I'm glad we know the whole thing was a sham. There's no big brother God watching, ready to hurl lightning bolts every time we screw up or decide to have a good time."

A few nodded and murmured in agreement, which only made Anna feel worse.

"I'll make this right," she promised.

"How?" the woman wanted to know. A long silence followed, dozens of accusing eyes piercing Anna's soul.

"I don't know," she finally admitted.

"It's just talk," said the woman. "Even if God's up there, I don't think he cares anymore."

Anna had no response. The words, only a short time before, had been her own, spoken in frustration and anger then as they were now. Amid the silence, the diners turned away almost as one, excising her in that gesture from their lives, their community. The waitress guided Luke away. Even as he returned to his seat, Anna could feel the unspoken censure in the room still pressing in upon her, stealing away the very air.

The sisters paid their bill and left. Anna dropped into the passenger seat of the car, her face buried in her hands.

"They don't understand," Bonnie tried to assure her, closing the door, sealing out the world.

Anna sat back, pushing her hair aside to reveal smudged makeup and wet eyes.

"Neither do I," she said, defeated.

"They'll get past it, Anna," her sister said hopefully, passing Anna a small box of tissues. "It'll just take time."

"No, they won't. And I wouldn't expect them to. Bonnie, I can't stay here. Not anymore."

"We'll go back to the house. It'll be okay."

"No, it won't. I'm a pariah here." She drew a breath. "They all know me, and right now I can use all the anonymity I can get."

"Where? Where will you go? You've been on television and in the papers for weeks now."

"I don't know. I'll find someplace. Color my hair … change my name …"

"Honey …"

Anna forced a weak smile. "Look, I'll stay another day or two. Okay?"

Bonnie nodded and started the car. As they drove down streets they had known since childhood, Anna became aware of a spiritual pestilence in the town, a creeping malady that had taken hold, swiftly, surely, lethally.

And its mortality rate, if left unchecked, would be total.

A couple of the town's church buildings, of different denominations, had been abandoned and vandalized. Spray-painted acts of fury and hatred, words cursing the name of Peter and the apostles, splashed their sides. Signage had been ripped away and smashed. Windows had been shattered. Statuaries had been toppled. Doors set afire now stood charred and black.

"Oh, Anna," Bonnie said. "I wasn't going to drive down here. You didn't need to see …" She grew visibly upset. "I meant to turn on Mariposa Way. I wasn't thinking. With all that back there at Rose's …"

"It's okay," Anna whispered, touching her arm to calm her. "Was anyone hurt when it happened? At the churches, I mean."

"Not that I've heard of. Not around here. Elsewhere … I don't know."

"They've been told everything they ever believed is a lie," Anna lamented. "The believer's whole world is centered on Jesus. Built upon him. When he's suddenly stripped away …"

"Some people are just quietly walking away from the faith, like zombies or something. I don't know if it's shock or just that they don't care. Some are pretending nothing ever happened. I don't know if it's denial or certainty … maybe both. Some are angry, feeling they've been made fools of all their lives, and others are crowing that they'd been too smart all along *ever* to have believed in God, or in Jesus in particular."

"The world's hated him since day one," Anna said. "It's like people are delighting in this, as if they finally see a chance to rid themselves of him once and for all."

"I can't believe how quickly so many self-proclaimed believers are turning their backs," Bonnie agreed."

"I don't know … I think for most it's just a matter of convenience. Going with whatever they think looks best in the eyes of the Joneses."

"But not for everyone. For a few I've talked to, it's as if they'd been waiting for an excuse to give up the faith all along. Or just never really believed."

Anna closed her eyes. She could feel her own back turning on God, her own faith slipping away.

So, is that it? Has my faith been rooted only in material things and physical proof all along? Do I have so little trust in God himself that when I don't understand what's happening, I can't trust that he's still guiding the outworking of some great plan?

She was shaken, wondering now whether she had ever known true faith, whether she had ever really believed at all.

Why do I feel this way? Why am I unsure of you, Lord?

She felt her confidence eroding, her faith evaporating, both being replaced moment by moment with a resentment toward God for letting her find the scrolls in the first place.

Merciful Father, if you're really in control of all things, please, in Jesus' name, tell me why you did this! Help me understand.

A cry of desperation, of agony. She fought to suppress her disappointment, her doubt, her rage, but it kept bubbling up, breaking past her heart and her intellect to claim her mind and drive a wedge permanently between the woman she had been and the one she felt herself becoming.

A woman she didn't know. And that woman terrified her.

◆ ◆ ◆

Dyson sat on the couch in his apartment, his shoes off, his stocking feet up on the cluttered coffee table. Before him, mounted on the wall, a widescreen television displayed the rapidly changing images and graphics of a news channel.

But his mind wasn't on the events flashing before him.

What will she say? How do I say it?

He replayed in his mind yet again the words he had chosen. They were brief, but their ramifications would send aftershocks through every facet of his life.

I've always wanted this, but what will she say?

Again, he pondered the phone in his hand. It had grown warm from his grip, cradled there for more than an hour, waiting as he wrestled internally with the situation thrust upon him.

How do I even ask her?

He was yanked from his reverie by a flashing red banner and a loud musical tone as the television declared a news alert.

Now what?

"We've just received word of a massive explosion in central Italy, southeast of the Naples area. While all reports are as yet unconfirmed and what information we have is sketchy, eyewitnesses as far away as ten miles have reported sighting a mushroom cloud rising from the site of the blast …"

He sat upright, his attention now laser-focused.

"We now have video from an Italian traffic chopper that, we are told, was five miles north of the blast site at the time of the explosion …"

Images appeared, shaky but settling down. Anxious voices in Italian could be heard over the din of the rotors as the camera swung around, acquiring a new subject. The countryside came into view, a quilt of vineyards and fields, villages and roadways. Vesuvius stood majestically, filling the left side of the screen.

And in the distance, so bright as to gouge purplish streaks into the image and light an area stretching all the way to the beach, rose what unmistakably was a mushroom cloud.

"Ladies and gentlemen, we're getting reports of a nuclear detonation in central Italy, along the A3 Autostrada south of

Naples, near the town of Ercolano. It appears to have taken place during the latter part of rush hour."

Dyson watched, unbelieving.

I was right there, he realized. *Right there on that stretch of highway ...*

"We'll stay with this story as the facts become clearer, but this much seems evident. There has been a terrorist strike near the western coast of Italy. As to why, at this point we can only guess."

Ercolano, he pondered. It was a small but densely populated town. A beautiful place.

At least, he worried, it had been.

◆ ◆ ◆

Anna dropped her purse on the sofa, still torn from her moorings, still feeling like an orphaned child.

Please—I need to be sure of you, to hear your voice ...please!

"Looks like rain," Bonnie commented, heading toward the kitchen. "Have you heard anything?"

"No," Anna said. "I haven't turned on a radio or TV all day."

"Ben's taking a nap. I don't want to wake him, poor dear. He's been on late shift at the plant. It would be nice if it rained ... It's so pleasant for sleeping."

Now alone in the den, Anna sat down, her thoughts distant. She fixed her eyes upon a framed photo atop the mantle, one of Bonnie and her on her sister's wedding day. She had been a high-school senior, and Bonnie a college junior. She walked over and picked up the photo, and a flood of memories came to her. The yellow bridesmaid's dress she wore, the bouffant hairdo, the dyed high heels that were a little too tight. The way her sister kept giggling right before the ceremony. The way their parents looked upon them both, so proud, so thankful. A soft smile blossomed on her lips. It seemed as if everything had been so simple then. So easy. So untroubled.

"Before I knew Sam," she whispered to herself. "Before we were married. Before I even knew what a shovel was …"

The ring of her cell phone sounded, its song filling the den.

"There's a room where the light won't find you, holding hands while the walls come tumbling down.… When they do I'll be right behind you …"

She crossed to her purse, found the phone, flipped it open, and heard Dyson's voice. She smiled.

"Hi."

"Are you watching TV?" he asked.

"No."

"You might want to."

She spotted the remote on the coffee table and turned on the screen.

"Which channel?"

"I don't think it matters."

At once she found coverage of the Italian disaster.

"—just east of the town of Ercolano. Reports on the ground tell of massive destruction at the site, with a significant loss of life and casualties numbering in the thousands …"

"When did this happen?" she asked, stunned. "How?"

"Less than half an hour ago. They don't know how or why. They say it must have been terrorism."

"But, why *there?* It doesn't make any sense."

"I don't know, Anna."

"How horrible," she said, seeing the panic, the chaotic rush of rescue personnel and fleeing citizens.

Bonnie walked in and saw the report. "Oh no …"

"Listen," Dyson said. "I know this isn't the best time, but I need to talk to you."

Anna turned from the television. "I'm listening."

"No, I mean in person. I can be there in three hours."

"You want to drive three hours just to talk?"

"Hey," he reminded her, "you drove six for me."

"Fair enough," Anna nodded. "You know where I am."

"See you in a few."

"I'll be here."

She closed the phone, dropped it back into her purse, and sat down.

"Jack?" Bonnie asked.

"How did you know?"

"You have a tone you only use with him."

"I do not."

"You do so." With a smile she handed Anna a cup of tea and took a seat on the sofa next to her. "So, he's coming here?"

"He says he wants to talk to me. Something serious, I think."

"Oh, *really?"* Bonnie said, a smile playing on her lips.

"Stop it," Anna said. "It's nothing like *that*."

"If you say so …"

"You're not going to be happy until I'm married again, are you?"

"And neither are you."

Anna had no reply.

They settled back and watched the screen, the reports now coming in rapid-fire fashion. The scene was horrific. Fires burned everywhere, sending black smoke billowing into blue sky. Burn victims wandered in search of medical help, which was agonizingly slow in coming. Law officials and government authorities worked to evacuate as many as possible from the blast zone, but resources were few, with the smaller roads so clogged they were impassable. Any rapid evacuation of the area was impossible.

"I barely recognize this world anymore," Bonnie said. "What happened to the one we grew up in?"

"I wish I knew."

How could you let this happen? Anna prayed, one frustration building upon another. *Aren't you in control at all? Are you even there?*

And suddenly, in a span of moments, something was ripped from within her, cast in tatters to the winds. For the first time in a very long time, she felt utterly alone, and what she had feared most settled upon her like a cold shroud. The dreaded woman once a stranger to her, whom she didn't know at all, had slipped in, wearing Anna's flesh like an abandoned shell, a vacant thing. A gasp escaped her. As she moved from the room into the hallway, her face turned from her sister, tears flowed.

She no longer believed.

Ten

Anna sat in the guest room, the light of a single bedside lamp bathing her as she looked through an old cardboard box. Inside were things of Sam's, things she had meant to sort through years ago, things she instead had shoved aside because pain still lingered among them, a rekindled thought away. She had brought them with her to Bonnie's, hoping perhaps that her sister could help her find the strength to finally get the task done.

But now, empty and alone, she decided that the pain living among the things inside the box was preferable to the spiritual hollowness she felt. She now sought solace in them, in the past, in him.

She reached into the box. Her eyes blurred with tears and struggled to focus on the scraps of paper—receipts from restaurants and car-rental agencies, now faded with age. A few she recalled, images rising of pleasant evenings out or working lunches eaten hurriedly.

A Reuben sandwich—how you loved those.

There were photos taken at various digs, most of them secondary in-situ shots of artifacts taken in case the first didn't provide enough information. A few, a very few, were candid pics of the team members, all smiles, their brows shaded by wide-brimmed hats.

She waded through university documents, travel papers, notes, and sketches. Sam's handwriting splashed everything, and it comforted her, its flows and scratches so familiar, so unique, so—*Sam.*

In every word I hear your voice.

Then, nestled at the bottom of the box, a small leather-bound book caught her eye.

His journal ...

She picked it up and found her fingers flipping to the last written page, only a third of the way into the book. An entry was there, written the morning of—

Written that last morning.

As she read, a puzzled scowl claimed her. The words revealed only now something he never had told her, something that made no sense.

I don't understand, Sam. We never found any such—

She read on and learned that her husband's last discovery hadn't been made while digging into the soil or exploring a cavern. It hadn't been an object of antiquity, but rather, something of a far more immediate nature. And he had uncovered it alone.

Sam had learned who had stolen the Aztec calendar of Oaxaca, so long ago. He had found solid evidence.

What was the evidence? Where is it? I went through all but this one box and never saw anything that—

The doorbell rang. She heard Bonnie moving down the hallway toward the foyer. Wiping her eyes, she placed the journal gingerly back into the box and closed the lid.

◆ ◆ ◆

"Come in out of the rain," Bonnie said, holding the front door wide open. "My, but it's pouring out there."

She closed the door behind Dyson as he stepped into the house. His gray overcoat glistened, dripping on the floor.

"Let me take that," Bonnie said, stripping the garment from him. "I'll go hang it up to dry."

As she disappeared down the hallway, Dyson walked in and found the living room empty.

"Hi," sounded a voice from behind him. He turned to see Anna standing in the opening to the hall.

"Hi," he said, visibly nervous.

She walked into the room and took a seat on the sofa. He sat down beside her.

"Was the drive okay?"

"Good," he said. "Good drive. Kind of wet, kind of long. But it gave me time to think."

"About what?"

"About the reason I wanted to talk to you. What I need to ask you."

Trapped by his eyes, she studied him. His discomfort level was visibly growing.

Surely this can't be what Bonnie thinks it is.

"Well," she said, "Here I am."

"Okay." Another pause, a longer one. "You know how when we first got to know each other, we'd sit in the university lounge and talk about all the things we wanted to do with our lives? About where we wanted to be in ten years? What we wanted to be doing? Who we wanted to be with?"

"Yes …"

Oh no! It is *what she thinks it is!*

"Well," he struggled, "I don't really know how to ask this, so I'm just going to come right out with it."

She held her breath.

No … I can't … I'm not ready …

"Anna," he began, "would you … mind if I took your job?"

"What?"

"Dean Mercer called me into his office earlier this afternoon and told me what happened yesterday, with you and the board of regents. I'm *so* sorry for what they did to you. It must have been terrible …"

She stared aside, thrown by the sudden change of direction.

"What?" he asked, concerned by her reaction. "What is it?"

She was silent.

"I'm sorry … I shouldn't have asked …"

"No," she said. "Go ahead. You were saying …"

"You sure you're all right?"

"Yes," she insisted. "Please."

"Okay," he said, without certainty. "Dean Mercer called me in and told me they needed to fill your position at Oldefield. He knew I had been looking to move up, either there or somewhere else, and—"

"Somewhere else? You never told me that. You were thinking of leaving?"

"No," he said quickly. "But I may have made a few noises to that effect along the way, the way I answered questions sometimes. I guess he thought I was."

"You … 'guess.'"

"So, anyway, the board offered me your old position, and I wanted to get your input and okay before I made a decision. I wouldn't hurt you for the world, Anna. I know how much that job meant to you. But they need my answer first thing in the morning, and I—"

"Jack," she said, taking his hand, "I think it's darling that you felt you needed to ask me first. You should take it." She smiled. "You could have asked me over the phone."

"No, I couldn't have." He smiled back, looking relieved. "And it's really okay with you?"

"Yes. You know all my students, and I know they like you. And I'd much rather have you teaching them than some stranger brought in from outside, no matter now qualified he may be. Besides, I know a few of the girls have a little crush on you, so you'd get their vote."

"They do?"

"Nothing serious," Anna assured him. "Don't worry. They just like having you around."

He seemed to see an opening. After a few moments, he took it.

"What about you?" he asked softly. "You like having me around?"

She wasn't ready, even as she found his eyes again. Her reply, but a breath, came slowly.

"Maybe."

"But, nothing … serious?"

She remained silent, her eyes searching his. She felt him squeeze her right hand just a little more tightly. She reached up with her left and lightly traced the front of his muscular shoulder. Through his shirt, she felt the scar there.

The spiritual emptiness within her ached, swelling in her throat, constricting her heart. So alone, so hollow, she reached out, clutching for him like a drowning woman, needing that emptiness filled by something, anything.

Help me …

He leaned in, and as the space between them narrowed, his bracing scent enveloped her, his aura of tender authority sweeping her away. She closed her eyes as his lips pressed into hers with a warmth both giving and firm, gentle and strong. Her throat tightened and a shiver ran through her, stilling a deep breath her body ached to take. Something like ice afire rushed within her, a weakness swirling throughout her being, dancing into her arms, her legs, her fingertips. She leaned softly into him, heightening the pressure between them, and lifted one hand to caress his freshly shaved cheek.

An ember ignited, flaring quickly beyond control, softening a wall she had built stone by stone, a barrier of guilt and pain fourteen years in the making. It had forged a distance, keeping danger at bay, forestalling any emergence of the kind of oneness she had known with Sam.

For to know it again, to treasure another man, would be a betrayal.

The wall had encompassed her for so long, its presence had become a part of her, an unquestioned companion she had come to accept as the years had slipped through her fingers. But in isolating her, it had forced a loneliness upon her she had never wanted. In shutting out love, she had shut out everything.

No longer. Now, in this man's arms, her freed heart ran

as wax. For the first time in too long, it beat with purpose, with another.

The kiss was deep and all consuming, an eternity. As it finally broke, the distance between them only slowly widened, an intangible electricity still arcing the gap. She felt his breath still upon her lips, the passion lingering there. Anna, adrift, kept her eyes closed, opening them only as finally she drew air. She found his eyes fixed on her own, her hand resting lightly on his jawline.

The barrenness still was there, the pain. But now she knew she wouldn't have to face the torment alone.

◆ ◆ ◆

Two hours later Bonnie, having heard a car depart, walked in to find Jack gone. Her sister was on the sofa cuddling a cushion, head thrown back, eyes closed, wearing a contented smile she had allowed herself.

"Did he leave?" Bonnie asked.

"He left."

Bonnie looked to the door, then back to the sofa. "He forgot his coat. Was he in a hurry?"

"He has an early meeting at Oldefield. We were talking, and time got away from us."

Anna's smile didn't fade as she leaned forward, her gaze finding her sister's. Bonnie canted her head, recognizing a long-lost gleam in those sparkling eyes.

You don't mean!

Anna squealed, the respite assuming a guise of joy, and she kicked her feet in a rapid burst as Bonnie drew quickly to her side.

"Did he?" she asked excitedly, taking Anna's hand, looking for a ring.

"Oh, stop that," she scolded, pulling her hand away. "No. At least not yet."

"Well?"

"He kissed me."

And then, with the whole night before them, they were as teenagers again. And the intimacy reborn between them, that singular closeness known only by sisters, was a joy they hadn't so fully shared in a long, long time.

Months passed, and the initial uproar over the scrolls settled as the world again sought an equilibrium, however cynical. The sanctuary of Jerry Orsen's Church of God's Providence, for the first time in a long time, was almost full. A buzz rose from the gathered congregation, laced with questions and speculation. Other than the addition of a modest arrangement of Christmas lights and garlands, nothing in the room indicated a particular change worthy of note. What had they come to see?

A special mailing had gone out, inviting the entire list of recent attendees to come back to church that Sunday morning to take part in a rebirth, to witness a transformation, to experience a meaningful evolution in their personal spiritual growth. A few came hoping to find a new way of serving something greater than themselves, something real and not mere falsehood. Some, still carrying anger from their disillusionment, came in the hope that they might regain that part of their weekly social calendar they had lost. Others came only to see for themselves what Pastor Jerry had up his sleeve, for he always had something.

The drone of subdued voices sharply ceased as Orsen entered through a side door at the front of the sanctuary. All eyes were on the man as he walked to the pulpit, dressed in his usual robe, his Bible in his hand. He mounted the three steps, took position behind the dais, and silently stood looking over the crowd.

I hope this works.

"Good morning," he said pleasantly, receiving a largely mumbled echo in reply. "I'm glad to see so many of you here with us this morning. I know the ordeal we've all been through has been a trying one, and I greatly admire your spirit in being open to our invitation."

He shifted his weight from foot to foot, glancing at the notes he had prepared and left atop the podium.

"As this holiday season approaches, I thought it might be a good idea to nail down a few things once and for all. When first I heard that the man we knew as Jesus was not exactly who we thought he was, I felt betrayed. I felt angry. I wanted to just pack up and leave this church. When I sat down and realized, on top of that, that the twelve men I'd most trusted to tell me how to live my life had lied to me, I wanted to walk away from this town altogether and not look back … to say good-bye to God and get on with my life, on my own terms."

A murmur rose. Orsen saw he had struck a responsive chord.

"But then," he said with his usual dramatic flair, "I got to thinking. 'Jerry,' I said, 'there was a God *way* before there was a Jesus. There was a God *way* before anyone ever heard of a Peter, or a Paul, or a Matthew.'" His voice grew louder. "'There was a God who stood on top of Mount Ararat and talked to Moses from within a burning bush, who led his people out of Egypt and into the Promised Land.'"

Nods filled the chapel, punctuated by rising sounds of approval.

"The Jews, bless 'em, they knew God back when there wasn't any Jesus." He held up his Bible. "Do you see a Jesus in the Old Testament? I sure don't! Do you see apostles or any other second- and thirdhand helpers out there doing God's business? I sure don't! All I see is God dealing directly with men … talking to them, giving them guidance, leading them with a pillar of cloud by day and a pillar of fire by night! I see a God talking to us himself or through first-string prophets of his own choosing."

He scanned the crowd.

Getting there …

"But you say, 'Pastor Jerry, God doesn't work that way anymore. He doesn't give us miracles and signs in the sky and prophets.' Want to know why? Because we abandoned him two thousand years ago, that's why! We left him for a lunatic we accepted on faith … a fellow we were told, by a bunch of confessed liars, was qualified to speak for him. Well, ladies and gentlemen, now we know better!"

The crowd was with him. Orsen saw it. He shook his Bible at them for emphasis.

"God didn't need no Jesus to talk to Adam, or to Moses, or to Abraham, and he doesn't need one now! He's called 'almighty' for a reason! And if Moses didn't need Jesus to get to heaven, then neither do we!"

He raised the Bible high with both hands and spread it open down the middle, gripping each half.

"All we need," he shouted, "is God himself!"

He ripped the book in two, held the sundered halves far

apart before him, then tossed the second part derisively to the floor.

"*This,*" he said, waving the first half in front of them, "this is all the God we need. It's all the God any of us needs, and it's all the God any of us has *ever* needed!"

The members of the congregation leaped to their feet. Some held their hands out or clutched them over their hearts, shouting out praises to the God their pastor had returned to them. Others just stood in appreciation of the fact that, once again, their Sunday-morning routines had been returned to them.

When the collection plate was passed, the throng showed their appreciation in a more tangible fashion. Afterward, as Orsen sat in his office running a tally, a broad smile stretched upon his face.

Gotta give the people what they want.

"Looks like the best we've done since I've been here," he observed. "I'd say the crisis has passed."

He looked up to find his secretary standing in the doorway. Her brow was furrowed a bit.

"Problem, Tiffany?" he asked, punching numbers into a calculator.

She stood watching him.

"Pastor," she said, "there's something I don't understand."

"Speak, my child."

"Well, you told everyone that Jesus isn't in the Old Testament."

"He isn't."

"Yes, he is."

"Darlin'," he said with a grin, "you go find me his name in there, and I'll give you this twenty-dollar bill."

"Not by name. That's not what I mean." She took a few steps toward him. "I was watching this cable news show last night, and this Bible expert pointed out, like, sixty prophecies referring to Christ in the Old Testament. The Jews never realized it. The way the tabernacle was built, the things they did in their sacrifices and at Passover, and even specific dates and places for when the promised Messiah would come. All of that foreshadowed him. He's all over that book. That's why this whole confessions thing is so weird. I don't get it."

"Just a matter of interpretation, sweetheart," Orsen said, hitting the grand total. "Not bad, if I do say so myself. This church is on solid ground again."

"I wonder."

"You're beating a dead horse, honey. So was the guy on TV."

She turned to leave. Focused on the calculator tape, Orsen didn't notice.

"And it's Sinai," she said, pausing at the last moment.

"What?" he barked, with a tone one would use when shooing a pesky fly.

"God spoke to Moses on Sinai," she said, "not Ararat."

"Whatever."

Tiffany rolled her eyes. "Merry Christmas," she said with no little sarcasm, closing the door behind her.

Orsen just shook his head.

"A mountain's a mountain," he mumbled, rereading the figures before him, delighted with himself.

◆ ◆ ◆

Vesuvius rumbled.

Dyson made his way down into the ruins of Herculaneum, barely feeling the movement of the earth beneath his feet. The quakes he had experienced thus far had been extremely minor, save for an isolated large event several days before, so his concerns were few.

Few, but not nonexistent.

The town, once a Roman fishing village, had shared Pompeii's fate that August of AD 79. She lay directly west of the volcano, only four miles from its summit, but hadn't suffered the initial, major ashfall due to strong northerly winds. Spared the heavier rains of volcanic material, she instead was buried in a series of scalding mud and ash flows, ultimately coming to lie beneath more than sixty feet of volcanic material. The flows had been so heavy, in fact, that the coastline at her shore had been completely repositioned, pushed fifteen hundred feet farther out to sea.

As time passed and an empire fell, Herculaneum was all but forgotten. The fact of its existence was all but lost to the ages. New towns rose from the rich soil, their founders and citizens little knowing of the streets and buildings buried beneath their feet.

And then, quite by accident, Herculaneum's theater stage was rediscovered by a peasant digging a well. Soon, a network of tunnels, less-than-carefully dug, wound through the area like those of an anthill, and the ancient town began to give up its first secrets. Much was looted, removed for display in museums, or sent to the private homes of the wealthy. Statuary, wall paintings, artwork, personal possessions—all taken, many of them never to be seen again.

It had been thought, following the initial excavations of the town, that all its residents had been given time to escape and few had perished there. No bodies had been found. It appeared that Herculaneum had been completely abandoned prior to Vesuvius's worst eruption. But eventually, excavations along what had once been the town's seacoast revealed hundreds of blackened skeletons huddled in boathouses. Mothers cradling children, husbands hugging wives, all trying to provide a protection beyond the ability of humankind. They had perished in the first pyroclastic surges of the mountain—ground-hugging torrents of ash, rock, and mud hurtling down at one hundred miles per hour, with temperatures exceeding thirteen hundred degrees.

Waiting in the night for help that never came, these people of Herculaneum had died instantly, touched by a searing violence they could never have understood. Now, another scorching blow, initiated this time by human hands, had struck the vulnerable site. Damage estimates had placed the blast at six kilotons, which had left nothing but a respectable crater where a mile-long stretch of the A3 had once been.

The confession of an Iranian national, extracted through the persuasion of Jordanian police officials, had provided information that the nuclear device had been brought ashore at the Port of Salerno and loaded onto a truck for delivery to the chosen target area. It had been a smaller weapon, one whose stated yield had been ten kilotons, but whose age had apparently diminished that yield by almost half. Its detonation, it now seemed, had been accidental.

Its intended target had been the Vatican, in retaliation for a perceived slight leveled against the Muslim people by the pope two years earlier. It hadn't been the first time such an "attack" by the Christian leader against Muhammad had occurred, but an incensed few were determined to make it the last.

"Islam," he simply had said in an interview discussing the world's religions, "is what it is."

Instead, the weapon had detonated one hundred twenty-five miles southeast of Rome, on the flanks of Vesuvius. The resulting firestorm, swept by erratic ocean winds, had destroyed hundreds of structures and killed thousands of people—close to seven thousand, one estimate had stated. Most of the buildings still standing were deemed unsafe, and the possible fallout and radiation hazards had yet to be dealt with. The Italian government had instituted a widespread evacuation of the entire coastal region south of Naples and north of Torre del Greco. In the span of a week, the whole area—including the municipalities of Ercolano and Portici—had become one massive ghost town.

Some had speculated that the slumbering volcano had been stirred to life by the nuclear detonation, resulting in the tremors now being felt in the area. Others, pointing to the data continually streaming from sensors on the volcano's slopes and to the fact that such minor quakes had been occurring for centuries, drew no such conclusion.

Dyson had returned to Italy to help in the survey of blast and quake damage at the treasured site. In the months since the blast, radiation levels had dropped well below the point considered safe, prompting Italian officials concerned with tourism and the well-being of their national historic sites to investigate and restore any damage done.

"'You owe me one,'" he mockingly quoted in good humor, imitating the native accent of Gianni Valerio, who had insisted that Dyson be part of the assessment team. "'Who got who shot?' I mean, how low is that? Hey, I got shot too, you know. Dragging me halfway across the world ... and at Christmas, yet."

He climbed over a partially fallen wall, pausing then in the middle of an ancient Roman street to compare the current state of the ruins with survey photos from the year before.

"Lost a whole wall right there," he moaned. "Going to take a lot of work to get this place back to its normal two-thousand-year-old ruined shape."

Dyson moved from area to area within his assigned coordinates, snapping comparison photos and detail shots and making notes. The blocks of structures, referred to as *insulae,* Latin for "islands," were divided by three *cardo*—north-south streets—numbered according to their position within the excavated portion of the city. Some buildings, to his delight, seemed virtually untouched. Others, the worst of the lot, had collapsed altogether and would require major restoration. A structure known as the House of the Deer had lost most of its tile roof, but its walls had come through intact. Another known in modern times as the House of the Neptune Mosaic, along with its adjoining wine shop, had suffered heavy damage, including the collapse of an entire interior room.

He turned down a side street and headed toward the southern portion of the city, which remained buried in volcanic soil because of the modern construction above. With the overlapping town of Ercolano above it, most of

Herculaneum might never see the sun again. He mourned for the treasures never to be uncovered.

Dyson paused at an intersection, seeing in the near distance an odd play of shadow that hadn't been there before.

What in the world?

Moving forward, his heart beat faster. Exhilaration rose, tightening his throat as he realized what he was seeing.

He pulled his walkie-talkie from his belt.

"Gianni," he called, "get over here."

"Where's 'here'?" came the reply.

"Just south of Cardo V, a little east of the House of the Relief of Telephus. Hurry."

He stepped forward, leaning in, laying his hand on something no one had touched since the reign of the caesars.

Man, I love this job!

Carols filled the air. Twinkling lights dotted trees and trimmed doorways throughout the mall, announcing the most wonderful time of the year.

For retailers, that is.

The secularized version of the holiday being showcased bore no mention of Christ, or of his birth, or of the fact that he had ever existed. Carols sang of snow and mistletoe and flying reindeer, but all spiritual significance had been sterilized away. Finally, after years of working toward the goal, the secularists had been given the ammunition they needed to erase the Christian Lord from the public consciousness forever.

Or so they hoped.

The recently swollen ranks of other religions had brought about a response from retailers, whose marketing strategies for the holiday season had expanded to include Hanukkah- and Kwanzaa-related merchandise as never before. Many converts applauded the newfound diversity, ignoring the purely financial motives upon which it was based as they embraced God, family, and culture in ways foreign to them.

Anna stood in a bookstore, barely able to believe her eyes. There, spread wide on a special display shelf near the entrance, were copies of a hardback publication produced by a major scientific organization and distributed by a major New York publisher. The title mocked her:

Heresy: The Confessions of the Apostles

She picked up a copy, shaking her head in disbelief as she thumbed through it. There for all the world to see, in exquisite detail, were all the papyri she and Dyson had found. Line-by-line translations of all thirteen leaves were there, running along the margins. Accompanying body text presented a simplistic account of their discovery, while omitting the involvement of Raphael or any of the other more unscrupulous persons involved.

She thought back over the months since they had made the find.

What we've lost is immeasurable!

But the devastation didn't end there … around her.

What I've *lost!* She recalled the auction the previous month when the original leaves of the second trove had been placed for bid. They had made world headlines, promoted by a giddy atheist organization as "the words that finally brought Christ to his knees."

They had sold for millions.

Anna and Mercer, upon learning of the upcoming book she now held in her hands, had fought against the first trove being included in its pages. For months they had tried to convince first the museum curator in Milan and then the Italian government to keep them hidden away, that at least in this one small way they might keep the damage from being total. But they had been overruled, due largely to the promised licensing and royalty fees and the number of zeros flashed before the eyes of the officials making the decision.

She, her students, Mercer, and the hired scientists in Switzerland had all been offered generous fees for writing their own accounts of the finding and analysis of the scrolls, as had anyone closely associated with the find. Anna, her students, and the dean had turned the offer down flat. The others, of course, had been all too happy to tell their stories.

Flipping through the book, she came upon the smaller individual leaves that had accompanied each trove, the treasure maps in each box telling where the other was located. She looked at them, studying the small diagrams as she had so many times when looking at the original formerly in her possession. She tried to imagine the hand that had drawn them, the author of each leaf, who so long ago had created a heartbreaking tragedy with a very, very long fuse.

Who were you?

She couldn't bring herself to imagine Paul himself sitting down and penning the things. Even if it was only wishful thinking, she still had far too much respect for him to believe he could have—or would have—done such a thing.

Why not just take the secret to your graves?

Her sorrow weighed heavily within her. Try as she might, she had been unable to convince herself that the entire thing hadn't been her fault. It had colored everything she had done, everything she had thought, every choice she had made since.

When a dozen universities around the world had come to her offering lucrative new positions, she had turned them all down.

I've done enough damage.

Her sister had implored her to reconsider, emphasizing the bright new start she would find in a new place, with new people. Anna, however, had been immovable in her decision.

I'm not destroying anyone else's name.

"I should have burned them the moment I laid eyes on them," she whispered to herself. "The past *should* stay buried. It's like a disease … infecting the present and destroying the future."

She considered the book in her hands, her mind falling back to a question she had never been able to answer. She flipped to the double-page spread depicting the so-called confession of Peter, and as she yet again read its perfect Greek, her ire rose.

Who leaked this in the first place? How did it get out of the lab?

There had been only one answer.

Raphael.

How many other antiquities are you going to steal from their rightful owners? How much more pain are you going to inflict?

She thought of the bullet scar on the front of Dyson's shoulder, still an angry pink, but healing.

Oh, Jack …

She thought of him. Of that first kiss. And of the many that had followed. She allowed herself the barest of smiles.

She had worked hard the last few months to put the past behind her, the pain, the guilt, the grief. She had walked away from her old life, her old school, her old responsibilities. A new apartment in a new town had helped alleviate the pressure of accusing eyes, but in its place a new loneliness had built as she avoided unnecessary contact with those around her. Her savings, consisting largely of the life-insurance settlement she had received following the deaths of her parents, had provided a measure of financial security so she wouldn't have to seek employment for some time. Given time to think and reflect, she was beginning to learn to let go, to put herself first, to realize there are things beyond one's control. She had almost convinced herself of it.

Almost.

Maybe I'll go back to teaching history somewhere, she allowed. *Someday.*

Anna placed the book back on the shelf. Even as she had stood there, two had sold.

How ironic, she mused, *and how typical of us. The number-one Christmas gift this year is a book denouncing Christ as a fraud. Who would ever have believed such a thing could happen?*

She walked the mall, knowing she no longer lived in the same world. This one was cold. Hollow. Joyless. Meaningless.

She sighed, a prayer drifting from her mind with no real destination.

If only you existed …

She passed the shop windows, finding no warmth in the gleaming tinsel and colorful ornaments that lined them. Clothing and electronics, jewelry and accessories, none held any appeal.

An empty holiday for an empty world.

She had seen quite enough for one day, and her feet were crying out for relief. She tried to remember where she had parked her car.

Did I park outside Creighton's? Or was it …

She paused, deciding she had gone the wrong way. She turned and headed up the opposite side of the mall, trying to remember.

And then she noticed something in the window of a trinket shop, on a clearance shelf. The object was resting in a cradle of molded acrylic, its color unmistakable. Its mottling unique.

A small oval piece of red stone, about five inches in diameter.

Travertine.

One whole side had been polished mirror flat, and into this, in flowing script, was engraved in silver a verse from Proverbs: *Trust in the LORD with all your heart and do not lean on your own understanding.*

Anna's breath caught. Her heart leaped. She rushed into the store, reached down, and held the stone in her hands. She clutched it to her heart, praying a silent thanksgiving.

"Can I help you?" a young salesclerk asked as he approached.

"I think perhaps someone just did," she said, wiping her eyes. "Where did you get this?"

He shrugged. "I don't remember seeing it before."

She paid for the stone. The clerk wrapped it and its display stand in white tissue and dropped them into a small bag.

"No returns on clearance items," he informed her. "Happy Holidays."

"Merry Christmas!" she replied with a smile as she left.

◆ ◆ ◆

The overcast sky grew dark. The biting wind intensified, its teeth sinking into all who had dared venture outside, sparing nothing and no one. Strings of colored lights swayed upon the eaves of homes, dotting the barren December landscape with splashes of pointless color.

Anna drove along, headed home. She would be receiving a call from Jack that night—he had promised.

I did so want to be with you at Christmas, she sighed.

She drove through the wooded countryside, the darkness all around her more than mere night. It seemed oppressive, heavy. The cold was dense, seeping in through every crack and crevice, trying to reach her. Feeling uneasy, she switched on the radio, hoping a carol or two might warm her spirits.

"—and we have long maintained just such as this," came a voice, tinged with the sound of a Hebraic upbringing. "Jesus, yes, did walk the streets of Jerusalem, but as a great moral teacher, not as the Son of God."

"But if he was lying about being deity," the host asked, "how could he have been a moral teacher? Would a man like this lie about such a crucial issue?"

"He never said he was deity," the rabbi insisted.

"Oh yes he did," Anna argued. "When the high priest asked him, 'Are You the Christ, the Son of the Blessed One,' he answered, 'I am.' But I forgot … We've tossed out the New Testament …"

"… thus, you can't lend the New Testament any credence," continued the rabbi. "It's now been proven false …"

"Figures," Anna moaned.

"… and I must say I want to thank Dr. Anna Meridian for finally putting this issue to rest," the rabbi went on.

"Don't thank me," Anna said.

"God's truth always triumphs," he promised. "And thanks to Dr. Meridian, the whole world now sees that we—"

She shut off the radio. The silence now seemed a comfort.

Snow began to fall. It glowed in the beams of her headlights, large flakes obscuring her view ahead. She slowed as the fall became heavier, wary of the deep ditches on either side of the street. As white obscured the woods around her and she began to lose sight of the road, she decided it might be a good idea to pull over somewhere, to get indoors and wait it out.

A light was shining ahead. As she drew near, a simple roadside sign appeared, which read Faith Bible Church—Unto Us a Child Is Born.

The building behind it was a small one, not too unlike the church in which Anna had been raised. Its steeple soared into the dark sky, vanishing amid the flurry and fog. Its snow-tinged roof and open shutters, all black, contrasted with its white clapboard siding. Warm light glowed from behind frost-veiled window glass. Smoke rose from a chimney and was swept immediately aside.

Anna pulled off the road into the parking lot gravel crunching beneath her tires as she came to a stop. She emerged from the car, hefted the strap of her purse over a shoulder, and glanced around as she shut the door.

She didn't notice that her phone had slipped from her purse onto the front seat.

Less than a dozen other vehicles surrounded her own. The wind had grown much colder since the mall, and more fierce, causing her to flip up the collar of her coat and hold it tight around her face. She made for the church entrance, the footing treacherous in high heels.

A sign above the door read Welcome, Stranger.

She climbed the wooden steps, pulled on the old brass handle, and entered. Inside the tiny vestibule, she found the air warm and filled with the fragrance of baking bread. Flowers in vases rested on a modest walnut table to one side. The door to the sanctuary was open, and a voice came from within.

She went in, taking a seat on a pew near the back. Few people were there, fewer than twenty, she estimated. One little girl several rows ahead turned to look at her, a lingering glance. She returned Anna's smile.

The pastor was an elderly man, fragile and gray, clad in a shirt and tie. He used no microphone, as far as Anna could tell. His voice was that of a much younger man, strong and vibrant.

"Jesus cannot be quantified," he said, "or measured, or captured in a laboratory. We do not need science to prove to us that we love our children. We do not need science to tell us our parents are real, or our wives, or our husbands. We know these things are true because we have experienced their lives in our own, every hour of every day … teaching us lovingly, touching us deeply, making us who we are. And those of us who are of the body of Christ experience our Shepherd and Lord every bit as vividly and every bit as surely. Yes, our faith is based first in fact, and that fact is sure, despite what some would now have us believe. But we also *know* Christ … We do not simply know *of* him.

"Those who speak of Jesus Christ as but a figure of history do not know him. They do not understand that he is as real and alive as *any* living person, speaking to us through his word *today,* in the present, as surely as we speak to each other. He is not just a figure of the past, like Christopher Columbus, or Abraham Lincoln, or even Moses …"

Anna smiled, delighting in every syllable. *Sound doctrine … How long has it been since I've heard it?*

"We know Christ lives. We know he rose from the dead, appeared to his disciples, and for forty days went among the people that all might see for themselves that he had conquered death. He did not leave them without evidence, and while we do not *need* the proof the world might demand, he has not left us without it. We have not seen his face with our own eyes or placed our hands into his wounds as did Thomas, but we know as surely as we know each other that he lives today. The noted Harvard Law School Professor Dr. Simon Greenleaf once stated that there is more solid historical and reasoned proof for the resurrection of Christ, as would be presented in a court of law, than for most of the unquestioned events of human history. Any fair and impartial jury, he asserted, would conclude *based only on the evidence* that Jesus indeed rose from the dead, just as the

Gospels tell us. And no one ever doubts whether Cleopatra sailed the Nile.

"My friends, he was raised by the Father and is alive. Through Christ, God stepped down out of that unimaginable, timeless realm beyond our own and became a man, entering the finite sphere he had created for us. He took on physical form and walked among us, and through death and resurrection was raised incorruptible, the firstfruits of us all. And so shall *we* be raised on that last, great day."

Anna listened, her eyes glistening.

The sermon ended. The gathered families rose, exchanged pleasant words, handshakes, and hugs, and moved toward the front of the small chapel where pies, cakes, and other refreshments waited.

Anna stood, smoothed her dress, and gently made her way up the outside aisle. The pastor, speaking with a young man, noticed her approach and paused to point him toward the dessert table. As she neared, the old gentleman was standing alone.

"Good evening," she said.

"Welcome, my dear," he said. "I'd guess life for you hasn't been easy of late."

Anna was surprised. "You know who I am?"

"Yes, Dr. Meridian."

"From the news," she surmised. "Of course."

"Perhaps."

"This whole thing has haunted me," she said. "I've felt terrible for what I've done to the world."

"Don't," he said with a comforting smile. "What has happened, had to be. And you have been greatly blessed, Anna."

"I don't *feel* blessed," she confessed. "I'm not even sure I believe anymore. A little while ago, earlier tonight, I found something that *could* be a sign, but—"

"Few of us are called upon so, my dear. Yours is a special part, set aside only for you. Be thankful."

"I don't understand."

"You will." He laid a hand on her shoulder. "The harvest is coming."

She looked into his soft eyes, wondering.

"What brought you to us tonight?" he asked.

"The snow," she said. "I came in to get out of it."

"Snow?" he asked.

"Oh yes," she said. "It's really coming down. I was lucky to get here. We may be stranded."

"Oh dear."

He went to a window and looked out. She followed.

The snow had stopped, leaving behind but a light dusting.

"But it was so much worse than this," she said, confused. "I could barely see. I've been in so many snowstorms … It was a bad one."

He smiled kindly. "Quite often, when in the midst of a storm, things seem worse than they are."

"Yes, but …" She pondered his words, pausing before she spoke again. "You're a good shepherd. These people are privileged to have you."

"There are many wolves. These few are my flock, entrusted to me. Many who were among us have left … These remain. It's my job to see them safely home."

"That's beautiful," she said, smiling.

"You're welcome here anytime, Anna."

"Thank you, Reverend."

He took her hand, silently thanked her, and went to the others. Her brow furrowed, she turned and looked outside again.

"I just don't understand …"

Mystified, she made her way toward the door. As she pulled her keys from her purse, she noticed a man in the back row, right where she herself had been sitting. He wore old clothes, long out of fashion—a gray suit with a fedora. Its wide brim obscured the upper part of his face. As she walked past, watching him, he subtly tipped his hat and gave her a pleasant smile. Anna, strangely drawn, smiled back.

Again, the comforting scent of warm bread hung in the air.

She went outside. The air seemed not as cold, not as harsh. The world smelled new.

She reached for the door of her car, pausing as it opened, noting only then that the man had followed her outside.

"Lovely night," he remarked from a short distance opposite her.

"Yes," she agreed.

"God causes all things to work together for good to those who love God," the man said, "to those who are called according to His purpose."

Puzzled, Anna looked at him.

"I suppose," she said politely.

"Answer the call, Anna."

At that moment, from within the car, her cell phone rang. She glanced down to find the illuminated readout of her phone bathing the passenger's seat in an electric blue.

By reflex she looked into her purse. "I thought …" The

cell-phone pocket was empty. Looking up again, she found herself alone. The man was gone.

"But …"

She glanced around, looking for him, finding him nowhere. The church door wasn't *too* far away.

I guess he went back inside.

She dropped into the driver's seat and picked up the impatient phone. Dyson's number filled the display.

"Hey," she answered. "The weirdest thing just happened …"

"What?"

She scowled, looking into her rearview mirror. "Oh, nothing, I guess."

"I tried calling a little while ago. Everything okay?"

"Yes, fine. I left my phone in the car."

"Listen," he said. "Are you busy?"

"Just headed home. How did Herculaneum fare? Much damage?"

"Why don't you come see for yourself?"

"What?"

"I've made a find, Anna. It's big, I think. I found a descending passageway. The quake shook loose a plug of hardened ash. Some kind of catacomb. There's stuff down there. Shiny stuff. I need your expertise."

"I'm out of the business, Jack. You know that."

"Come on, Anna," he implored her. "Ancient Rome is your thing, not mine. My strong suit's Central and South America. I'm just here to survey damage, not to evaluate a whole new find. Gianni and I have been down there once already, but I know you're going to want to experience this in situ."

Images of the buried town filled her mind. She had been there many times and had loved each experience. Time had frozen there, preserving forever a window into the past that never should have been, capturing a magic not possessed by any other place of antiquity, even Pompeii.

"My treat," he further pleaded with her. "And you know you love it here."

She remained silent, thinking as she looked toward the spot where the strange old man had stood.

"Answer the call ..."

"Hey, I did it for *you,*" Dyson said with an audible grin.

"All right," she yielded with a smile. "Just for you."

Twelve

Anna, dressed for the somewhat warmer Italian climate, stepped through the glass doors leading from the tarmac into the passenger lobby of Naples' Capodichino Airport. She looked very much the native Campanian woman, wearing a white, half-sleeved, ruffled peasant blouse and gray capris she had bought just before the flight. A northerly gust from outside caught her from behind at the last moment before the doors closed, blowing her hair in front of her face. As she swept the tangled tresses back, clearing her field of view, she saw a sign being held high at the back of a large knot of people. It read, And the Rest.

She smiled, hurrying forward, and found Dyson there waiting for her. He bent down, and they shared a lingering, breathtaking kiss.

"Oh," she said, her arms around him, "I've missed you so much."

"When we get home," he said, "we're both going to do a lot less missing. I promise." He breathed in her scent, her neck, her hair. "Wow … you smell great."

"Thank you."

She laid her head against his chest and closed her eyes, just letting him hold her. For a moment the crowds around them simply went silent and faded away.

If only I could stay here forever, she wished.

She felt a kiss on the crown of her head.

"Well, lovely lady," he said. "Are you ready to get out of here?"

"More than ready."

"Do you want to go to the hotel, or straight to the site?"

"The hotel," she said. "Please."

He took her ever-present purple gym bag and led her down the concourse.

"Looks like somebody went shopping."

"Who, me?" she asked, smiling.

"I like it," he said. "That outfit. Very … carefree."

They stopped at the baggage claim, waited until her suitcase appeared, and departed the terminal for his waiting car. In minutes they had left the airport behind them and were winding their way along narrowing roads toward the hotel.

"Man, I hate driving here," Dyson barked as a car suddenly swerved in front of him, missing his bumper by less than a foot. "These folks just don't believe in the concept of the safety cushion."

"Better you than me," Anna said, clinging to the seat-belt shoulder strap. "Eyes on the road."

They managed to reach the hotel in one piece minutes later. It was a relatively new place, its sign proudly declaring its heritage: Hotel Neapolis.

Dyson retrieved her luggage from the trunk. "I got you the room next to mine. You want to take a nap or anything? I could kill some time in the café."

"All those hours in the air gave me plenty of sleep

already," she said. "I would love a hot bath, though, and maybe something to eat. Then Herculaneum."

He smiled and bowed. "Your wish is my command."

◆ ◆ ◆

Her bath had been a delight of soft plumeria, jasmine, and warm oils. The light lunch of pasta and fruit that had followed satisfied them both, immersing them in the romantic flavors of the region. Now, fully refreshed, Anna held her breath as Dyson wove his way through constricted streets planned and built long before the advent of motorized traffic.

"The roads south are closed," he explained, his foot constantly switching from pedal to pedal. "Everything's impassable for miles around the blast site. What the shock wave didn't get, the fires did. Highway's gone altogether. The smaller roads are filled with toppled masonry, abandoned cars, you name it."

"All that history lost," Anna mourned. "All those people. It's so sad."

"Yeah," he agreed. "It's kind of a shock to see the place so still, so quiet. No sounds of traffic, or voices, or kids playing. Just the wind. Really eerie."

As he passed a pair of oil storage tanks, Anna realized they had entered an industrial district. Buildings to their left were constructs of rusted metal and badly faded paint. To the right, the Mediterranean sparkled.

"Not the prettiest part of town," Dyson commented.

"At least, the traffic's a lot lighter."

He turned to the right, pulled the car into a space, shut off the engine, and pointed.

"Here we are," he said. "The other marina's nicer, but this one was a lot closer."

He climbed out of the tiny vehicle, and she followed, the straps of her purple gym bag over her arm. Inside were a Windbreaker, a camera, a few excavation tools, and a flashlight.

"Two if by sea," he quipped, slipping on a pair of sunglasses pulled from the breast pocket of his denim shirt. He zipped his jacket against the ocean breezes. "There she is, right down there."

They descended a ramp and walked out onto the dock. Anna loved the scent of the ocean and drew of it deeply. Dyson led her to a slip occupied by a new white boat with a maroon sun canopy. "Twenty-three-footer," he beamed. "She's fast and easy to handle."

"It's lovely," Anna said, her hair tossed aside in the breeze. The air was cool but not cold, though that would be changing later as the mercury dropped with the sun. Knowing this, she had worn a blue V-necked sweatshirt and jeans, with a jacket in waiting.

"It should be," Dyson said, after taking a moment just to enjoy seeing her standing before the sea. "She's costing Gianni's boss a tidy sum."

He climbed aboard first, then helped Anna in. As he cast off the ropes, she took a seat just forward of the pilot's station. The engine roared to life, and they were off. As Dyson maneuvered around the sea break, he pointed out a short row of small boats that had taken on water and sunk in a recent storm.

"Free parking," he commented.

They passed the coast on their left as the boat headed south. Ahead and to their left loomed Vesuvius, ominous in its sheer size. The mountain had always made Anna uncomfortable, but its presence was a necessary evil if one wanted to visit Herculaneum, as she often had.

Behave yourself, she warned it.

"I have a Vespa scooter waiting onshore," Dyson shouted above the sound of the waves and roar the engine. "We won't have to walk."

"Thank you." Anna smiled.

Never venturing more than a few hundred feet from shore, they covered the two-mile distance in just minutes. Again he maneuvered around a sea break, cut the engine, and dropped anchor just as the prow of the boat came to rest against the rocky shoreline.

Anna looked up at the modern apartment buildings just off the beach, homes now as vacant as the entire area. The sea thundered behind them, while before them, chained to an electrical pole, waited the scooter Dyson had promised.

He helped her out of the boat and over the rocks, then handed her a bike helmet. After crossing a triple row of railroad tracks, they reached the scooter. It was a pale metallic blue.

"Pretty," Anna commented. "Nice choice."

"I figured we only needed one," Dyson said with a grin as he unlocked the bike.

"You would."

"Wanna be my biker chick?"

"Do I get a cool leather jacket?"

"Probably not."

Anna pouted, teasing him, and slipped her helmet on. Dyson pulled the scooter clear of the pole and swung his leg over the seat. As he put on his helmet and fastened the chin strap, Anna climbed on behind him, sidesaddle, and wrapped her arms around his waist.

"Hang on," Dyson said, starting the motor.

He turned, clearing a small stand of trees before winding his way through the claustrophobic streets and alleyways west of modern Ercolano. Covered vineyards to their right spread far to the south, overlying much of the newer land once laid down by the volcano. He wove along the northern side of a stone wall, beyond which Anna knew Herculaneum waited.

And then, with a sudden sweep to the right, they passed through an opening in the wall, and the twenty-first century vanished. Now they were surrounded by stone hewn by men whose lives had passed before the star had shone over Bethlehem.

It was AD 79 all over again.

Dyson guided the scooter down a cross street, past ancient homes and businesses whose owners had been forgotten, places now named for their most prominent features.

The House of the Beautiful Courtyard. The House of the Wooden Partition. The House of the Corinthian Atrium. The House of the Carbonized Furniture. Such were what remained of a place once deemed a flowering paradise by its tens of thousands of residents—a paradise on the shoulders of the Mediterranean.

On the shoulders of a colossus patiently waiting to destroy everyone.

They slowed. Before them rose a sixty-foot wall of volcanic material, its strata sharply defined in shades of gray. Along its crown ran a double row of pines, isolating the excavation's timelessness from the modern streets and vineyards beyond.

Dyson stopped at an intersection, alongside what once had been a community drinking fountain. The aqueduct that had fed it was gone, swept away in the cataclysm. Anna climbed off the scooter and looked at the town immediately around them, where the daily lives of so many had once unfolded.

A thermopolium, she recalled, the Roman equivalent of a fast-food restaurant. Ceramic pots were still sunk into the rectangular marble counters, from which hungry Herculaneans had made their selections.

And beyond that, just to the south, stood a place where appetites of a different sort had been satisfied. A brothel.

Oh well …

"Where's Gianni?" she asked.

"Had to go back to the museum for some equipment. He'll be back tomorrow morning. He stationed a couple of his guys to watch the site."

"You can trust them?"

"Sure," Dyson said. "Gianni's the most careful man I know. He trusts no one who hasn't earned it. And I trust his judgment."

"So, out here I'm all alone with you?" she teased. "I may be safe from the big bad mountain, but you, on the other hand …"

"Yeah," he said, grinning, "you're in trouble now."

The silence was oppressive. Save for the two guards, she and Dyson were the only people for miles. The wind, shifting northeast, whistled through the stone, howling in a plaintive voice.

"Ground zero is a mile due east," Dyson mentioned, removing his shades. "We're safe here, from a radiation standpoint."

"Where's the site you found?"

"Just over there," he pointed. "Behind the—"

A low rumble filled the air, breaking the silence. Anna felt a vibration in her feet and ankles as the ground moved almost imperceptibly for a moment.

"That's been happening a lot?" Anna asked, concerned.

"Yeah," he said. "Minor stuff, though. Window rattlers."

"How often?"

"Few times a day. I've been on the phone with the Geological Institute, though, and they say there's nothing to be worried about yet."

"Yet?"

"The quakes don't seem to be in any hurry to get stronger. Ol' Italy's just relieving a little stress, that's all."

"What if the nuke shook something loose?"

She was more than a little concerned. That was clear.

Dyson smiled and took her into his arms. "They don't think so. We're fine. Come on."

He led her toward his discovery. Anna glanced up, unable to see the volcano for the solidified ash wall. But she knew it was there.

And she had an odd feeling *it* knew *she* was there too.

At the entrance Dyson greeted the two guards in Italian.

They smiled, eyeing Anna for a little longer than he was comfortable with, scrutinizing her from head to toe. Once the couple had passed by, Dyson looked back over his shoulder, as did Anna, who caught them watching her from behind as she walked away.

"Classic," Dyson muttered. "Can't trust these guys for a minute."

"Jealous?" Anna teased.

A dark opening appeared before them, edged by hardened ash on one side and masonry on the other. Crumbled volcanic detritus made the footing hazardous. "This is it," he said. "Near as we can figure, it was a temple of some sort. Seems to have been better built than just about any other structure excavated here. The roof took the weight of the ash flows."

"Amazing," she said, reaching into her bag for her flashlight. She switched it on, then they passed through the opening and found themselves standing on polished white marble. Ornate columns of the same stone surrounded them, numbering more than one would expect, given the size of the room.

"This architecture isn't Roman," she observed. "I don't know what it is. I've never seen anything like it."

"Good," Dyson said. "Then it isn't just me."

"I'd say these pillars are why the roof stood up. Four rows in such a confined space. And the walls aren't just cemented stone. Those are heavy slabs. Blocks, maybe. The place was built like a bomb shelter."

"Maybe to survive the volcano," he theorized. "As if whoever built it knew it would have to someday."

"The Romans thought Vesuvius was extinct," Anna said. "Looks like someone else knew better."

"This way," Dyson said. He led her to a passage at the back of the main chamber. A large, heavy wooden door, carbonized and still in place, stood half open.

"Took both Gianni and I to get this open yesterday," Dyson told her. "The metal bracing helped hold it together. Looks like it used to be heavy oak, but it's just charcoal now."

"It must have been an oven in here," she noted. "Hundreds of degrees, for who knows how long. Months, maybe."

They passed through the opening. At the other side of a short landing, leading downward, was a flight of stone steps, vanishing into the darkness.

"I have *so* been through this before," she said, her tone wary.

Please, Lord, she prayed. *No more surprises.*

He led her down the stairs, past heavy archways carved in marble. They were well underground now. When the bottom step was finally behind them, and they had reached their destination, Dyson flipped on a work lamp.

Its white light gently bathed the room, revealing a place like none Anna had ever seen. Apparently carved out of the bedrock, the chamber had been bedecked with supporting structures of sparkling crystalline stone. Columns of an unknown type supported an elaborate network of deep-set beams high above, into which figures of men, women, and animals had been carved.

"This is Penteli marble," Anna marveled, running her fingertips up and down one column. "What the acropolis was built of. The Parthenon. In sunlight, when polished, it gleams golden."

"I didn't know the Romans used it," Dyson said.

"They didn't, Jack," Anna puzzled. "Never, that I'm aware of. This comes from a single quarry a long way from here, north of Athens. It's as fine as glass but stronger than most other types of marble. The sculptors of ancient Greece used it almost exclusively."

"So what's it doing here?"

She shook her head in amazement. "I have no idea."

"These figures," Dyson wondered, shining a flashlight at the ceiling beams. "Who are they?"

Anna looked up, her gaze following as he shifted the beam from one place to another until it fell upon tableaus of powerful men battling bizarre serpentine beasts and embracing voluptuous women.

"I don't know," she admitted. "Look at that armor they're wearing … They certainly aren't Roman. But they're not Greek, either."

In complete wonderment, Anna stepped farther into the room, letting it surround her. It was roughly rectangular, its walls curvaceous in form with deep horizontal recesses cut in groups of three throughout. A raised, circular platform with tapered sides, something like an altar, rose in the center of the room.

"These could be loculi," Dyson said, indicating one of the recesses. "Except—"

"Except for their length," Anna finished. "They aren't long enough for a human body. At least, not one over four and a half feet tall."

Another rumble sounded, so low as to be felt more than heard. The floor, for an instant, shuddered beneath them. Anna's discomfort quickly grew.

Qumran …

"So," Dyson pressed on. "What are they? They're all empty."

"I don't like this, Jack," Anna said. "We should go. I'm not risking a cave-in. I'm not risking losing you."

"Just a few more minutes, Anna," he insisted. "Please."

With a terse nod she assented but wasn't happy about it.

"The notches in the wall?" he asked again.

"Display alcoves of some sort, I'd guess. But what was meant to go there, I haven't a clue."

"Funerary urns?" Dyson ventured.

Anna shrugged. "Let's just get some pictures and leave."

"We already got a few general views. If you see anything you want detailed shots of, focus on those."

She reached into her bag, fishing for her camera. As her fingers probed, her interest in the altar mounted.

"It's amazing, Jack," she said, slowly circling the structure as she continued digging blindly in her bag. "This altar definitely isn't Roman. The whole place, whatever it is, doesn't seem to belong here. It's as if—"

She screamed and jumped back, her attention locked on something low and in shadow. Dyson reflexively lunged forward, placing himself between Anna and whatever she had seen.

It was a skeleton, clothed in the tattered remains of a robe.

"I'm sorry," she said. "It startled me is all."

"We didn't see it before," he apologized. "We just gave the place a quick once-over. We mostly focused on the temple upstairs."

She stepped forward, holding her light toward the skeletal

remains. The man had huddled in a niche, a hollow formed where the wide base of the altar flowed into the wall. Beside him, on the floor, rested an oil lamp of bronze, its original luster long since lost to a green and gray patina. In his lap rested an object Anna immediately recognized. It was approximately one square foot and crafted of leather, with a shoulder strap that hung loosely on the floor. She lowered herself to one knee, set her gym bag aside, and, foregoing her gloves, carefully picked up the artifact.

"This is a writing pouch," she said, turning the tooled antiquity in her hands. "He was a scribe."

She looked at Dyson.

"Open it," he suggested. "It *is* Christmas."

She lifted the cover flap, wary of its brittleness. Peering inside with her flashlight, she saw a small bronze inkpot and split-nib pens of both reed and bronze.

"Pens and ink," she told him. Pulling an inner flap forward, she saw many sheets of papyrus tucked neatly away.

They all had writing on them. In Greek.

Anna gasped.

"What is it?" Dyson asked, directing his light toward the site so she could work with both hands. Reaching into the bag, Anna pulled the leaves free of the pouch and gently returned it to the man's lap.

She stood, her light spilling onto the tawny pages, and began to read. Just a few lines in, tears began to stream.

"Anna?" he asked. "What is it?"

She stared at the papyri, her hands shaking, and felt a warmth clutch her heart, knowing something precious had been returned to her. In one searing flash it swept her, filling her even as her fingertips filled deep imprints wrought by cruel iron nails.

"We have to get out of here," she said, her voice breaking as she reached for her bag. "Right now."

"Anna …?"

"Now!"

She rushed toward the stairs, the papyri in her hands. Dyson was close behind.

"Anna! What is it?"

She stopped abruptly. Someone suddenly was there, standing before them.

"Neil?" Anna asked, surprised to see her former student at the foot of the steps. "What are you doing here?"

The ground rumbled as Neil Meyer stood before them, blocking the way.

"Hello, professor."

"I don't understand," Anna said. "How did you know where I was? And why are you here in the first place? You went home back in May."

"I came back," he flatly stated. "Unfinished business."

"This whole area is closed off, son," Dyson said, sensing something very wrong. "How did you get through?"

"We need to leave here," Anna said, but Neil didn't move.

"I don't think so," he said.

Gunshots rang out in the temple above, the echoes repeating down the stairway. A shadow appeared at the top of the stairs. A figure descended, one Neil didn't seem surprised to see.

Raphael.

Anna backed away a step or two, coming to rest against

Dyson. She clutched the papyri to her chest, then tried too late to hide them behind her. They had been seen.

"Ah, Dr. Dyson," the tall man said, smirking as he leveled a gun at them both. "How lovely to see you again. How *is* the shoulder holding up?"

Dyson glared, working to contain the hatred bubbling within him.

"You're with *him?*" Anna asked the student, incredulous.

"This young man has been quite a help," Raphael said. "Every move you've made the last year or so has been relayed to me. And every move you planned to make as well."

"What?"

"I tapped your phone," Neil bragged. "Soon after I joined your class. I heard every call you placed or received."

"Why?" Anna demanded. "Why would you do that, Neil?"

Neil took a step forward, glaring at her.

"You don't know who I am, do you?" he said. "You never did. You have no idea."

"What are you talking about? Of course, I know you."

"Look closely," he said angrily. "You should know me, but you don't."

"Neil," Anna said, "that's enough. You're making no sense."

"No?" He stepped closer still. "Here's a clue. You killed my father."

What?

"You're crazy, kid," Dyson said.

"Hardly," the boy insisted. "My last name wasn't Meyer then. It was Grant."

Anna, shocked, stared into the face before her, finally finding a likeness hidden by the years.

"Scooter?" she asked, barely able to believe it.

"It was Neil, always," he said. "You never even bothered to ask my given name."

"What's he talking about?" Dyson asked Anna.

"His father," she said. "He died with Sam at Qumran."

"You killed him," Neil said. "You took him out into the desert, and you killed him. I'd already lost my mother. Then you took *him* away from me. He should never have been in that cave at all. We were supposed to have spent that day together."

"It was an accident, Neil," Anna said, her heart breaking for him. "I lost my husband too. I liked your father very much. He was a good man."

"He was all I had!" Neil shouted.

For more than a decade, an irrational hatred had festered and grown in Neil's heart, untethered by rational thought. It was a rage feeding upon itself, growing, burning hotter as the years passed.

"Do you know what it's like to grow up in a strange city with someone you hardly know?" he asked. "Someone who only took you in for the social-security check, whose husband resents your being under the same roof? I was abused. I was beaten. All because you robbed me of my father. When I got old enough to leave and found out you were still at Oldefield, I had to find you. I had nothing, but my grades were good enough to get me enrolled on a hardship grant, using my mother's maiden name."

"Neil," she said with curtained eyes, "I'm so sorry. It must have been terrible, what you went through. But what happened to your father—"

"Wouldn't have happened if you hadn't dragged him out into the desert!" The more Neil shouted, the angrier he became.

"All right," Dyson said, lightly gripping Anna's shoulders as he stared past her at the student. "Enough!"

"Shut up!" Neil snapped, his eyes fixed on Anna. "You think you're so smart, but you never suspected a thing. Never! I was the one who told Raphael about the dig at Rome. I stole the papyrus from the box that first day, after you kicked us all out of the lab and went to make a phone call."

"You couldn't have. The lab was locked."

"I overrode the access code with an electronic gizmo Raphael gave me. I gave him the leaf and told him about the second set of scrolls in Pompeii."

"So, why didn't you just take them all?" Anna demanded.

"I would have … but I was interrupted by that stupid security guard. I'd paused to look at one of the leaves when suddenly there he was, at the door. I'd left it open. I ducked down and was afraid he'd seen me. But he hadn't, and after he came in I managed to slip out behind him. I was lucky to get the one scroll shoved into my shirt."

"So," an amazed Anna said, "this has all been about some twisted vendetta against me?"

"Not just *you!*"

"Who else, then? Who else have you hurt?"

"God!" he seethed. "He *let* my father die. He let you kill him! So when those scrolls appeared, I couldn't let you hide them away. With those, I could destroy you *and* God *and* all those who believed in him, with one fatal blow. It was perfect!"

"Oh, Neil," Anna mourned, crushed that hatred had so fiercely consumed him.

At that moment a brief tremor, more powerful than the others, shook the chamber.

"We should get out of here," Dyson said. "The quakes are getting worse."

"You aren't leaving," Raphael said, recentering the aim of his gun.

"She deserves to die," Neil said. "In a cave-in. Like my father."

"Trifles," the robber gloated. "Ancient history. First, I must thank you, dear lady, for the lovely silver cross we found in that room you excavated. Fetched a pretty penny. Too bad we failed to look behind the rotas square … Could have saved us all a lot of trouble."

Anna glowered at him, her anger rising. "It was you! You stole the Aztec calendar at Oaxaca."

Raphael only smiled.

"Sam knew," she went on. "He found proof. I found a notation in his journal, written the morning he died."

Raphael laughed. "And where is this proof?"

Anna looked down. "I don't know. But it was there. He wrote that he had it with him at Qumran …"

"Ah …" The thief smiled with glee. "'I don't know.' The eternal excuse of the almost-great."

And then, looking into those cold eyes, she knew.

"It was you."

"Was it now?"

"At the cave. You knew he'd found you out. You followed him …"

"Hardly. I was in a Mexican jail at the time for, shall we say, an unconnected indiscretion."

"And Sam knew that, didn't he? If he'd gotten that evidence to the Mexican authorities with you already in custody …"

"You see? I was indisposed … thousands of miles from Qumran."

"You sent men," Anna accused him in an even tone, her eyes wide. "They followed him. They stole the evidence from him before he could use it against you, and then …"

A visible shudder ran through her, and Dyson held her more tightly. Anger burned as the horror clawed at her flesh.

"They caused the cave-in!"

"Did they now?" Raphael toyed.

"You killed Sam and Grant!"

A laugh burst from the man's throat. "If true, I'd imagine the plastic explosives used in the cavern would have made for an impressive display, wouldn't you think? Such a clever bunch might even have made it look like an accident, so no suspicion could possibly fall on … well, whoever it was who sent them."

Anna looked up at Dyson, her eyes glistening even as anger flared behind them.

"I must say," Raphael added, "I'm grateful to whatever kind soul devised that mission of mercy. Being where I was at the time, it would have gone very badly for me had your dear departed husband's evidence come to light."

"You?!" Neil shouted. "All along, it was you?"

He charged at Raphael. The gun fired, its report echoing sharply throughout the chamber, and Neil crumpled to the floor.

"Neil!" Anna cried, dropping to the young man's side. She cradled his head as he shook, spasms rocking him. Blood spilled from beneath him, spreading in a wide pool.

"I'm ... I'm sorry," he said weakly, his eyes searching, unable to find her face.

She felt him die in her arms.

Raphael leveled the gun at Dyson. "Please back away, Doctor. A nice comfortable distance."

"Do it, Jack," Anna said.

"But ..."

"It'll be okay," she said. "Trust me."

"I beg to differ," Raphael said.

Dyson stepped back and to the side, stopping at a point as far from her as Raphael was. Suddenly the professor jammed his hand into his jacket pocket and pointed it toward his enemy.

"Drop it, Raphael," he barked.

"Very dramatic, Doctor," the man said. "But I happen to know you don't have a gun. My sources tell me you haven't carried one since Pompeii." He aimed squarely at Anna. "Shall I put my information to the test?"

After a tense moment, Dyson pulled out his hand to reveal a closed pocketknife.

"I'm sorry, Anna."

"And now, *Miss* Meridian," Raphael said, "I'll take those papyri."

She rose to her feet, her eyes widening in horror.

"*Now,* if you please," Raphael insisted. "Obviously, you were trying to protect them ... How important you must consider them to be. If they are what I think they are, were they to become public, they would cost me millions. And, suffice it to say, some of my more unforgiving buyers would seek a very unpleasant retribution for my having provided them with false antiquities."

He held out his hand, but Anna didn't budge.

"The papyri," he said with calm venom.

"No."

He stepped forward, lifting the gun higher.

"The papyri," he demanded again, more chillingly. "Please don't make me shoot you. I would so hate to ruin such a lovely face."

She knew he could just kill her and take the leaves from her lifeless fingers. But she also knew he wanted her to surrender, to yield to him, to lose to him one final time. He wanted that final victory. She clutched the papyri more tightly and, that merciful fire rekindled, silently prayed.

He stepped forward again, pressed the tip of the gun barrel against her forehead, and cocked it.

"Last chance," he said.

Anna stared into his cold, unfeeling eyes.

"No," she repeated, the word final, tears coursing.

"Pity," he said.

Dyson lunged. In that instant a tremor violently rocked the chamber, knocking them all off their feet. The hammer of the gun slammed home, the report swallowed by the din as the bullet harmlessly struck overhanging stone and ricocheted away. Dyson fell hard into one of the wall alcoves before struggling to his feet. Anna clung to a pillar, hanging on for life as the floor buckled violently beneath her, undulating like the ocean's surface. The rumble was deafening, the upheaval prolonged, as if the world itself were coming apart. Rock and dust rained down. Raphael, unable to regain his balance, lost the gun, stumbled over Neil's body, and landed sprawled upon the altar.

The air was a choking haze. Dyson ran through the shower of debris and found Anna. The papyri were no longer in her hands.

"We have to go!" he shouted, though she couldn't hear him. She whirled to see a mass of stone fall from the ceiling, pinning Raphael to the altar, crushing him. With a seemingly defiant spasm of dying muscle, he clutched at nothing and went still.

Dyson grabbed her hand and pulled her up the stairs. No daylight shone from above. Struggling to keep their footing, they were thrown repeatedly against the walls of the passageway.

They burst into the temple above, only to find it, too, crumbling under the strain. To one side, amid the cloak of dust and falling debris, Anna saw a robed figure, huge in stature and surrounded by light, his upstretched arms holding a massive beam that alone now supported the heavy ceiling above. The stone glowed red where his hands gripped it. He turned amid the chaos, and his piercing eyes met Anna's.

Those eyes. That smile. The face, no longer crowned by a time-worn fedora, was one she knew.

You answered the call, she somehow heard him say, though his lips never moved.

Her mouth fell open, and again she became aware of being pulled roughly toward the crumbling doorway. Time seemed to slow, to flow like thickened oil. When they were finally through and into the open air, they saw it had grown dark.

Too dark, too soon.

The temple completely collapsed behind them, tiny fragments of shattered stone pelting their arms and legs. The guards they had met on the way in were lying on the ground, dead from gunshot wounds. Running for their lives and barely able to see, Anna and Dyson barreled ahead, toward the Vespa. He focused on the scooter, pulling her behind him. She glanced upward.

The sky was filled with shadow, a deep, brutal gray that spread like a cancer above them, churning and growing darker each second. Its weight pressed down on them, descending, threatening to consume them. In the far distance, miles to the west, blue sky still shone beneath its widening edge.

Forsaking their helmets, Dyson jumped on the scooter, dragging Anna onto the seat behind him. The headlight flared and they were off, coursing back through the trembling city streets, headed at top speed for the beach.

Anna allowed herself to look back. The terror she found behind them was like none she had ever known. She cried out, her scream unheard, drowned in the roar of the cataclysm.

Vesuvius had erupted. A massive column of smoke and ash billowed upward from the crater, spreading to fill the heavens, promising death. The sound it made engulfed everything else, filling her being, passing through her, jarring bone and sinew. Lightning flashed everywhere, a continual barrage of uncontained rage. She slammed her eyes closed, shutting out the crushing horror, barely able to hear herself think.

Father! Not now! It can't happen now!

The continually moving earth threatened to toss the scooter from the street, but Dyson somehow kept it on the road. Anna kept her eyes closed, not knowing just where they were, praying the beach would appear at any moment. She felt them accelerate and knew they had reached a straightaway.

Anytime now … anytime now!

A rain of tiny hailstones began to fall, odd in the force of their impact. She allowed herself a peek.

It wasn't hail. It was hot pumice.

She wanted to scream.

Then suddenly they came to a screeching halt.

"Let's go!" Dyson shouted, tearing her from the bike. They ran through the line of trees and across the railroad tracks, finally coming within view of the rocky shoreline.

Except, it wasn't the shoreline anymore.

The waters had receded. As if in fear, the Mediterranean itself had pulled away from the land and was still in flight. The boat's anchor cut a narrow, jagged swath across the dark, wet sands, and in the distance, at the other end of two hundred feet of anchor line that had paid out to its limit, the boat bobbed in the still-retreating surf.

The pseudonight grew blacker and heavier, descending like an unearthly hand. The drying air grew acidic and sulfurous, making it hard to breathe. Dyson pulled Anna across the rocks, and they broke into a dead run across the sand, toward the only salvation they had. Her heart was pounding, both from fear and exertion. Pumice rained down, the stones larger now.

Finally, Anna felt water splashing around her feet, and when it was knee-deep, she saw Dyson climb into the boat, whirl around, and drag her aboard in one adrenaline-charged motion.

Anna fell into the forward seat as Dyson severed the anchor line with his pocketknife and flew to the controls. Her eyes shut hard against the looming terror, she felt the boat come to life beneath her as it swung around. She couldn't hear its motor.

All she heard was the thunder of Vesuvius.

As she put her hands over her ears, she was pressed back into her seat by the forward acceleration of the vessel. Faster and faster it leaped through the water, putting behind them a distance that seemed too little too late.

A loud crack sounded, rising above the encompassing roar, slamming against them. Anna feared the moment had come.

Father, she prayed, *accept me into your hands.*

And then she felt something warm against her face, her hands.

She opened her eyes.

Sunlight.

The aural assault had diminished slightly with distance, falling away to a tolerable level.

"I think we made it," she heard Dyson shout.

In her lap and around her feet lay pebbles of pumice stone. In her hair were flecks of volcanic ash. She turned to find Dyson behind her at the wheel, and beyond him, beyond the maroon canopy covering the stern of the boat, Vesuvius roared like an insane beast. Lightning still cut cruel arcs across the sky, more intensely now. The pillar of cloud issuing from the mountain's maw spread wide, climbing twenty thousand feet into the darkening sky. Flame and sparks rose from the summit as if from the anvil of a gargantuan blacksmith.

"We're about five miles out and headed northwest," he added. "I'll make for the other marina. It's only a mile or so ahead."

"Can it reach us?" she asked, eyeing the dark cloud.

"The ash cloud looks to be headed southwest. I think we're safe. There isn't supposed to be another shift in the wind today."

Her eyes were glued to the volcano, still so large behind them.

"The man," she began. "The man in the temple … Did you see him?"

"What man?"

She paused, suddenly unsure. "Nothing. Nobody."

"Anna," Dyson said, standing over her, "marry me."

The words easily penetrated the rumbling of Vesuvius. Her gaze snapped to him.

"What?"

"Marry me," he repeated.

She rose from her seat and went to him. Wrapping her arms around his neck, she stood on tiptoe as he kissed her, running his fingers through the ash-speckled swirls of her windblown hair.

"Yes," she whispered in his ear, her cheek caressing his.

And he heard her.

She knew she finally was free. Free of the shadow of the papyrus scrolls, the guilt of their release. Free of the shadow of Qumran, the guilt of two deaths she hadn't caused.

Free.

They stood together at the wheel, his arm around her waist, as Naples spread wider and nearer before them. After a few minutes she turned and looked back, Lot's wife very much on her mind.

"Jack," she said, awe choking the words. "Look."

The western lip of Vesuvius had collapsed. A malevolent roiling of gray, black, and hellish crimson, part of the fiery column rising from the caldera, was coursing down the slope, funneled narrowly toward the coast. Its speed didn't seem great, but Anna knew that was just an illusion—it was hurtling at almost one hundred miles per hour, a flow of fiery gases and choking ash of almost fifteen hundred degrees.

A pyroclastic surge, the most lethal child of Vesuvius. It had buried Herculaneum once before, long ago.

Now, it would do so again.

She watched as it swept inexorably over the town. She mourned for Ercolano and the other villages of the region, already mortally wounded by humankind. She mourned for Herculaneum, its history and its beauty, lost once more, perhaps forever. She mourned for those caught in the path of the flow, should anyone still have been in the evacuation zone.

And she mourned for Neil Meyer.

Great plumes of steam rose in the distance as the surge slammed into the sea. A new shoreline was being created, upon which children would one day play, and fishermen yet unborn would earn their livelihoods. The fertile soil, soon to overspread the whole of the western slope, would bring forth abundant vineyards, bountiful crops, and fruit-laden trees for those choosing to risk life in the shadow of the mountain.

Expended, Vesuvius would sleep. But it would not die.

As Anna looked on, watching the brutal outpouring, she realized that something else had not died; it had only been asleep.

Her precious faith, in loving grace and mercy, had returned to her.

Thirteen

They took new rooms, this time at the Hotel Splendid in western Naples. After checking in, Anna collapsed on the bed. Dyson ran into the bathroom, something he had needed for a while.

He walked back into the room to find her sitting there, shaking uncontrollably.

"Anna?" he worried, rushing to take her into his arms. "Are you okay?"

"I think so," she said. "I guess … it's just all hitting me now."

He sat beside her on the bed and held her, rocking her, cradling her head on his shoulder.

"A little later, after you've gone to sleep," he said, "I'm going to be a basket case. I've already got it penciled into my appointment book."

Fifteen minutes passed. Twenty. He felt her calming in his arms. Her pulse slowed, as did her breathing. For almost half an hour they sat silently, sharing the moment, there for each other as they came to terms with what they had survived. Anna drew strength from him, her sanctuary in the storm, her refuge.

Finally, she spoke.

"You really meant that? What you said out there?"

"Every word," he said, smiling. "I love you, Anna. I always have."

She drew a deep breath. He kissed her forehead.

"Did *you* mean it?" he asked. "When you said yes?"

"Mostly," she teased. "Yes!"

Thunder sounded outside, distant and rolling. His arm still around Anna, Dyson reached for the television remote. "We'd better take a look and see how she's doing."

Live coverage of the event wasn't difficult to find. An image of the churning Vesuvius, the sun glinting off its heaving back, immediately filled the screen.

"The ash is still headed away from here," he noted, studying a graphic. "Naples should come through fine."

"Did you reach Gianni?" she asked, referring to the call Dyson had placed from the lobby. "Is he all right?"

"Yes. He's going to run me over to the Hotel Neapolis to get our things. I'm sorry we lost your other stuff at Herculaneum."

"No problem." She smiled with a measure of relief. "I'm quite happy with the way that turned out."

"I'm also sorry you lost the papyri you found in the pouch," he said, hugging her a bit more tightly. "What was on them? Why did Raphael want them so badly?"

"Because of what they said."

"Which was?"

"Something wonderful."

"Why did you refuse to hand them over?"

"Because of what they said," she repeated.

"He really would have shot you, you know. He shot *me.*"

"I know," she said, reaching up to caress his shoulder. "I'm sorry."

"Anna, what did they say?"

"Look away," she said, an impish smile playing on her lips.

"What?"

"Look away."

Intrigued, he did as she asked. Anna plunged a slender hand deep into the V-necked collar of her sweatshirt, her fingers slipping beneath the band of her long-line bra. Then, after a moment, she pulled her hand free.

Along with the papyri.

"Okay, you can look," she said, holding them out with a giggle.

Dyson smiled, tickled at her ingenuity. "You little …"

"I couldn't let him have them," she said. "Even if he would have killed me, I couldn't. I knew God hadn't put these into my hands just to lose them again. I knew something would happen to ensure they reached the world."

"And that something was Vesuvius?" he asked.

"Turned out that way."

"So what's the big secret? What do they say?"

"I only read the first few lines," she said, carefully unrolling the leaves. "But that was enough."

She feared she might have damaged them in the escape, but they seemed not too much worse for having ridden it out beneath her top. Still, they felt more fragile to her fingers than had those from the travertine boxes.

And then she read.

"I, having served as the scribe of the apostles of Christ, do here

with these my last words confess that it was I who authored their denials of our Lord, they who were my brethren; that I did so without their knowledge, my hand guided by the Evil One, as I now, too late, have come to realize ..."

Dyson stared in wonder. "You've got to be kidding."

"The handwriting's identical," Anna said, her eyes misting with happy tears. "So is the language, the structure, everything. I'd be willing to bet the ink and paper match too."

"Incredible," he said, looking closer. "The odds that you'd find both those *and* these, and all within a year? Buried *under* Herculaneum? And the only reason we found that temple chamber at all was because a nuclear bomb went off in the neighborhood! This is impossible."

"It's not impossible," Anna said, smiling softly. "It's God."

He fell back on the bed, his mind awhirl as he stared at the ceiling.

It really is *you?*

"Read some more," he said. "Read them all. The whole thing."

There came a knock on the door. Dyson rolled off the bed, crossed the room, and looked through the peephole.

"Gianni," he said, smiling at Anna.

He opened up and invited his friend into the room. Anna rose to her feet and shared in their embrace.

"You were so lucky," Gianni said, hugging them both and patting his friend on the back. "I can't believe you got out of there alive."

"We had help," Anna observed.

"That is one angry volcano out there," he said. "The eruption isn't as big as it could have been, and we're not in the shadow of the ashfall, but they're suggesting everyone be ready to leave, just in case the winds shift out of the south."

"Not likely in December," Dyson said. "The cloud's headed out over open water."

"And Sorrento. I know. But I didn't issue the warning. The volcano blew all of a sudden … things change."

"How much time do we have?"

Gianni checked his watch. "We can run by the other hotel if you still want to, but after that I say we all get out of here. The traffic is going to be pretty bad."

"What else is new?" Dyson said.

"I have the museum van downstairs. It's only a couple of miles each way. If we hurry, we can be there and back within an hour."

Dyson took his new fiancée into his arms and held her close.

"Wait here," he told her. "Keep those papers safe. You seem pretty good at that. We'll be right back."

"You be careful, Mister," she said, his warmth mingling with her own. As he kissed her, she melted into his embrace, wishing it could go on forever.

Finally, he released her, grabbed his phone, and hurried to catch up with Gianni. She followed him to the door and watched the men disappear down the hallway, then she went back inside the room and locked herself in.

Walking over to the window, she gazed out at the woodlands and aged pastel buildings spread wide before her, extending to the horizon. People scurried in all directions, some carrying what possessions they could as they heeded precaution and headed north. The room was on the side of the hotel facing away from Vesuvius, which suited Anna just fine. With her, the mountain had more than worn out its welcome.

Hey, I didn't break a nail, she realized, holding a perfect ten before her. *And there's not a thing wrong with that.*

◆ ◆ ◆

The quiet hillside surrounded her, the budding trees swaying gently in the cool breezes of a welcome and approaching spring.

Anna sat on the balcony of her apartment, reading over the translation she had completed. Though she had already informed the archaeological community and the press of the gist of the document, she had checked, rechecked, and verified that her word-for-word analysis was correct before sending it to Dean Mercer at Oldefield, for release the following day.

"Do I get to hear it now?" Dyson asked, emerging from the doorway. "It's finished, right?"

"Right," Anna said with a smile. "Pull up a chair."

She glanced down at the sparkling diamond on her finger. He had given it to her the very day they had arrived home from Italy, telling her he didn't want to waste a moment in formalizing his proposal. The ring had come wrapped in a brand new purple gym bag, which now rested at her feet, far from empty.

Their wedding would soon follow. The final arrangements were in place, and the invitations had gone out. Bonnie would be her matron of honor. Albert Mercer had agreed to give her away.

And her students would be there too. All but one.

"You're going to love the ending," she promised, waving the translation in front of him.

"I love it already," he said.

She straightened the computer printout, took a breath, and began.

"I, having served as the scribe of the apostles of Christ, do here with these my last words confess that it was I who authored their denials of our Lord, they who were my brethren; that I did so without their knowledge, my hand guided by the Evil One, as I now, too late, have come to realize.

"As I traveled with my teacher Paul, once Saul of Tarsus and student of Rabban Gamaliel the Elder, I found the favor of a Roman girl named Jessana, whose attentions I found desirable. Her family had great wealth, her father great influence. We spent much time together, and I did fall in love. She spoke harshly in my presence of Paul and the brethren, convincing me that their intentions were not honorable, and their aims political more than spiritual. She filled my pockets with silver and my head with notions alien to me, and after a time I did listen.

"A place of meeting was provided the brethren in Rome, a secret room beneath the country house of a noble named Septimus. He had been swayed by the powerful words of Paul, whom he had heard speaking upon the occasion of one of our first ventures into the city, and had commissioned the building of the room without the sanction of Rome. There, we gathered in safety and in numbers, knowing the danger presented by Nero, who opposed our teaching. But as our peril increased and the girl Jessana spoke sweet words into my ears, put money into my pockets, and brought earthly pleasures I had not imagined, I came to

believe I could no longer trust my brethren, that I should leave their company.

"I departed my teacher Paul, telling him that my family needed me, that I intended to return to my native Thessalonica. But after my departure, I instead remained in Rome, with Jessana. She promised to agree to marriage if I proved my love for her by helping to stop the political revolution she said was being sought by the brethren, an upheaval that she feared would being great harm to her family.

"To this end, with Jessana's encouragement, I formulated a plan whereby their message would be weakened so as to prove impotent against the emperor. Although the plan was intricate in conception and difficult to execute, I became certain it would bring the desired result. Using those materials with which I had written so many letters for my teacher Paul, I devised a set of writings in the names of the original Twelve, as well as that of my teacher, setting forth that they had knowingly falsified the glorious resurrection of our Lord, that they denied his rightful claim to the throne of the kingdom everlasting, that they had continued in professing the miracle, not because it was truth, but because the power of its message would result in changed lives and the overthrow of Rome, that which had taken hold of Judea.

"And having thus created the denials, I placed them inside two stone boxes made for me by an artisan in the city, half the writings in one box and half in the other. I placed into each of the boxes directives for finding the other, and I sealed the boxes with wax, warming them first as we learned to do in preserving food in jars of clay. And I placed one, late at night, within the house at Pompeii where I had taken a room, inside a wall being rebuilt, for it had been all but destroyed in an earthquake. And

the second box I placed in the wall of the gathering place beneath the home of Septimus the noble, behind the remembrances of the birth of our Lord ..."

Anna paused, a huge grin on her face. "I'll come back to this part."

Skipping slightly ahead, she continued.

"And I sealed up the wall and awaited the deaths of the Twelve, after which no one would remain to deny my account; then to inform the authorities of Rome of the proof of their insurrection, and of Christ's falsity.

"But soon thereafter, Septimus passed away, and so that he might protect the believers, his brethren, he ordered with his last breaths that his house be destroyed and the hidden stairway be filled with earth, sparing the hidden room itself out of respect and love for the faith, that no future owner of the house might discover its secret and endanger them. The denials I had hidden there thus were lost to me, and to all beyond reach.

"After this, Jessana, mocking me for my failure, departed me, first revealing to me that she and her father had devised a strategy from the start, by which I had been used against the brethren, and that she never had loved me ..."

"Ouch," Dyson said.

"And I began to regret my evil deeds, and I determined to return to Pompeii and there destroy the first box as well. Along the way, as I stopped for dinner at a thermopolium in Herculaneum by the sea, I met a young man whose family lived in an upstairs room in the house of Calatoria, widow of Gaius Petronius. As we spoke, I came to realize he was of the brethren, and when I confessed a lost faith in our Lord, he took me to his room, where he showed me a small wooden altar he had built.

Above this, embedded in the plaster of the wall, was a cross also fashioned of wood, and there he prayed for me."

"He's talking about the House of the Bicentenary," Dyson noted.

Anna nodded. "Isn't that exciting?"

"Go on."

"And there I wept, realizing the enormity of my sins against God, our Lord, and my teacher Paul, and I did plead for forgiveness. My guilt became like a millstone, a burden such that I dropped to my knees and could not rise again. Within the hour, the mountain of Vesuvius began to disgorge the wrath of hell, and I knew it was a judgment upon me for what I had done. The people of the city did flee, but I, knowing the wrath of God would only follow wherever I ran, remained. Travelers from Pompeii, escaping to the north, told of their city being buried already beneath a rain of brimstone; indeed, the same had begun to fall upon Herculaneum. Therefore, resigned to the imminence of my death, I went into the ancient Temple of the Old Ones, therein to wait, and discovered this catacomb, where now I lie.

"Old Ones?" Dyson wondered.

"I know," she said. "No wonder it didn't look Roman. Apparently, it was there before Herculaneum was."

She paused, emotion taking hold.

"Are you okay?" Dyson asked, reaching for her hand.

"Yes," she said, wiping a tear. "This next part is … difficult."

"So, the denials I hid away in Rome were buried by man, and those I hid away in Pompeii were buried by God, as now I myself am. I have heard the rumbling and have felt the ground shudder around me and know I am entombed. The fires of hell

lick at the door; the air grows oppressive and bitter, searing my throat, and I cannot bear it much longer.

"I cannot undo what I have done, for the heinous works of my hands are beyond my reach; I pray that the Father in his wisdom has hidden them away forever, that the eyes of no man ever find them, and my wicked act bear no deadly fruit.

"I, Demas, student of Paul, have written these things. May the risen Lord Jesus Christ bear mercy toward my soul, that in that mercy his glory be shown."

Anna laid the printout on the table, her eyes wet. She was sniffling.

"Demas?" Dyson quietly wondered, the weight of the words like none he had ever heard. "*The* Demas?"

"Yes," Anna said. "It's tragic."

"He was seduced into walking away from a faith he knew was true. Even as he sat at the feet of Paul, he let the world come between himself and God."

"Not the first time someone yielded to temptation," Anna said. "And it sure wasn't the last."

"The part you skipped before," he reminded her. "Go back. What was it?"

With a smile, she flipped to the earlier page.

"And the second box I placed in the wall of the gathering place beneath the home of Septimus the noble, behind the remembrances of the birth of our Lord, sweet spices and gold, which were kept in three vessels; one Roman, one Hebrew, and the cup of acacia wood used by our Lord at that last Passover supper."

Dyson's eyes grew as large as saucers as he realized what she had said.

"No way," he uttered, his voice failing him. "No way!"

Anna reached into the gym bag on the floor beside her. From it, she produced the polished wooden cup she had found in the vault, now emptied of the precious yellow metal it had held.

"Yes way!" she said, smiling broadly, holding up the wooden chalice.

He reached out and took it into his hands, knowing whose hands had once held it during that last earthly night before the ultimate sacrifice brought to pass the final and everlasting redemption of humankind. The cup's inner surface was darkened by a reddish stain.

As if from wine.

"I can't believe it," he said breathlessly. "I just can't."

"I know," she squealed.

"We weren't even looking for it," he said in amazement. "For all those centuries … all throughout the Crusades. The Arthurian legends, the Knights Templars. Then the Nazis, and thousands of treasure seekers. All those years they were searching in all the wrong places."

The Holy Grail.

"And the whole time," Anna said, "it was buried under a hill in Rome. Paul must have carried it there with him." She ran a fingertip lightly along its rim. "Everything else from the vault is still in the safe-deposit box. It never left Italy."

Dyson studied the cup's featureless contours. "How did you get this through customs?"

"They didn't look at it twice. It was just a plain wooden cup to them. It doesn't look valuable or particularly old, so they didn't even ask about it. But I wasn't going to let it out of my sight … not before I was sure."

Dyson shook his head, unable to tear his eyes from the acacia goblet. "It's going to take me a while to absorb this, Anna."

"I still can't believe it."

"How in the world did you keep this to yourself?" he asked, visibly astonished. "I'd have burst wide open trying to keep that inside."

"Because I knew this moment would come. You and I, together, alone, now."

For several long minutes they sat quietly, pondering what Demas had written and trying to convince themselves of the chalice Dyson held in his hands.

"We can't keep it," Dyson said with a measure of reluctance. "It has to go back."

"I've already called Albert. I didn't tell him it was the Holy Grail, but I did tell him I had an artifact I wanted him to escort back to Milan."

"Carlo will be beside himself," he said, smiling. "His museum is about to acquire the single most valuable artifact in the world."

"What do you think they'll say when they hear all this?" Anna wondered. "The world, I mean. What will people say when they learn that the lie they embraced *was* a lie, that all of it was the work of a single misguided man?"

"I think," Dyson replied, "God only knows."

Epilogue

The world took the news as it had the first reports. Those willing or wanting to believe did. Those unwilling to believe did not.

And those who had moved on, who had dropped their faith like a hot rock, never looked back.

Worldwide, the number of those who called themselves Christians had fallen by two-thirds. Everywhere, across America and the continents, former churches had become synagogues, mosques, lecture halls, social clubs, libraries, schools, markets, or laundries. In the eyes of some, the faith had lost a credibility it could never regain. For others, whose conviction had seen them through, the crisis had only made them stronger.

As the final written confession of Demas became known, a few did come back into the fold, truly penitent for their lack of faith. Only a few. But this time, word of the discovery had to spread without help from the media. No stellar book deals were signed. No science- or faith-based television specials were made. No blockbuster movies were released.

There was just no commercial, worldly interest to be found in Jesus Christ, after all, being God.

◆ ◆ ◆

No hat.

As Orsen scanned the crowd before and below him, his hands gripping the pulpit as if to steady a shaky foundation, a sense of relief rose. Nowhere did he see the fedora-crowned man who haunted him even in absence, whose words, absurd though they were, would not cease to echo:

"He will tear down what you have covered in whitewash and will level it to the ground, and when it falls, you will be destroyed in it."

"Crazy old man," the pastor uttered, barely audibly.

Most of those gathered were new to the church, though a few holdovers from his father's days remained. And there was, as always now, one conspicuous omission among those present.

We've moved on, Pop. I know what you believed, but there's just no money in clinging to that old-time religion. A church can't survive by hanging itself on Jesus … we've turned a corner and there's no going back. Maybe he was real and maybe he wasn't, but if there's a God in heaven, he won't turn away a good soul. No way. Christ or no Christ.

His father's face hung before him, a countenance shining with a silver light Orsen did not recognize. The worth of faith, Son, the man once had said, is measured not merely in its quantity or existence, but in its object. It isn't what you believe, but in whom you believe.

Never had Orsen agreed. Believing is an end in itself. It doesn't matter what you believe, so long as you believe in something.

"And judging from the till, I believe I've saved this church," he whispered.

He turned on the microphone and began to speak, a wolf before the sheep, leading a flock that never had known the shepherd.

◆ ◆ ◆

Mr. and Mrs. Jack Dyson walked through a city park, watching the falling leaves scatter in the autumn wind. Streaks of red and gold and orange swirled around them, a clatter set to the music of the winds. His arm was around her, holding her close as he treasured her. Her hand rested lightly upon the generous curve of her belly.

She was with child.

"How about Nicole if it's a girl?" Anna suggested. "And William if it's a boy."

"Or," Jack returned with a smile, "Angela if it's a girl, and Roger if it's a boy."

"I can see we're miles apart on this," she laughed.

"We still have two months to decide. Quite a Christmas present we have to look forward to. Was Willowdale okay with extending your maternity leave?"

"Yes," Anna said. "Professor Winsett will sub for me starting the second week of November."

"Are you still happy to be back into history? No regrets over hanging up your shovel, giving up the thrill of discovery?"

"Not one. I'm very happy to be in the classroom, especially now. I've had quite enough on-site thrills for one lifetime."

"I guess I can't blame you there."

"Besides," she teased, "one archaeologist in the family is plenty. How was Oldefield this week?"

"Same as ever," he said. "And enrollment's up. Seems the publicity you generated led to good things, after all."

"I'm glad to hear that."

"And," he added, "the shiny new computer labs don't hurt, either."

They continued along the sidewalk, watching children at play in the cool of the day, knowing they would soon share in the joys of family. Anna looked down at the deep wine maternity dress she wore beneath her open car coat, remembering how many times she had dreamed of such a moment.

Oh, Father, if only there were words enough to thank you for this gift.

Her thoughts drifted back. Not to the horrors of Vesuvius, or of that day in Herculaneum, but to the entirety of her ordeal.

"What was it all for?" she wondered aloud. "I mean, I trust God that he knew what he was doing, but what was it all for? Why the pain that came upon the church?"

"I've been thinking about that," Dyson said. "A lot. And I think I figured it out."

"Oh, did you?" she said, smiling up at him. "Just over a year as a believer, and you have all the answers?"

"Not all," he said. He kissed her on the forehead.

"So, tell me."

"Think of the things that happened, that taken by themselves seem tragic, even cruel. Presenting to the world evidence that Christ was a fraud. A violent nuclear detonation, without warning, in a populated area. An even more violent volcanic eruption. Seems at first glance that God was asleep at the switch."

"Okay, go on."

"But take everything together," he proposed. "Look at the events as pieces of a larger puzzle."

"I love when you do this," she said.

"You find the scrolls. They become public. Two-thirds of all self-described Christians leave the church, their faith swept aside by an unproven assertion because that faith was rooted not in Christ but in worldly things. Convenience. Social needs. The approval of those around them."

"I'm with you so far."

"Then a nuclear bomb goes off. Not a huge one, but bad enough. Creates a zone of destruction a mile wide. You know, I looked at aerial shots of the detonation point. It went off *exactly* at the spot along the road where it needed to for the death toll to be minimized. Small rural area. Just another mile or two farther along or farther back, and tens if not hundreds of thousands more would have died. And then, the whole region, including several towns with narrow streets and no viable means of rapid flight, gets evacuated over the next several days because of spreading fires and fallout.

"And the nuclear blast kicks off the seismic force necessary to move uncounted tons of volcanic sediment and reveal, beneath Herculaneum, the truth about Demas and his forgeries."

"A force only Vesuvius could provide," Anna said with a nod of understanding. "And when it erupted, once the truth of Demas had been uncovered and physical proof secured for all the world to see, the wrath of the volcano was unleashed against *an abandoned area.*"

Dyson's astonishment played on his face. "Instead of the few thousand lives the bomb took, more than a *million* would have died had Vesuvius suddenly erupted with the normal population in place.

"It's hard to accept, but in the outworking of God's design, seemingly horrible things sometimes have to happen in order for wonderful things to follow. He uses the deeds of evil people for good, as we saw with Joseph's brothers. Millions died in the Holocaust, but that was what it took for the world to be sufficiently moved to allow Israel to exist as a nation once again ... as the Bible said would happen. And then there was Darfur, and 9/11 ... You just have to trust that God knows what he's doing.

"It's amazing the way he uses even the actions of terrorists. The volcano was set to blow at any time, and without warning. Seismologists have known it for years. It would have gone up anyway, just like it did in AD 79, and in 1631, and in 1944, and dozens of other times. The way it worked out, who knows how many lives were saved?"

Anna stopped as they passed a bench and gingerly took a seat, pausing to consider her husband's words it all. She watched a cluster of tiny sparrows just across the walk as they fed on a generous scattering of seed, tossed on the ground for them by an earlier occupant of the bench—sunflower, millet, cracked corn, safflower.

How like them we are, she thought. *They found that food lying there, thinking they just came upon it, that it was a lucky accident of nature. Yet they were fed by a deliberate hand, providing for them with compassionate forethought, with a loving desire that they flourish. Don't we all too often credit our own cleverness for the blessings that come into our lives? Don't we praise our own devices, our own hard work, or even simple good fortune for the things that sustain us each day?*

Her husband took a seat beside her. And at that moment, as if in welcome, Anna felt the baby kick.

"Oooh, she knows you're out here," she said, smiling. "She loves her daddy."

"Or *he* does," Dyson grinned. "Sure you don't want to know?"

"I'm an old-fashioned girl. I love a surprise."

They watched the leaves fall all around them, drifting down, coming to rest as they covered the world in a blanket of color. They brought to mind another more fearsome blanket, one of stark gray.

"Another thing," he said, "I looked at a volcanological map online, up at Oldefield. The surge from Vesuvius traveled a relatively narrow path down the mountain before reaching the sea. I'm sorry to see Herculaneum buried again, but the flow stayed within the evacuated area. Same with the ashfall. Torre del Greco and points south suffered a pretty good dusting, but that was it. They had a mess to clean up, but there was no death toll to speak of."

"Providence," Anna recognized.

"I'd say so."

"But why did the first scrolls have to become public at all?" she still wondered. "I know there was a reason, but why put the church through that?"

"Maybe to purify it," Jack offered. "To separate the wheat from the chaff, true faith from apostasy. Those who are Christ's are Christ's. They can never be lost. Now, those remaining can look at one another and know the wolves are no longer among them."

"'Wolves,'" Anna whispered, remembering words spoken the night a snowstorm had driven her to take shelter. "The reverend at that little church I told you about … he mentioned wolves. He said a harvest was coming. He knew, Jack."

"In hindsight, you can begin to see it," he said, holding her close. "A manipulated scribe named Demas, and a group of hate-driven terrorists, and a greed-driven looter, and an angry, misled, deluded young man"—he looked into her face, a countenance aglow with impending motherhood—"and one very loving and very determined Anna Meridian. All were called upon to fill key roles in the outworking of a divine plan put into motion before this old world was created."

She leaned into him, overwhelmed by it all.

"Anna *Dyson,*" she corrected. Her eyes glistened in the soft light. "For whatever time is left before the Lord comes."

She melted into him, cradled in his strength.

"I take it back," she said. "You *do* have all the answers."

"Naahh," he insisted. "I got lucky."

"I love you," she whispered, reaching up to caress his face.

They kissed, their souls a wondrous singularity, forevermore. As he held her, she again placed her hand gently over the beating heart of her unborn child.

We're three, and yet we're one.

"Maybe," she said, "Angela would be a nice name after all."

Author's Note

"Who do you say that I am?"

This question is the very foundation of Christianity, for in its answer lies the spiritual condition of each of us. Too many of us don't seem to understand what it means to be a Christian, believing that in our good deeds—our "Christian charity"—lies our salvation.

Yet even though Christ's love bathes our hearts and souls with a compassion beyond our understanding, Christianity in its essence isn't about being nice to one another.

Nor is it about building larger sanctuaries and drawing larger congregations each Sunday.

Nor is it even about feeding, clothing, or sheltering the poor.

All these things are wonderful and present a pattern for us to follow for the duration of the earthly portion of our lives. Through them we love others and show but a measure of the kindness our heavenly Father has shown us. But they don't save anyone.

Nor is Christianity about displaying "tolerance" and being accepting of others wherever they happen to be. Jesus Christ was considered by those around him to be one of the least tolerant men they'd ever met. Consider that he didn't say, "Come to the Father by whatever road you choose." He didn't say, "It doesn't matter what form your faith takes or what you believe in, so long as you indeed have faith."

He said, "I am the way … no one comes to the Father but through Me" (John 14:6).

No one.

Believe in him, believe he is God, or die in your sins.

One or the other.

To the worldly mind, trusting one's eternal destiny to Someone who last walked the earth more than two thousand years ago isn't simply difficult, or unlikely, or far-fetched.

It's impossible.

This is why Jesus specifically told those who would follow him, "You did not choose Me but I chose you … no can come to Me unless the Father who sent Me draws him."

Our power to believe comes not from within ourselves but—like life and love themselves—from God.

Christianity isn't about behaving our way into heaven. It isn't about eating the right foods or wearing the right fashions or doing the right things. It isn't about our own knowledge or will or persistence leaping in to save us from a destiny separated from God.

It's about an act of self-sacrifice set into motion before Adam ever drew his first breath upon this earth.

It's about God reaching down and setting foot among us, and dying in the place of a largely ungrateful people who have always hated him—because, for whatever unfathomable reason, it pleased him to do so.

"While we were yet sinners, Christ died for us" (Rom. 5:8).

Some well-meaning, self-proclaimed Christians have taken to insisting that God saves everyone. They say his love is such that he could never allow any of us to be lost. Those who believe this have no idea what it means to be a Christian, nor do they understand what Christ accomplished on the cross. When challenged, they ask, "Why wouldn't God save everyone?" Unfortunately, that's the wrong question.

The right question is, "Why does God save *anyone?*"

Yes, God is love. We see that every day as we hold our families and our children and our loved ones close. But God is also justice.

And, thankfully, he is mercy. We're saved because *he* reached down to *us*. We're saved according to his plan, his rules, his judgment. We were told specifically and unequivocally, *Die without believing in Jesus, and you die in your sins.*

So, what does it mean to believe? *What is faith?*

This question has been answered in many ways through the years. Some mistakenly think that faith must be blind. However, Christians are told to love God with all their hearts, souls, and *minds.* We're to know *what* we believe and *why* we believe it. But we shouldn't root our faith exclusively in the evidence of the intellect. The tangible facts behind our faith—while important in helping us "make a defense to everyone who asks [us] to give an account for the hope that is in [us]" (1 Peter 3:15)—should never be its sole basis. We should never rely solely upon worldly wisdom in judging the merit of what we believe, for the things of the Spirit are but *foolishness* to the world and are *spiritually discerned* (see 1 Cor. 2:14). True faith is rooted in many realms, from the physical to the historical to the experiential. God has touched our lives in many ways.

The deity of Christ and the reality of his resurrection lie at the core of saving faith. If Jesus wasn't God—*if he wasn't raised from the dead*—then believing in him saves no one, and God finds no glory there.

I wish to recommend a few books that deal with the deity of Christ and with the "many infallible proofs" (Acts 1:3) we have of his resurrection that Sunday morning. *More Than a Carpenter* and *Evidence That Demands a Verdict*, by Josh McDowell, detail both historical evidence and reasoned affirmations that enable believers to rest secure in their faith. *Who Moved the Stone,* by English journalist Frank Morison, is unique in that the author originally set out to refute once and for all the Christian case and to prove Jesus a mere man. Yet, after more than a year of painstaking research, he reached the opposite conclusion and came to believe. The knowledge contained in these volumes can add much to one's witnessing arsenal, and to the surety of one's faith.

To *believe* in Jesus Christ is to believe that he is God in the flesh, who lived among us and died to satisfy the justice of the Father. It is to believe that Jesus died in our place, suffering our just penalty, so that we need not know spiritual death. It is to trust in him *and in him alone* for salvation, depending not on ourselves, or on our good works, or on any other means of humankind's devising.

We're saved only because God has chosen to save us through his Son. We *receive* salvation. We don't buy it. We don't pursue it. It's a *gift*. There's one narrow bridge by which we may reach God, a bridge he built because, otherwise, there could be none between us.

And if we place our trust in any other, if we try to cross that chasm by any other path, we just won't get there.

—Shane Johnson
Summer 2006

Author's Interview

1. How did you start writing? What was your first piece of writing like?

My first writing was a joint effort between myself and a close friend, a novel based on a creative writing assignment he had done in high school. That joint effort, more than two decades later, finally became my first novel, *The Last Guardian*. Please see http://www.shanejohnsonbooks.com/tlg/origin.htm for details on how all that came to pass.

2. Why do you write fiction?

That's part of the above history, a posthumous promise kept.

3. Why do people remember a story more easily than a sermon?

Generally, I think having characters and events to whom one can relate makes it easier to remember a story. Sermons tend to feel more like lectures or lessons, carrying with them an inherent distance.

4. What do you hope readers will take away from your book?

The knowledge that, no matter now unpleasant or even tragic some events may seem at the time of their occurrence, all are being made to work together for the glory of the Lord.

5. Which character in the book is most like you?

That's hard to say. As I write I become every character, expressing concerns and speaking as he or she would in turn. In many ways I'm most like the main character despite her experiences and losses, which are quite severe and lead to a crisis of faith. She ultimately believes and comes away with a stronger faith than she'd had before.

6. What actor would you picture playing (your main character) in a movie?

I wrote the book picturing Jennifer Love Hewett as the main character—she has the same playful quality as Anna yet can be focused and intense. In the prologue of the book Anna would be the age the actress now is, while the bulk of the story takes place many years later. Jack Dyson, the male lead, was Dennis Quaid from the start—his sense of humor, speaking voice, and overall character traits are perfect for the man I envisioned.

7. Which writers have influenced you most?

Charles Dickens, George Clayton Johnson, Hal Lindsey, and Charles Ryrie

8. Describe your writing process.

As I write line-by-line, I jump from character to character "becoming" each in turn, seeing and feeling the unfolding events through his or her eyes and responding accordingly. In a very real sense my characters write my novels—and I'm sometimes surprised at where they take the story. And, as always, my wife's input is invaluable—what a blessing she has been to my writing career. Without her, it would never have been possible.

9. Can you share a particularly memorable encounter with a reader?

No one face-to-face encounter stands out above any other, but I did once correspond via e-mail with a college student who had promoted *The Last Guardian* on her blog and considered it her favorite novel. I sent her copies of some of my later work, thanked her for her support, and over the following months exchanged several encouraging messages with her.

10. What is one fact about yourself that readers might find most surprising?

I was agnostic throughout my teenage years and early twenties, approaching the level of atheism a few times along the way. I was convinced that science had (or would have) an answer for every problem facing us all, and I was very much a humanist. But God saw fit to send a very good friend into my life who was Christian and knew *why*—the first such person I'd ever met. Along the way and as the years passed, others were placed into my path who helped me to better understand just how God had chosen in grace to deal with a mankind who had abandoned him.

Invite Shane Johnson to Your Book Club

Transport your book club behind the scenes and into a new world by inviting Shane Johnson to join in your group discussion via phone. To learn more, go to www.cookministries.com/readthis or e-mail Shane directly at demasauthor@aol.com.

Additional copies of *The Demas Revelation*
are available wherever good books are sold.

If you have enjoyed this book, or if it has had an impact on your life,
we would like to hear from you.

Please contact us at

RiverOak Books
Cook Communications Ministries, Dept. 240
4050 Lee Vance View
Colorado Springs, CO 80918

Or visit our Web site
www.cookministries.com